SATHOW'S SINNERS

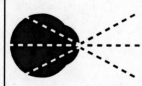

This Large Print Book carries the
Seal of Approval of N.A.V.H.

SATHOW'S SINNERS

MARCUS GALLOWAY

WHEELER PUBLISHING
A part of Gale, Cengage Learning

GALE
CENGAGE Learning·

Farmington Hills, Mich • San Francisco • New York • Waterville, Maine
Meriden, Conn • Mason, Ohio • Chicago

LIBRARY OF CONGRESS CATALOGING-IN-PUBLICATION DATA

Galloway, Marcus.
    Sathow's sinners / Marcus Galloway. — Large print edition.
        pages cm. — (Wheeler large print western)
    ISBN 978-1-4104-7697-5 (softcover) — ISBN 1-4104-7697-9 (softcover)
    1. Large type books. I. Title.
PS3607.A4196S28 2015
813'.6—dc23   2015001855

Published in 2015 by arrangement with The Berkley Publishing Group, an imprint of Penguin Publishing Group, a division of Penguin Random House LLC

Printed in the United States of America
1 2 3 4 5   19 18 17 16 15

SATHOW'S SINNERS

1

Missouri
1886

Some folks thought the world was a stage. For Nate Sathow, it was a madhouse. One big, sprawling madhouse. That didn't necessarily make the world a terrible place to be. The sun rose and set in the sky above a madhouse. Cool winds blew around it. Any walls could provide shelter, warmth, or be filled with the scents of freshly baked pies. But make no mistake. It was still a madhouse. The moment a man lost sight of that, he allowed himself to be locked away with the other lost souls.

"What's the matter, Nate? You look troubled."

The man who'd asked that question rode a tired gray mare that most other men would have sold or put out to pasture long ago. But Francis Waverly didn't give up on any living thing, no matter how poorly regarded by others. As far as Nate could tell, that was the reason Frank associated with those who might be called dregs or unsavory characters by more respectable portions of the world. It's also why Frank wore the plain black shirt and white collar of a preacher whether he had a congregation listening to him or not. His wasn't a blind or childish sort of hope. It had been tempered by fire, which was why Frank also wore a gun. Two of them, in fact. A man could have buckets of faith in his god or fellow mortals, just so long as he didn't let it impede his common sense.

Nate hacked up a breath that had been festering in the back of his throat since his last cigar had gone out, looked over at Frank and told him, "Ain't troubled. Just thinking about madhouses."

Frank nodded while looking up at the clear Missouri sky. "Suppose it's as good a time as any for that sort of thing." He savored the touch of a passing breeze against his cheek before shifting his gaze toward a sprawling old mansion at the end of the trail. "Perhaps it'll be a short visit. He may not even be here."

"He's here. Not like this is the first polecat I've tracked through a field."

"Three fields," Frank corrected. "And

don't forget the two towns, four camps and three rivers in between."

Smiling didn't come easy to Nate Sathow, or perhaps it just didn't come often. Most folks didn't spend enough time in his company to decide which. Wide through the shoulders, he filled out his battered duster like a hastily piled stack of bricks. Callused hands gripped the reins of a spotted gelding he'd purchased with the profits he'd made hunting down a pair of escaped killers from Wichita. A .44 Remington was holstered across his belly where it could be quickly drawn in a pinch. The smirk on Nate's face parted a sea of salt-and-pepper stubble on his chin and bent the scar that ran from the corner of his left eye, along his cheek and around to the lower portion of his ear. "He did give us a run, didn't he?"

"Nothing we're not used to. I recall a couple of robbers who led us through every bayou in Louisiana."

"The Frimodt brothers," Nate groaned. "Crossed paths with them within a few days of meeting the fellain that house up yonder. They put the fear into an entire county when they busted out of that sorry excuse for a jail in Baton Rouge and shot at you every chance they got."

Frank looked over to the man beside him

and asked, "Why is that? You were there just like I was. In fact, you were the one riding up front with the shotgun in your hands the first time we caught sight of the Frimodts. Why was I the one in their sights?"

"Maybe they don't like preachers," Nate replied.

Scratching at his white collar as if it had suddenly gotten a little tight, Frank said, "What kind of nonsense is that? Why would they hold a grudge against preachers?"

"I may be the one shooting at these dogs, but you're the one tellin' 'em their souls will burn afterward."

Frank recoiled as if he'd been struck. "I make it a point to say nothing of the sort!" After a hard glare from Nate, he added, "Not on a regular basis, anyway."

The grin left Nate's face once he spotted a large sign posted alongside the trail that read *McKeag Sanitarium — Visitors report directly to front desk. Do not approach patients.*

"Perhaps I should be the one to go inside," Frank offered.

"I've tracked down worse than this one," Nate said. "After all the trouble we been through to get this far, I ain't about to hang back now. Besides, you should be outside in case there's trouble."

"Only trouble you're likely to find is the trouble you make. I've visited plenty of sick folks. They don't need someone coming in and —"

"The only sickness those folks got is between their ears," Nate snapped. "And I ain't about to ruffle any feathers. I'm the one in charge of finding this fugitive, so I should be the one to speak to whoever's running this asylum."

The trail widened a few yards beyond the sign. Judging by the ruts worn into the dirt veering to the right toward a large carriage house, plenty of wagons made the trip to McKeag Sanitarium. Frank reined his horse to a stop and allowed Nate to continue on his own. "If you don't want to ruffle feathers with the staff, you probably shouldn't call this place an asylum," he called out as Nate was still moving down the path leading to the mansion's front porch. "It's a hospital. Better yet, don't call it anything. Just be respectful. You hear me?"

"Yes, Ma," Nate grumbled under his breath so just his horse could hear. "Every loon in this damn place can hear you."

After swinging down from his saddle, Nate tied his horse to a hitching post next to a watering trough, patted the gelding on the neck and climbed the steps to the sprawling

11

front porch. Rocking chairs were situated along the front of the house, one of which was occupied by a young woman with stringy hair and vacant eyes. Nate tipped his hat to her as he strode toward the front door. She watched him for a moment, lowered her head and curled herself into a ball between the rocker's arms.

Inside, the place looked like anything but a mansion. The wide, luxurious spaces of the original design were now smaller rooms partitioned by walls that smelled of freshly cut pine. The desk, a few paces in and to the right of the main entrance, reminded Nate of one that would be found in a hotel. He stepped up to it, removed his hat and addressed the large, stern woman seated behind it who was dressed in a simple, starched dress.

"Pardon me, ma'am. I'd like to have a word if I may."

She looked him up and down with eyes that had seen more than their share of just about everything ugly in the human condition. "Are you visiting someone?"

"Not as such. I'd just like to ask a few questions." Although Nate's years as a lawman were well behind him, he'd hung on to a few relics from those days. Most were badges he'd stolen from the lawmen who'd employed him. Those tin stars weren't just handed out like candy, so he would explain their loss by claiming once they were ripped from his chest lost in a fire during a bloody shootout that was still talked about in parts of west Texas another time. He reached into his inner coat pocket for one of the smaller pieces of tin with the word deputy engraved in simple lettering. That one, he'd pocketed after riding with a posse in the Dakota Territories. After the hell he went through in the Badlands for so little pay, he didn't feel the first twinge of guilt about the theft. Today, it served to grease the wheels with the woman behind that desk.

Her face brightened somewhat and she sat up while asking, "What can I do for you?"

"I'm here to inquire about someone that may be in your care. Probably only just got here in the last few weeks and might have mentioned spending some time in —"

"Stop that man! He's armed!"

Nate instinctively reached for the pistol in his holster when the voice shattered the calm within the fancy house. He quickly realized, however, that the stomping steps rattling the floor were coming from above his head instead of from anywhere close to him. The woman behind the desk came around to push him toward the door.

"You'll have to step outside," she said. "We can handle this."

"But I . . ."

"We don't need any heavy hands in our sanitarium. We are well versed in keeping our patients in line."

Once the stampede had worked its way to the left side of the house, Nate could pick out the sounds of bare feet slapping heavily against stairs. He allowed himself to be pushed toward the door, if only to get a look into the next room that was filled with more rockers, bookshelves that reached all the way to the ceiling and a wide staircase with a sloping polished banister. A skinny man wrapped in a flimsy cotton gown came down those stairs in a jumble of bony arms and legs. Even though he somehow remained upright, he stumbled in such a rush that it was impossible for Nate to tell if he was racing down to the ground floor or falling.

"Stop right there!" another man shouted from higher up the staircase. "This is just soup! I'm bringing you your lunch. No need for any of this."

Extending a long arm up the stairs, the man in the gown pointed up at whoever had spoken and shrieked, "I know what you

14

monsters put in that soup! It'll twist my mind! It'll put me to sleep! And when I'm twisted and asleep you'll . . . you'll . . . there's *no telling* what you'll do!"

A young man wearing plain black pants and a rumpled white shirt eased his way down the stairs, closely followed by reinforcements that outweighed him by no fewer than forty pounds each. "Take it easy now. Aren't you hungry?" the smallest orderly asked.

Nate had almost been tossed outside when the screaming man at the bottom of the stairs pulled a paring knife from where it had been stashed beneath his gown. "None of you are gonna get your hands on me!" he shouted before snapping his wrist and sending the knife whistling through the air to skip along the wall. While the men coming down the stairs ducked to avoid the flying silverware, the man in the gown pulled another knife and several other pieces of cutlery from wherever he'd been hiding them.

"I'll burn this corner of hell down before I let one more atrocity get committed here!" the lunatic screamed as he threw another knife.

The young orderly was shoved aside as one of the bigger men vaulted down the stairs, launching himself toward the ranting patient with both arms outstretched. Somehow, the man in the gown managed to hop back and gain enough footing to perch upon the sill of the closest window. He remained there for less than a second before gravity dragged him down again. By the time his feet touched the floor, the second big fellow was coming at him.

"You'll have to leave, sir," the woman from the front desk said as she continued herding Nate toward the main entrance. "We have a situation here."

"Sure as hell do," Nate grunted as he put his back to her and raced outside on his own. The door was immediately slammed shut behind him, which did nothing to mask the sounds of struggle from within the house.

"Need a hand?" Frank asked from his saddle.

"Just stay put and watch the road," Nate shouted as he stomped past the girl in the rocker to run along the wide porch toward a corner of the mansion. "Make sure nobody gets to that carriage house!"

Before Nate could round the corner, two men shattered a window and spilled outside. One of the big orderlies landed heavily on his back with the man in the gown on top

16

of him. Nate drew his pistol and roared, "Both of you stop!"

Neither man was listening. The slender one in the gown thumped a fist against the orderly's shoulder and cocked his other hand up over his head like a hammer he intended to drop. His raised fist was wrapped around a shiny fork with three wickedly long tines. Nate sighted along his barrel for as long as he dared before squeezing his trigger. The Remington bucked against his palm, sending its bullet through the middle of the crazy man's improvised weapon.

Before Nate could follow up, a heavy hand dropped onto his shoulder and spun him around so he could look into a pair of dark eyes set within a red face atop a thickly veined neck. "No guns around the patients!" a muscular orderly said. "Hand it over, or you'll be hurt worse than him."

The woman from behind the front desk came outside, hollering, "He's a deputy!"

The orderly let Nate go and grunted, "Just step aside and let us do our jobs."

Suddenly, something poked Nate in the shoulder. It was a sharp, jabbing impact from something much narrower than a fingertip. When the object fell onto his boot, Nate looked down to find the severed handle of the fork that had been in the patient's hand. Less than a second later, something else hissed through the air. The orderly let out a surprised yelp and twisted around to reach over his shoulder. Lodged in the thick meat a few inches below the back of his neck and just out of his reach was another fork from the same set that had been stolen by the patient.

Another orderly climbed through the window and was promptly dispatched by a spoon. Its tip cracked solidly against the bridge of the orderly's nose, causing the young man to stagger. The patient shoved him back through the window and then bolted for the carriage house.

"To hell with this place!" the escaping madman hollered. "And to hell with all of you!"

By the time Nate yanked the fork from the orderly's back and shoved him aside, he was nearly tripped up by the one with the spoon welt on his face, who was tentatively climbing through the window again. "I'll handle this," Nate said as he sped by. That was enough to convince the orderly to climb right back inside again.

2

The crazy man rushed toward the carriage house, his hands outstretched and his fingers clasping in anticipation of opening the door to get to a horse. A rifle shot cracked through the air, spitting a round to knock a hole into the upper corner of the wide wooden structure. Still in his saddle, Frank levered another round into the Winchester he'd just fired and sighted along the top of its barrel.

"I knew it!" the crazy man shouted without even taking the time to look in Frank's direction. "Everyone at this place wants me dead!" He changed his direction faster than a jackrabbit and darted around the carriage house.

"He's making for the woods," Frank said.

Nate was already running to catch up to the escapee, leaving the sanitarium and its workers behind. "I see him, damn it."

"Want my help now?"

"No! Just stay put."

Knowing that Frank was surely grousing about how stubbornness was some kind of sin, Nate kept moving. About twenty yards ahead of him, the escaping patient ran, his loosely fitted gown flapping around his legs. Bare feet dug into rich soil warmed by the ever-present humidity of a waning Missouri summer. Insects darted through the air, growing thicker in the short distance between him and a dense patch of trees that stood like a wall at the edge of the McKeag property line.

"Stop!" Nate shouted.

The crazy man didn't spare the time it took to look over his shoulder. Instead, he pumped his arms even harder to build up steam before vaulting over a log that lay half-buried in a mess of weeds and dirt.

Nate fired a quick shot into the air, which did nothing to slow the other man down. Even a lunatic would most likely know that anyone who had a prayer of gunning him down wouldn't be able to do it while at a full run. Unwilling to holster the pistol, Nate pushed himself until the muscles in his legs started to burn and made certain to keep an eye open for that log. He launched himself over the obstacle, clearing it with significantly less space than the man who was just about to reach the cover of the trees.

Skidding to a halt, Nate stretched out one arm so it could be used to steady the Remington. His breathing was heavy enough to be a problem, so he swallowed a gulp of air and ignored the pounding of his heart while taking aim. The first time he squeezed the trigger, he knew his shot was wide. Nate kept track of where the crazy man was headed using the edge of his vision. Then he shifted his aim a bit and fired again.

Although his bullet struck exactly where it was supposed to, it still wasn't enough to get the job done. Nate fired again, blasting through the rest of the branch he'd picked out until the entire gnarled length of wood toppled from its tree. Its thicker end dropped to form a rough barrier in the path the crazy man meant to take.

The man in the gown leapt without breaking stride and for a moment, it seemed he might actually clear the branch in front of him. Although his right leg made it over the obstruction, his left snagged on the branch and brought him down amid a storm of flailing limbs and foul language.

Nate put everything he had into his strides. His boot twisted at a painful angle thanks to what could have been a rabbit's hole, but he kept charging forward. Even when something silver whistled past his head, he kept going. The crazy man had gotten to his feet by now, so Nate ran even harder.

Having chased more fugitives than he could count, Nate could feel all the way down to the marrow in his bones when he was close enough to capture another one. The rest of the world and all of its other inhabitants faded away as he focused on the skinny man in the filthy cotton gown. That man headed deeper into the woods, moving faster than most creatures on two legs could despite the limp marring every other step. Nate didn't waste time in firing another shot or taking the breaths needed to form any more words. He simply tore after his prey as if it was what he was put on God's earth to do.

Sunlight barely touched this stretch of wooded ground, stabbing through between a leafy canopy the wind was constantly moving and the birds that called those boughs their home. Nate could tell the crazy man was catching his second wind and would eventually find a way to prolong this chase or make it a whole lot worse. Slowing to a jog, Nate aimed his Remington from the hip and fired two shots. They hissed wide and to the right of the fleeing lunatic but were enough to convince him to circle around the other side of the tree directly in front of him toward a much harder path.

The man in the gown had to leap over another log, and once he was airborne, it was too late to dodge the stump behind it that was partially buried in mulch. Screaming like a banshee, the lunatic hit the stump and landed in the bushes.

Nate rushed forward to leap over the log headfirst. It wasn't a graceful landing, but most of his weight dropped onto the thrashing lunatic's back. Before the crazy man could get his bearings, Nate grabbed one of his wrists and jammed it up tight against his back. Just as his elbow was reaching its limit, the patient attached to it twisted around to relieve the tension and pull his arm loose. He squirmed out from under Nate's weight then scrambled to his feet and started to run again, unmindful of the fact that Nate still had a hold of his gown.

Using the crazy man's momentum to help pull him up, Nate tightened his grip on the muddied garment and dug his heels into the ground. When the man's gown snapped taut, Nate hauled back and pulled him to a halt. No matter how fired up the crazy man was, he couldn't outmuscle his pursuer, and when it became clear that the man in the gown was still going to put up a fight, Nate dragged him around and swung him into the nearest tree. The lunatic bounced off its trunk and fell awkwardly onto his back.

Nate took a knee beside him, placed the Remington's barrel against the other man's forehead and thumbed back its hammer. There wasn't anything better than that metallic click to catch someone's attention.

Breathing heavily, the escaped patient blinked and smiled up past the revolver. "As I live and breathe," he said with a hint of a Virginia drawl, "is that Nate Sathow?"

"It sure is. How's life treating you, Deaugrey?"

"I seem to have found myself in a bit of a pickle right this instant, but I'm sure that's about to improve."

Nate stood up but didn't holster his .44. "Don't be too sure about that. After all the trouble I went through to find you, it might be better for me to just hand you over to them doctors back at the hospital."

Now that he wasn't flinging utensils or scampering like a rabid squirrel, Deaugrey Scott conducted himself with quiet composure. Accepting Nate's assistance to stand back on his feet, he straightened up to a height that was just shy of average and dusted off a lean, wiry frame. The fact that he was still wrapped in a cotton gown soiled with blood, dirt and sweat didn't make the slightest bit of difference to him as he straightened it like a gentleman tugging at the lapels of an expensive overcoat. "Considering the food they serve in that hellhole, I'd consider it more of a zoo than a proper hospital."

"Looked nicer than any house I ever owned, but I guess you're the expert on being locked up."

"I suppose you were summoned here to talk me into staying?"

"Not at all," Nate replied while walking back through the trees. "I heard you were thrown in here after running some sort of swindle in Jefferson City and came to offer you a proper job."

"We're a long way from Jefferson City," Deaugrey pointed out.

"That's right, because you pissed someone off there and then scampered all the way across the state before ending up in a hotel near the Arkansas border."

"Nice hotel. Excellent breakfasts. I recall you're fond of breakfast."

"I sure am, but I can do without being forced to pay for some crazy man's hotel bill just because I let it slip that he is a friend of mine."

Deaugrey smiled even wider while moseying along as if he were merely out to stretch his legs. "You said that? I'm touched."

"*Was* a friend of mine," Nate amended. "Them cordial notions turned mighty sour the longer I had to follow your crooked trail all the way up here."

Pressing a finger to Nate's chest, Deaugrey said, "You went through an awful lot of trouble to find me. That's the sort of thing a friend does."

"It's what a partner does and, God help me, I could use your talents for a job being offered to me and Frank."

"Frank's here?"

"He fired the rifle at you," Nate told him. "You might have seen as much if you would have slowed down long enough to look. Come to think of it, if you would have taken a breath somewhere amid all that running and screaming you might have seen *me* before throwing all of that damn silverware."

"It was a spoon," Deaugrey scoffed. "Surely you can't have gotten so soft that a spoon worries you?"

"You stuck a fork into one of them boy's shoulders."

"He was the one trying to feed me that god-awful soup." Having followed Nate far

enough out of the woods to sight the repurposed mansion, Deaugrey stopped and
placed his hands upon his hips. Only now
did he show the first signs of fatigue.
"What's this job you mentioned?"

"It's big."

"Do I get to hear more than that?"

"Not before those orderlies catch up to
us, and I'd rather get you away from here
than think of some excuse for the doctors
to turn you loose."

"You'd do that for me? I knew you still
called me friend."

Nate holstered the Remington and shoved
Deaugrey along, limp and all. "I'll get you
away from here because the pay for this job
is enough to make up for the trouble."

"What's my cut?"

"You get out of another asylum."

Deaugrey stopped and twisted his face
into a contemplative expression. "What happens if I refuse? These jobs of yours are
rarely without their dangers, and the worst
I get at McKeag's is bad soup fed to me by
lummoxes in smocks."

"If you refuse, I'll shoot you in the leg to
make sure you stay at McKeag's without
making such a pest of yourself."

"Would you honestly do that?" Deaugrey
gasped.

Nate's smirk could barely be seen. "What are friends for?"

3

The man who greeted Frank and Deaugrey upon entering Weslake's Finery was none other than Monty Weslake himself. He made that much clear the moment he spotted Frank from behind the tailor's frame that was being used to hold a silk waistcoat while it was being altered. The tailor's enthusiasm waned a bit when he saw Deaugrey step inside the shop wearing his filthy, rumpled and torn dressing gown.

"A good day to you, sir," Deaugrey said while tapping his fingers to his brow as though doffing a hat.

"Um . . . yes," Weslake said. "What can I do for you gentlemen?"

Frank stepped forward while adjusting his long black coat so it covered his guns while allowing his black shirt and starched white collar to be clearly seen. "My friend here is in need of some clothing."

"Recently discharged from McKeag's?"

the tailor asked.

"That's right. I suppose it's fairly obvious. A simple shirt and pair of pants will suffice."

"And a hat," Deaugrey added. "Don't forget the hat."

"Yes," Frank said. "Something simple."

Weslake approached a table of assorted selections folded into neat piles. "I hate to be one to question a man of God, but these items you're asking for . . . do you expect . . ."

Before the other man was forced to struggle even more with his words, Frank stepped in and told him, "While donations are always appreciated, I do have money to pay for these items."

"That's good to hear, Father," Weslake said. "Business has been rather slow lately."

Frank smiled and nodded once. "I understand."

"So do I," Deaugrey said. "I understand most folks only want to give to the poor when it suits them. They talk about charity only when they're in a room filled with a congregation that can appreciate what they've done out of the kindness of their hearts."

Weslake's brow furrowed. Looking down, he selected a shirt from the bottom of a pile and held it up to Deaugrey. "This is about your size. The collar is frayed and a few of the buttons are missing. I can let you have it for half price."

"Much obliged, sir," Deaugrey said with a slightly thicker Virginia drawl. He hiked up the bottom of his gown like a saloon girl showing her wares and added, "I can also use some knickers, if you don't mind."

Such a lewd display in his shop could only be greeted by disgust or uncomfortable laughter. Opting for the latter, Weslake selected a pair of dark brown pants that matched the shirt in quality. When he handed over a pair of long underwear, he added, "You can have these for free if you put them on immediately."

"Consider it done, my good man." With that, Deaugrey went completely against the shopkeeper's intent by stripping out of his gown and dressing himself in the middle of the store. He'd barely had a chance to button all of his buttons when he was distracted by a display of hats arranged on an iron rack.

Since he was the only one who took notice of Weslake's discomfort, Frank stepped up to him with cash in hand. "Here you go," he said. "I greatly appreciate your generosity."

When he saw how much money he was being given, Weslake brightened up a bit. "And I appreciate yours, Father. This here is enough to cover those clothes along with a hat from the lower part of that display."

"Excellent. What about boots?"

"And a gun!" Deaugrey chimed in.

"The shop next door sells any kind of boot you might need. Shoes too," Weslake said. "As for the gun . . ."

"Never mind the gun," Frank cut in. "You've been a great help. Thanks again."

Barefooted, his shirt open to display a pale bony torso, holding his pants up with one hand, Deaugrey said, "I can use some suspenders too."

Frank handed over a bit more cash to cover the request.

Deaugrey wasn't in much of a hurry to finish dressing. In fact, he seemed to lose interest with each task once he was slightly more than halfway through with it. They walked to the neighboring leather goods store to quickly purchase some boots. The owner of that place was more amused with Deaugrey than the tailor had been and sent them on their way with a mismatched pair of boots that had been pulled from a bin. Upon seeing the sign above the bin, Deaugrey laughed. "Irregulars," he said.

"How appropriate."

Frank paid for the boots without further explanation and showed the other man to the door. Once outside, Deaugrey was still hopping into his boots while Frank patiently followed behind with the newly purchased hat in hand.

"I owe you for these clothes and such," Deaugrey said.

"You owe us for a lot more than that if I recall."

"Oh, I suppose there was the matter of getting me out of that wretched sanitarium. I imagine Nate already has plenty of ways lined up for me to repay that debt."

"If you don't like that sanitarium or any of the others you've seen, then perhaps you shouldn't put yourself into them."

"I'm not the one who makes that arrangement," Deaugrey replied. "It's not like a hotel, you know. The folks who work there are usually quite insistent."

Now that Deaugrey was mostly dressed, Frank handed him the hat, a dented bowler that looked as if a small animal had chewed on the left section of its brim. "What was it this time?"

"Looking for a confession, Preacher?" Deaugrey said with disdain.

"Only if you're looking to give one."

Deaugrey stopped at the corner of the boardwalk and looked at the crossroads in front of him. He stood up straight, buttoned his last button and placed the bowler on top of his head as if he were about to address a small audience. "I've had quite my fill of those looking to dig around behind my eyes, thank you very much. Did that one there ask you to rake me over the coals?" he inquired while nodding a bit farther down the street where Nate stood leaning against a fence. Beside him was a hitching post where two horses and a mule were tied. "Having known him longer than you, I'd suggest you put your foot down with him every now and then before you become just another one of his dogs."

"Dogs?" Frank scoffed. "Is that what you think of the men who work with Nate?"

"Not all of them, but there are plenty."

"I can agree with that," Frank said. "Partially, at least. But you've known me for a while as well. You must know that I'll always want to know what causes a man to sin or what demons may be whispering into his ear."

Deaugrey smiled wide and said, "When those demons talk to me, padre, they sure as fuck don't whisper."

Frank wasn't about to flinch at the claim

34

or react in the slightest to the turn of phrase that was so obviously meant to jab at his sensibilities. Instead, he turned to look down the street intersecting with the one where Nate was waiting. "There'll be a posse coming for you eventually. That could be them right now."

When he saw the small group of men gathering at the other end of the block, Deaugrey shrugged. "It usually takes a bit longer for the assholes running those sanitariums to give up on their search and ask for help from the outside. I'd say we've got another hour or two at least."

"Then do you have a place to recommend where we might get a bite to eat?"

"Come now, holy man. There was a guiding hand that allowed us to take our leave from McKeag's house of horrors. I'd call it luck, but you may call it by a more fanciful name. Whatever name you prefer, I think we'd both agree it's best not to test its limits."

"If you think any sort of divine presence had a hand in what happened at that sanitarium, then you are more confounded than I'd imagined. It was undeniably luck," Frank sighed. "And it's best not to push it when it comes your way."

"On that," Deaugrey said, "we can agree.

There's nothing for us in this town anyway. Shall we take our leave?"

Frank threw an easy wave at the group of men who were now looking in his direction. "Sounds like a good idea," he said quietly. "And if you could resist the urge to raise your voice until we're gone, I'd be very appreciative."

"I suppose I can do that."

Both men strolled toward Nate at a brisk pace without appearing to be in a rush. "Since you're feeling so agreeable," Frank said, "perhaps you could answer a question for me."

"Depends on what the question is."

"Where were you keeping all of that silverware?"

Deaugrey looked over at Frank with a vaguely surprised grin on his face. Draping an arm over the other man's shoulders, he said, "There are some questions with obvious answers and some with answers you truly don't want to know. That question, my friend, is both."

Frank accepted that with a slow nod, which quickly built into heartfelt laughter. By the time they'd reached the spot where Nate was standing, Deaugrey had joined in the merriment as well. Nate took one last pull from his cigarette, flicked it on the ground and stomped it out beneath his foot. "I see you two are getting along better than usual," he said.

"At least he's good for a bit of conversation," Deaugrey said. "You've barely said two words to me since I agreed to come along."

" 'Agreed'?" Nate grunted. "I suppose you'd rather be rotting in that sanitarium."

"Not hardly." Stepping up to the tired gray mare standing next to Nate's gelding, Deaugrey patted the animal's flank and said, "She's not much to look at, but I suppose she'll do. I like the color."

"Thanks," Frank said. "Hopefully you like that one's color as well."

Glancing in one direction and then the other as if he didn't even see the mule, Deaugrey asked, "Which now?"

Frank pointed at the mule, but Deaugrey grimaced as if he'd just been asked to eat it raw. When he looked over to Nate, all he got was a nod. "You expect me to ride this out of town?" Deaugrey asked. "This?!"

"That or walk," Nate replied, "because you sure as hell ain't riding in the saddle behind me. The only ones who get to do that are a whole lot prettier than you."

"Don't look at me," Frank said. "My charity only extends so far."

"That's fine talk from the two of you. Especially since you expect me to offer my assistance on whatever treacherous outing you've lined up."

"You don't have to offer your assistance," Nate said while climbing into his saddle. "I'm taking it all the same."

"There's not even a saddle."

"We'll pick one up in the next town we find. This one's about to get too hot for us. There's a posse forming to hunt down the lunatic that escaped from McKeag's earlier today."

"Imagine that," Deaugrey mused. "Almost as frightening as the prospect of a man needing to ride across this great sprawling land of ours on the back of a mule."

"We're not crossing the country," Nate told him.

"Still . . . no saddle?"

"Do you have a blanket?"

"No."

Nate made a sound as if he were trying to suck something out from between his teeth. "Then I guess there's no saddle. Come along with me like we agreed or stay behind to face the music. Your choice." Without another word, Nate pointed his horse's nose away from the hitching post and flicked his reins. The spotted gelding took even less interest in Deaugrey's predicament than his rider had and ambled down the street with a casual swish of its tail.

"Here," Frank said, tossing a bundle to the man who stood watching Nate in disbelief.

Deaugrey caught the bundle as it unfolded to reveal itself as the dressing gown that had been wrapped around his body when he'd started his very eventful day. Despite all the hard times that utilitarian piece of clothing had seen him through, Deaugrey was none too appreciative for its return. "What am I supposed to do with this?"

"You take what you're given," the preacher said, "and be thankful you weren't forgotten altogether."

"Aw, to hell with this."

Shifting in his saddle, Frank swept aside his coat to show one of the .38s holstered at his hip. "Watch that tongue of yours, boy. Some of the Lord's servants are more forgiving than others."

Frank got his horse moving at a pace that would catch up to Nate's in roughly two miles. The expression on Deaugrey's face was a mix of aggravation and smugness. The latter threatened to overtake the former when it became clear that neither of the other men was going to turn around and force him to follow them. Elsewhere in town, a commotion was brewing that had the promise to become quite a storm. Among the shuffling of hooves against packed dirt, the words "capture" and "drag back" could be heard interspersed with "beat him to a pulp."

"God da—" Wincing as he looked at Frank's back, Deaugrey threw his old gown across the mule's back and climbed onto the tired animal. "Damn it," he grunted. "Just . . . damn it."

4

Kansas
Two days later
The clatter of shod hooves against dusty rock sang out behind Nate in an uneven staccato entwined with heavy, grunting breaths. By the time Deaugrey's mule caught up to his horse, Nate swore the sorry thing was going to flop over and die on the spot. At first, it overshot him. Then, after several frantic tugs on a set of old reins that had been coiled at the bottom of Frank's saddlebag for the better part of a year, Deaugrey fell behind once again.

"Jesus H. — Sorry, Reverend," Deaugrey said.

"I'm not a reverend," Frank said.

"Whatever. Will you let me catch up, Nate?"

"I'm not trying to stop you, Grey."

Finally pulling alongside Nate and then matching his speed through concerted effort and sheer force of will, the mule plodded next to the gelding like a duck trying to keep pace with a bobcat. "How much farther to that town you mentioned?" Deaugrey asked. "I think this animal you provided is about to drop."

"Shouldn't be far now."

"I hate to sound contrary, but didn't we pass a town just before we made camp last night?"

"That's not being contrary," Nate said. "That's just asking a question."

Flustered, Deaugrey twisted around to get a look at Frank. The man in the black coat and shirt nodded. "He's right. Being contrary means you go against most everything that's being said."

When Deaugrey looked back to him, Nate said, "You can look it up if you like."

"If you ever wonder why I sometimes lose my mind, all you'll have to do is think about moments like these."

"Speaking of that, how'd you wind up tossed into the bin this time, Grey?" Nate asked. "I heard about Jefferson City, but that would have landed you in a jail cell. What'd you do to convince folks you were too crazy to roam free? Burn down another restaurant?"

"I'm not talking about that. And in case

42

you've lost your memory, my name isn't Grey. It's Deaugrey. Dooooohgraaaay."

Nate shifted back and forth in his saddle, expertly acclimating to every movement of the horse beneath him. His head swayed ever so slightly and when it swung back toward Deaugrey, he raised an eyebrow and said, "Talking to me like that, like I'm an idiot child, it's a real good way to get yourself hurt."

"So's taunting a man who was, until very recently, considered dangerously unstable."

"Fair enough."

"So what's the job that was so important you came all this way to break one Virginian out of incarceration?"

Nate Sathow had seen many different brands of incarceration. Not one of them included renovated mansions, clean dressing gowns and rocking chairs. Rather than debate the finer points of misery with Deaugrey, Nate said, "I'd rather not get into it until we're all in one place."

"Can you at least tell me who 'we' are?"

"Sure. You, me, Frank and Pete."

After thinking for a few seconds, Deaugrey asked, "Pete who?" Suddenly, his eyes widened. "Not Pete Meyer."

"The same."

"That oaf knocked me unconscious the

last time we were forced to work on the same job!"

"Which is something damn near anyone who knows you has wanted to do at some time or another," Nate said.

When he glanced back at Frank, Deaugrey got an affirming nod from the preacher. Since he was getting no help there, Deaugrey said, "Well, I can't guarantee I won't lose my normally cheery disposition once we're in too close of a proximity."

"I'll roll those dice."

"What's the pay?"

"You'll like it just fine," Nate said.

When Deaugrey pulled back on his reins, he nearly slid out of the saddle they'd purchased the previous day. They hadn't been able to find anything priced within the pittance Nate had been willing to spend, so Deaugrey wound up sitting on a collection of leather scraps stitched together with twine. He didn't know the materials for certain, but the sore spots on his rump told Deaugrey that they surely hadn't been chosen by a true craftsman. "We've known each other a long time, Nate," he said. "And yes. I do owe you for getting me out of McKeag's but I'm not an indentured servant! I insist on knowing what I'm in for."

Since it was clear that the mule's rider

was even more stubborn than the animal itself, Nate brought his horse to a stop and turned it around. He approached Deaugrey, glaring down at him with enough fire in his eyes to make the mule shift nervously on its tired hooves. Finally, he said, "You're right."

"Yes," Deaugrey said in a valiant effort to keep from looking as if he'd dodged a bullet. "Of course I am."

"The pay is guaranteed to be at least two thousand each."

"Two thousand? I would think it would take a bit more than that for you to go through all the trouble of collecting me."

"Plus bonuses," Nate added.

Deaugrey's smile would have been just as fitting for a starving wolf. "Now you're talking! What kind of bonuses?"

"The man we're after has been on the run for a time and has plenty of men who want him brought back. If we can make a list of the names of anyone willing to help this son of a bitch, we'll be paid extra. If we bring in the sons of bitches themselves, that's even more."

For the first time in quite a while, Deaugrey didn't have a response cocked and loaded. Far from stunned, he merely nodded slowly as the wheels inside his arguably derailed mind began to turn.

"And then there are the acquaintances," Frank said from the rear of the small procession.

"Acquaintances?" Deaugrey asked.

"Oh yes," Nate replied with a similarly wolfish smile. "Between the man we're after and the bastards lending him a hand in remaining free while killing anyone he pleases, there will be plenty of assholes trying to join up with them. The sorts of assholes who commit their own list of sins."

"The kind of sins that put a price on a man's head," Frank said.

"Well now," Deaugrey said as he turned in his saddle to get a look behind him. "That's something you'd know all about, Preacher."

"Indeed it is."

"Is that enough to get your ass moving again?" Nate asked.

Deaugrey reached out to pat his animal's neck. "Oh! You mean the mule?"

"Whatever floats your boat."

When Deaugrey snapped his reins, he barely caught the mule's interest. After a few taps of his heels against its sides, the mule started walking again. "How long will we be out and about looking for these miscreants?"

"As long as it takes to find 'em."

"And I don't suppose you know where to find Pete . . . exactly?"

"He should still be in a town called Marlonn no more than another half day's ride from here."

Deaugrey's avarice lit him up from within like a candle inside a lantern. "What are we waiting for, then?" he said while snapping his reins. "Let's proceed!"

Although the proclamation would have been more dramatic if his mule clopped forward at more than a purposeful walk, Frank and Nate still followed his example.

5

Marlonn, Kansas

By the time they arrived in town, the sun was nowhere to be found. Its warmth had remained for a short amount of time before being dispersed by the shadows that had rolled in to claim the barren Kansas landscape. Marlonn was a simple cow town and not a very impressive one at that. As he rode from one street to another, Nate barely took time to look at the darkened windows or take notice of the faces staring out from behind them. Frank rode close to Deaugrey where he could occasionally tell him to remain calm and keep his mouth shut.

"Don't you tell me to stay calm," Deaugrey snapped. "There's eyes watching us from everywhere and they're not the sort that them doctors tell me about. You should be able to see 'em too!"

"I do see them," Frank assured him. "So long as they keep their distance, they offer no threat."

"You may be accustomed to the presence of unseen spirits, but I assure you they don't all answer prayers and turn water into wine."

Under most circumstances, Frank could let Deaugrey's words roll off his back. This wasn't one of them, and the preacher reared up to unleash all the fire and brimstone he could muster. Knowing all too well what was coming, Nate cut him off in a hurry. "Enough of that, the both of you," he said.

Frank and Deaugrey bit their tongues.

"We're to meet Pete at that saloon right there," Nate said while pointing to an establishment that had more activity flowing in and around it than the rest of the town combined. "If you're gonna insist on squabbling like children, then go rent a room and stay in it!"

"You'll let me go into the saloon?" Deaugrey asked.

So far, Nate had insisted that the crazy man stay away from any of the saloons they'd passed. There were plenty of good reasons for that, the least of which was Deaugrey's tendency to flap his gums.

"Yes," Nate said. "You can go into this one. Just try not to get too drunk too fast."

"I'll need a gun," Deaugrey said. "In case things get rough."

"Give him a gun, Frank."

Drawing one of his .38s, Frank spun the pistol around to slap the grip into Deaugrey's hand.

That kept everyone satisfied for the time it took them to ride up to the Three Dog Saloon and tie their horses next to a water trough. As the animals slaked their thirst, Nate walked inside the saloon. When Deaugrey started to walk forward, he was stopped by one of Frank's outstretched arms.

"Hang back for a spell," the preacher said.

Deaugrey nodded and stared at the front window as though he could see all the way through to the exact bottle he meant to bring to his lips.

The Three Dog was a large place with a bar taking up one wall and a small stage situated against the opposite wall. In between were at least two dozen tables, the largest of which were being used for card games of all sorts. Clusters of drunken cowboys bucked the tiger at one of three faro tables near the back and women of all shapes and sizes wandered through the crowd until they were summoned by a wandering hand or hungry stare.

Nate strode to the bar and was jostled along the way by a stumbling drunk. "Watch where you're walking, asshole!" the drunk snarled. When he got a good look at the gruesome promise etched into Nate's eyes, the drunk was all too happy to turn his attention elsewhere and stagger away.

Upon reaching the bar, Nate rapped his knuckles against the polished wooden surface to catch the ear of one of the two tenders on duty. The woman who responded to his summons was a stout lady in her late forties with long dark hair and a bosom that spilled up and slightly over the top edge of her corset. She smiled warmly at him and asked, "What's your pleasure, mister?"

"I'm looking at it," Nate said.

Although she clearly wasn't new to being propositioned in any number of ways, the lingering smile on her face showed she didn't exactly mind it this time. "Why don't you start with a drink?"

"Gladly. Set me up with the house specialty and a cigar."

She turned around amid the rustle of skirts so she could reach for a bottle on the shelf behind her. When she bypassed the expensive labels for something with a handwritten label, Nate suspected she might actually be filling his request instead of passing off a brand of liquor that would demand the highest price. Once she poured the drink, she reached beneath the bar to give him a lingering view down the front of her dress.

The whiskey was smooth and cut nicely through the trail dust that had gathered in the back of Nate's throat. He exhaled as it continued to burn all the way down to his stomach. Before he could lift the glass again, another scent caught his attention. It was the combination of a fine cigar and the perfumed hand holding it. "Thanks," he said while taking the cigar from the bartender.

She was quick with a match and snapped her wrist to extinguish the little flame as soon as the tip of Nate's cigar began to glow. "Anything else I can get for you?"

"Sure. You wouldn't happen to know anyone named Pete, would ya?"

"Can you be a little more specific?"

"Pete Meyer."

Her eyes widened a little and she nodded. "Oh yes. I know him all right. If you're a friend of his, you might want to loan him some money. He needs it."

"He always needs it," Nate sighed. "Where is he?"

She pointed toward a section of tables near the back of the room within spitting distance of the faro games. No more than that was needed since it would take a blind man to overlook Pete Meyer in just about any sort of crowd. The man's wide back, thick shoulders and shaggy hair made him stand out even more among the group of well-dressed gamblers sitting at his table.

"How much is he in for?" Nate asked.

The barkeep picked up some dirty glasses and started wiping them off. "Couldn't tell you about the gambling losses, but I hear they're considerable. He owes me for a whole lot of drinks though."

Nate thought back to the last few times he'd drank with Pete and sorted through the cash that was in his pocket. Handing over his closest guess plus a bit more, he asked, "Will this cover it?"

Taking the money, flipping through the bills and depositing them in the bank between her large breasts, she said, "Almost."

"Damn. How long has he been playing?"

"Better part of two days."

"Shit."

"Yeah," she chuckled. "That about sums up his run of luck."

After downing the rest of his drink, Nate made his way through the saloon. He wasn't about to lollygag but also didn't stride right up to Pete's table and demand a moment of his time. He'd had plenty of hard nights at the card tables, and Nate knew the last thing he would want is someone coming out of nowhere to give him a lecture or try to pull him away when his luck might be ready to take a turn for the better.

Pete's face was covered in thick whiskers, which did next to nothing to hide the solemn frown he wore. That might have been somewhat telling if Pete weren't so known to rarely do anything but frown. All Nate had to look at for the rest of the story were the stacks of chips in front of each man. Pete's wasn't the shortest stack, but two of the other men had enough chips in front of them to buy a sizeable portion of Texas.

Standing behind one of the empty chairs, Nate asked, "Mind if I sit in for a hand or two?"

The man who answered him sat directly across from Nate. He was slender, somewhere in his early thirties and had the chiseled features of someone who'd never had to do much to win a woman's attention. He wore a suit cut from expensive dark-blue silk and spoke in a steely, subdued tone. "As long as you can cover your bets, you're welcome to stay."

To Nate's right was a short man with

thick, powder-white hair and a bulbous nose. Small, beady eyes gazed out at the world through thick spectacles. He wore a dark suit and matching top hat which gave him a stately air. Pete sat between him and the handsome younger fellow. To Nate's immediate left was a man with a wide face, earnest eyes and tousled blond hair. Nate was suspicious of him almost immediately after having been burned too many times by baby-faced poker players.

While the blond man shuffled the cards, the gentleman in the blue suit said, "What's your name, friend?"

"Nate Sathow."

Pete had yet to respond to Nate with anything other than a half-interested glance.

The well-dressed man in blue said, "I'm Jim. The fellow beneath the top hat is Wilson. Sourpuss next to me is Pete and the dealer's Owen."

"No last names?" Nate asked.

"This ain't a social gathering," Pete growled. "We're here to play cards and that," he added while pointing a warning glare in Nate's direction, "is all I care to do."

"Seems like you're doing pretty well for yourself," Nate said.

"He would be doing just fine," Owen said,

"if he hadn't borrowed all that money in front of him from me to cover his losses."

Jim added, "And he'd be doing even better if he hadn't also borrowed from me to cover his losses from before Owen sat down."

Nate raised his eyebrows and looked over at Pete with genuine surprise. "Damn. You really aren't doing too well."

"What do you care, mister?" Owen asked. "You two know each other?"

"We've done some work together," Pete said before Nate had a chance to say a word. "Ain't nothin' more than that."

"Perhaps I could have a word with my friend here," Nate said. "And then I can leave you gentlemen to your game."

Jim slowly shook his head. "Afraid not, mister. You sat down, so you're going to play."

As he stared into Jim's eyes, Nate saw a whole lot more than he'd seen a few moments ago. In fact, the longer he sat there, the more he felt like he was looking up at everyone else from within the jaws of a trap that had just been sprung. "What are you going to do if I get up and leave?" Nate asked.

"I'll have my boys at the next table gut you so fast you'll be staring down at your own innards before your ass leaves that chair."

Nate's hand was close to his holstered Remington. His body remained coiled like a spring as his eyes slowly surveyed the nearby tables. Sure enough, there were two men sitting at the one to his left who glared right back at him. Three more that were seated behind Pete shifted to look at Nate while showing the pistols laying across their knees.

"You come along to help Pete here?" Jim asked.

Nate shook his head and laughed uncomfortably when he said, "I just got into town. If you have business with him, I can leave you to it."

Owen smirked. "That's a real shitty way to treat a friend."

"Yeah well, friend or not, you're staying put," Jim said like he was already holding a winning hand. "When our business is through, I'll decide whether you walk out of here or get dropped into the same hole I've already dug out back for Pete."

6

They were biding their time. The methods may have been heavy-handed and their precautions somewhat extreme, but that was all it boiled down to. In Nate Sathow's line of work, he gained the most ground through a simple talent of getting to the root of something and figuring out what needed to be done. Of course, one of those tasks was often much simpler than the other.

"I need to get up," Nate said.

"Why?" Owen grunted as he sorted the five cards in his hand.

"To stretch my legs. I've been sitting here for over an hour."

"We been sitting here a hell of a lot longer than that!"

"Then you must have chamber pots under your chairs because I've got to take a piss."

"Why didn't you say so?"

Nate slapped his cards facedown as if he meant to shove them through the table and into the floor. "Because I'm not in the habit of explaining myself to the likes of you!"

"For Christ's sake," Jim said. "There's an outhouse in the alley. Avery will show you."

"I don't need an escort," Nate said.

"And we don't need to let you leave this table," Jim hissed.

After a small bit of consideration, Nate shoved his chair back and stood up. "Fine then. Let's go."

Jim's eyes darted down to Nate's holster and back up again. "You've gone this far without trying anything stupid. Don't get any ideas now."

"You've got me covered front, back and at least one side. What the hell am I supposed to do?"

Whether Jim took any comfort from that was unclear. He eventually nodded to Avery who stepped over to Nate like the good attack dog he so obviously was. "This is nothing against you, Nate," Jim said. "You just have bad timing is all. This thing here is almost over. Stick it through without a fuss and I may even pay you for your time."

"Just let me keep my winnings. That should suffice."

"Winnings?" Jim said through a chuckle. "That's funny."

When Nate turned away from the table,

Avery was on his feet and standing directly behind him. Not only did Avery outweigh him by at least sixty pounds, but his pistol was already drawn and held in an easy grip that kept the weapon near his side so as not to attract much attention.

"Your gun," Avery said. "I'm taking it."

Since there were still at least four other gun hands around him, not counting the other players at the table, Nate held his arms out to the sides and let the Remington be taken from him. "I was wondering when you might get around to that," he said.

Avery stashed the Remington under his own gun belt and holstered the pistol he'd drawn. "Thought you might save me the trouble and do something stupid. Makes a mess, but at least I wouldn't have to drag you to no shit house."

"Well ain't we both just inconvenienced?"

Pushing Nate in front of him, Avery herded him through the saloon toward a side door. Along the way, Nate spotted at least one familiar face sitting at one of the other poker games. He kept that bit of information to himself and quickly opened the saloon's side door before he was shoved through it by the hulking gunman behind him.

The outhouse was large enough to serve

the needs of a place the size of the Three Dog. It was wide as a closet and about four times as long. As Nate discovered when he pulled open the only door into the structure that meant it could contain four times the stench of a regular outhouse.

"You coming in with me?" Nate asked.

"If you wanna crawl away through one of them holes in the floor, be my guest," Avery replied. He then stepped back so he could get a look at a pair of saloon girls tempting passersby while also watching the alley.

Nate entered the outhouse and shut the door. One quick glance was all he needed to confirm that there was only one easy way in or out. Half of the squalid chamber contained a long bench sectioned into a row of five holes. Two men sat doing their business. One of them appeared to have fallen asleep sometime while answering nature's call. The other fellow stood facing the opposite wall which wasn't much more than a low trough with a long slit at the bottom that emptied into a ditch beneath the shack. After draining his bladder, that man wheeled around to walk past Nate and get back to whatever pleasures he'd put on hold inside the saloon.

The conditions were far from ideal, but at least Nate had a moment to himself so he could think. Also, it wasn't just a ruse that had drawn him away from the table. He stood at the trough and stared at the rotting wall directly in front of him. Within seconds, the entire shack rattled on its base as the door was opened so another man could step inside. He was dressed in black and stood directly beside Nate between him and the door.

"Naturally," Nate grumbled. "A man can't get a moment's peace."

"If you'd rather," Frank replied, "I can leave. Thought you might appreciate a word. Isn't that why you came out here?"

"Partly."

"What's going on in there? At first, I thought it was an ill-advised impulse that brought you to that card game but when I went to check on you I saw the armed men watching that table."

"Pete's in trouble," Nate said. "The men running that game don't want him to leave for some reason and I'm fairly certain they intend on killing him after they're through."

"Through with what?"

"Don't know yet. But I'd wager those men inside are the only ones we need to worry about."

"I didn't see anyone overly suspicious outside the saloon," Frank said, "but that doesn't mean they aren't there."

"If they had more men, they wouldn't be so hell-bent on keeping us at that table."

Frank knew better than to question his partner's instincts on such things. Those instincts were what separated Nate from the common variety of bounty hunter. "I sent Grey in for a look as well," he said.

"I saw him in there," Nate replied. "Playing poker. Tell him to be ready."

"For anything in particular or just the general readiness?"

"When I make my move, I'll need you both to follow my lead. We'll have to move quick and bring them all down at once before they get a chance to put a bullet into me or Pete. Or you, for that matter."

"That saloon is a fairly public place for an execution," Frank said.

"All those dandies will have to do is accuse me or Pete of cheating and they'll be justified in shooting us."

The entire shack trembled as an impatient fist thumped against the door. "Hurry it up!" Avery said from outside.

The thumping was enough to rouse the man who'd fallen asleep. He snapped to attention, stood up and started grasping clumsily for his britches. "I'm comin', Margaret, I'm comin'!" he slurred.

Although the drunk seemed to be in a hurry, it was the man who'd been sitting on the bench to his right that got to the door first and hurried outside.

Having finished his business, Nate made himself presentable for the outside world and whispered, "Whatever happens, see to it the man in the blue suit stays alive."

"I'd prefer if you all stayed alive," Frank said earnestly.

Nate gave him a quick pat on the shoulder. "I know, Shep. That's what makes you a better man than me." He left the outhouse and was immediately grabbed by Avery who slammed him against a wall.

"Just checking to see if you grabbed anything other than your pecker in there," Avery said while patting Nate down. Once he was satisfied that Nate hadn't found a weapon hidden somewhere amid the filth, Avery spun Nate around and shoved him toward the door that led back into the saloon.

Without wasting a second, Nate spun around and slapped aside Avery's hand before delivering a sharp jab to the other man's stomach. Having already sized up his opponent, Nate knew better than to think that single blow would do the trick so he followed up with three more. His fists landed in a series of solid thumps against muscle that felt like bricks wrapped in a shirt and vest. Avery grunted as he absorbed the punches, which didn't stop him from reaching for his holster.

Not only did Nate get to Avery's gun first, but he also retrieved his Remington from where it had been stashed. Jamming both barrels into Avery's midsection, Nate said, "Tell me what's going on with Pete and those assholes at the card table."

"Go to hell."

"You really want to die for a dandy wrapped in a blue suit?"

It didn't take long for Avery to come up with an answer to that. Sneering down at Nate, he said, "The owner of the Three Dog hired Pete to find who's been stealing from every saloon in town. He found out who it was, but not before he got caught."

"Caught by Jim?" Nate asked. "He's the one running the outfit, right?"

"That's right."

"And Jim caught Pete while Pete was tracking him down?"

"Yeah."

Nate scowled at the other man. Even more questions were coming to mind, but he knew he didn't have enough time to ask them all. "What's going on at that card game?"

"There's one more saloon robbery on Jim's slate," Avery said. "It's a big one and he's not about to let Pete ruin it by talking to any law or causing a ruckus that will draw attention to what's going on."

"And what happens once the job is through?"

"Hell if I know."

Nate jammed the gun barrels in deeper as if he meant to dig two holes through the other man's torso. Thumbing back the hammers to get his point across, he said, "The hell you *don't* know. You aim to kill him."

"It's Jim's idea," Avery spat. "His plan. His call on whether Pete lives or dies. What's important is that plenty of folks see him at that game when the robbery is taking place so nobody can pin it on him and haul him away to jail."

"He's getting hauled away, all right," Nate growled. "If not to jail, then his carcass will be shot full of holes and hauled into a grave." Before he could get much further along those lines, Nate felt a hand come to a gentle rest upon his shoulder.

"Easy, Nate," Frank said. "Let's not attract any undue suspicion ourselves."

"Too late for that."

"Not as such. So far, we can be passed off as three men settling a disagreement. You go into that saloon guns blazing and we'll have to come up with a few answers of our own."

"I can handle that," Nate assured him.

"That tin you carry may not cut it if you show it while surrounded by a stack of dead bodies."

Avery was starting to show some hope thanks to Frank's intervention, but Nate put a stop to that by pressing one of the gun barrels beneath his chin. Nate's glare left no room for doubt that he would pull the trigger if it came down to it.

"Who hired Pete to track down your employer?" Frank asked.

"The barkeep," Avery replied. "That woman with the nice, juicy —"

"I know the one you're talking about," Frank cut in. "And where is the place that's set to get robbed?"

"Across town," Avery said. "Place called the Wagon Rut."

"I saw that saloon when I came into town," Nate said. "Didn't look like any sort of place worth robbing."

"No, but the card game held in the back room sure is."

"We can go there to have a look for

ourselves," Frank said. "And if this one is lying . . ."

Nate took a step back from the larger man. "If he's lying then he won't ever wake up." With that, he snapped the pistol beneath Avery's jaw straight up and followed up by cracking the pistol against his temple. Avery dropped like a sack of rocks and Nate holstered his Remington. "They'll be expecting us back inside soon."

"I doubt we'll be gone long," Frank said. "Since you seem to scout every place that serves liquor as soon as you ride into a town, I'm assuming you know a quick route to the Wagon Rut."

"I do."

"Then you'll go there and brew up some trouble for your friend Jim."

Nate's eyes narrowed suspiciously. "What sort of trouble?"

"Remember how we brought in the Lowell gang up in Oregon a few years back?"

A smile crept onto Nate's face. "Ahh, yes. I see where you're headed."

"You go take care of those robbers and I'll set things up here. Grey is already making himself comfortable inside, so it shouldn't be too difficult."

"If I'm not back in a few minutes, you and Grey get out of town as fast as you can.

I don't meet up with you in an hour . . . you'll ride on without me."

"Things would be a lot simpler if I'd found a nice quiet congregation somewhere," Frank grumbled.

"Yeah, but you'd be bored out of your skull in a matter of days."

The preacher may have stalked away wringing his hands, but he didn't deny a word of what his partner had said.

7

As a testament to truth in advertising, the Wagon Rut was built in a large ditch. Despite the number of horses tied outside, Nate only found two men drinking inside the saloon when he stepped through the batwing doors.

"What can I get for ya?" the scrawny bartender asked.

There were three card tables in the place and enough dust caked on them to choke a buffalo. When he spotted the unmarked door at the back of the room, Nate strode past the bar and said, "I can help myself just fine, thanks."

"Hey! You're not allowed back there!"

Nate ignored the bartender's protests. Before he got to the back door, however, he heard heavy footsteps approaching him from behind. Pivoting on the balls of his feet, Nate waited just long enough to read the harmful intent on the faces of the two men who'd been sitting with their drinks just a few moments ago. He snapped a straight punch to the closest one's nose, sending a spray of blood and a stream of obscenities from that one's face. The second reached for a pistol at his side, but wasn't quick enough to clear leather before Nate brought his Remington to bear. Even though the man in front of him knew better than to make another move, Nate smirked and took his shot anyway.

All three men flinched reflexively when the gunshot exploded through the saloon. The man standing in Nate's line of fire paled considerably. It wasn't until he felt the patter of wood splinters and grit from the ceiling against his face that he realized Nate had shifted his aim to send his bullet into the rafters overhead.

Nate stepped to one side while drawing the pistol he'd taken from Avery from under his belt. A heartbeat later, the door at the back of the saloon was pulled open so a small group of men could spill into the main room.

"What the hell?" bellowed a man with a round face and a mustache that had been waxed into a straight line below his nose. Upon seeing Nate, he said, "You'd best have a damn good explanation, mister."

"These men are here to rob you," Nate said while glaring intently at the group that was still inside the back room. The group stood gathered around two card tables that were piled high with chips, cash, a few gold coins and several other trinkets that had been tossed in to cover some major bets.

"Which men?" asked the fellow who'd been first to step through the door.

Staring into the next room as though he could see into the soul of every last one of its inhabitants, Nate said, "Jim sent them. The tracker hired by the barkeep at the Three Dog found out that him, Wilson and Owen all threw in together to clean out the lot of you."

The round-faced fellow wheeled around to get a look at the group behind him. "I know it ain't the two of you, since you're my kin and . . ."

Nate didn't need to worry about figuring out who Round Face was talking to. A surprise visit from a stranger combined with the gunshot, some already highly strung nerves and guilty consciences were more than enough to flush out the ones he was after. Three of the gamblers who'd remained in the room separated from the group and drew their pistols.

Round Face turned his back on Nate so

he could look directly at those three when he said, "You sons of bitches."

One of the other men who'd stepped out of the back room with Round Face hadn't forgotten about Nate. He carried a shotgun in both hands, which he kept aimed at Nate's belly. Since it seemed he'd done more than enough already, Nate was willing to drop his guns and keep both hands held high.

"My cousin Jerry recommended you," Round Face snarled. "I knew he needed money, but . . . robbing *me*?"

"It was Jim's idea," one of the three bandits said. "This don't have to get bloody."

"Jim means to see to it that you're run out of town with your tail between your legs!" Nate said.

After glancing over his shoulder at Nate, Round Face looked back at the bandits and asked, "That true, McNabb?"

Although McNabb had been the spokesman for the bandits until now, he suddenly seemed to be at a loss for words. "I don't — that's not — we ain't even seen that man before!"

"Bullshit!" Nate hollered. The plan was to stir things up at this saloon and all he had to do to make that happen was twitch just enough to be noticed, but not so much that it caused the fellow with the shotgun to pull his triggers.

Whether McNabb and the other two were responding to that movement or working on a schedule of their own would remain unknown. McNabb reached for his pistol and the other two bandits were quick to follow. After that, Round Face and everyone else who'd been inside that back room pulled their pistols and unleashed four kinds of hell.

Nate kept his hands where they could be seen and waited for the man with the shotgun to shift his aim toward the back room. By the time Round Face dropped, two of the bandits and half of the remaining gamblers were down as well. McNabb fired a shot a split second before the shotgunner could defend himself. Lead burned through the air to clip the shotgunner's upper arm and send him staggering back. Another shot came soon after, but didn't finish the shotgunner off. Instead, Nate had picked up his Remington and drilled a fresh hole through McNabb's head just above his left eye.

The shotgunner brought his weapon around while blinking in confusion. Although he could have been shot several times over by then, he was only worried about the deep gouge in his arm. Nate was still on one knee after scooping up his gun. He holstered the Remington and raised his hands once again.

"Goddamn it, God*damn it*!" Round Face hollered.

One of the surviving gamblers helped him to his feet. "You all right, Daniel?"

"Caught a bullet through a rib, but I suspect I'll live." Looking around until he spotted Nate, he pointed his pistol at him and snarled, "You!"

"He's the one that finished McNabb," the shotgunner quickly said.

"I know that! I just . . ." Suddenly realizing he wasn't just pointing a finger at Nate, Daniel holstered his pistol and asked, "How the hell did you know about this?"

"I'm a friend of the tracker that was sent to sniff out Jim and his men," Nate explained.

"Well give him my thanks. If he wants to point me in the direction of the bastard who tried to steal from me, there'll be a payment coming."

"That," Nate replied, "will be no trouble at all."

8

Four men stormed through the front doors of the Three Dog saloon. Since all of them already had their guns drawn, they attracted plenty of attention from the men hired to keep the peace among the drunks and gamblers. When one of the saloon gun hands approached him, Daniel spoke to him in a voice that couldn't quite be heard. Whatever Daniel said was enough to get the other man to quickly back away.

Nate, Daniel, the shotgunner with the bleeding upper arm and one more of Daniel's men walked past the bar on their way to the card tables.

Frank watched all of this from his spot at the far end of the bar. Upon making eye contact with Nate, he waited for the signal before doing anything more. He got the nod right away and eased his hand down to one of the .38s holstered under his black coat.

"I see you back there, Jim Harrold!" Daniel shouted.

Still sitting at the table that was now in Daniel's sights, Pete turned to get a look at what was going on. There were still two of Jim's boys sitting behind him. When one of those gunmen made a move toward Pete, he was stopped by a short, narrow blade that suddenly poked him between two ribs. "Not another move, friend," Deaugrey whispered as he tightened his grip on the knife in his hand. With a motion that was almost too quick to see, he reached over to snatch the pistol from the gunman's holster. Pointing the gun at the next closest of Jim's men, Deaugrey added, "You neither. Just sit back and keep still. Real, real still."

A good portion of the customers within the saloon had stopped what they were doing. After getting a look at what was going on, many of them found somewhere else to be so they wouldn't be caught in an untenable position if things went from bad to worse. Frank navigated through the milling crowd to get closer to the poker table at the eye of the storm.

Jim leaned back in his chair with his hands flat on the table. The expression on his face made it seem as if he were simply enjoying a show instead of looking down the wrong end of several guns. "That you, Daniel?" he asked.

"You know damn well who it is," Daniel replied. "I'm the man you meant to rob."

"I've been here all night long. The only men I can rob are the ones who try to bluff me in this here game."

"We don't want any trouble," the barkeep said. When Nate walked over to her, she began to reach beneath the bar.

"Whatever weapon you mean to retrieve," Nate said as he placed his Remington on the bar so it was pointed at her, "just leave it where it is while this plays out."

She held her trembling hands where he could see them.

"What did you tell these men, Sathow?" Jim asked.

"Don't worry about him," Daniel said. "Worry about *me*! Is it true that you sent those boys to rob me?"

"Get the hell out of my sight before I have my men burn you down." When he didn't get a response from any of those men, Jim stood up and turned around to look behind him. Avery's seat was still empty, and one other sat with a shotgun across his lap. "Wake up, damn it," Jim snapped as he swatted the shotgunner with the back of his hand.

Nate could already feel the tension in the air, and when the shotgunner behind Jim started to get out of his seat, one of Daniel's men didn't take too kindly to it and fired at the poker table, which sent everyone in the saloon scattering for cover. The gunmen sitting with Deaugrey tried getting up and turning to face the skinny man between them. Deaugrey was no stranger to using a blade, and he stuck it deep between one man's ribs to skewer his heart. He then grabbed the dying man's arm to swing him around and catch a bullet fired from a holdout pistol that had been kept in the second gunman's pocket.

Owen stood up and overturned the card table so it could be used as a barrier. Unfortunately, Wilson wound up on the wrong side of that barrier and caught the lion's share of a barrage of lead sent by Daniel and his men.

"Pssst," came a voice from over Owen's shoulder.

When Owen turned to look, he was greeted by the sight of a madman crawling toward him like an animal. He squeezed off a shot, but was too rushed to hit its skinny target. Letting out a shrieking laugh that could barely be heard over the general insanity filling the saloon, Deaugrey grabbed a handful of Owen's hair, yanked his head back and slit his throat.

"Holy Lord!" Jim said when he caught sight of all that blood. "What the hell is happening?"

The shooting was over. The air inside the saloon was heavy with smoke that churned slowly around the heads of the men who were still on their feet. Everyone else was either huddled beneath something solid or would never stand again.

Nate was still at the bar with his gun resting on the polished wooden surface pointed in the general direction of the lady barkeep. He'd been ready to defend himself, but hadn't needed to move a muscle. "You happy with what you started?" he asked.

The woman behind the bar stood frozen with her hands stretched toward whatever weapon was stashed nearby. "I didn't —"

"Don't give me that. I just rode into town, but I can see clear as day that you're the one who put all of this into motion. Your place was probably the only one that wasn't robbed. That means not only do you get a cut of the haul from the robberies, but this saloon becomes the place where everyone wants to spend their money."

"It . . . wasn't supposed to be like this."

Daniel had stepped up to the bar as well,

announcing his presence by slamming down his still-smoking gun. "McNabb is dead."

Those words shattered her spirit just as surely as a brick shatters a plate-glass window. The expression on the bartender's face shifted from sadness all the way into fury as she said, "You shouldn't have started your own games, Daniel! I warned you not to draw so many gamblers away from the Three Dog and look what happened!"

"The gamblers go where they go, Rita. It's always been that way." Daniel walked around behind the bar and helped himself to some whiskey. "That's why you sent Jim after me and mine?"

She didn't say anything to that, but the way she hung her head spoke volumes.

"And I suppose you were intending on backing any story Jim gave as to his innocence when it came time to hand someone over to the law?"

The barkeep hung her head so low that it seemed she would never find the strength to lift it again.

Jim was shoved forward by Pete who had the other man's arm locked behind his back. "I've been sitting here playing cards all night!" Jim said. "I've got witnesses!"

"Shut your mouth, Jim," Daniel sighed. Looking past him to Pete, he asked, "Ain't I seen you around here the last week or two?"

"Probably," Pete replied.

Waving a tired hand at the barkeep, Daniel asked, "Is this the woman who hired you?"

"That's right. After the second robbery in town, she put me on the trail of Cal Worsham. Took me just a day or two to find him holed up outside of town in a shed that could barely stop a passing breeze."

"What did Cal do to anyone?"

"Not a damn thing," Pete replied. "Near as I could tell, he didn't even drink, but Rita swore he was the man behind all of them robberies as well as the ones that happened later on. The only use Cal had for a saloon was to buy himself some company of the feminine persuasion, but he went to a cathouse out near the train station a few miles from here when the urge struck, and that place was never even robbed."

"How do you know all that?"

"I tracked him there," Pete replied simply. "It's what I do. Didn't take much to realize that was about the only place he ever went. After looking a bit closer at some things, it wasn't too hard to find out Jim was the man committing them robberies and someone from this saloon was setting them up."

Keeping her head low, the barkeep turned

so she didn't have to look at any of the men in front of her. Daniel wasn't having any of that and lunged over the bar to grab her chin and pull her around. "There was plenty of business to go around, you greedy bitch!" Daniel roared. "We all had a good thing going and you had to get greedy!"

"Here," Pete said as he shoved Jim toward one of Daniel's men. "I was hired to find the ones responsible for robbing those saloons, and there's one of them. She's the other. I'm done."

Daniel surveyed the saloon with careful eyes. "Where's the rest of your boys, Jim?"

"Forget about them," Frank said while emerging from the crowd of customers that were leaving their various hiding spots. "If there's any more, they're too yellow to be a concern to us." He held one of the men who'd been guarding Jim's table at the other end of his .38. Not only did the hired gun have no more fight in him but he seemed ready to face whatever indignity fate had in store for him next.

"Leave him," Daniel said. "Is he the last one, Rita?"

"Does it matter?" she sighed.

Staring at her with cruel satisfaction, Daniel replied, "No. I suppose it doesn't."

Slowly, Nate and Pete stepped away from

the bar and headed for the front door.

Slowly, the rest of the customers in the saloon resumed whatever it was they'd been doing before the interruption.

Not so slowly, Frank handed his prisoner off to Daniel's man and snagged Deaugrey by the collar.

"What are you doing?" Deaugrey asked. "I'm about to get dealt back into my game!"

"We're leaving."

"Do you know how long it's been since I've sat down to a decent game?"

"If we don't go right now I suspect we won't be able to go for quite a while," Frank told him. "Men were killed here and questions tend to follow a thing like that. Unless you fancy being in yet another cage, settle up and come with me."

Covered in blood and looking every bit like someone who'd elbowed his way through a brawl, Deaugrey looked at each of the gamblers at his table one by one. "Sorry, but I suppose I should leave. Are these my winnings here?"

"Yep!" one of the men said as he shoved some of the scattered coins and bills toward him. "That about does it."

After scooping up the money, Deaugrey allowed himself to be led away from the table. Leaning over to Frank, he whispered,

"I think I got more than my share."

"I don't think they mind," the preacher said while taking back the .38 he'd lent him.

Indeed, like many folks who found themselves suddenly not having to deal with Deaugrey Scott, the remaining gamblers at that table seemed much happier than they'd been before.

As the general commotion inside the saloon rose back to a normal roar, Nate and the rest of his group drifted toward the front door. Once outside, they wasted no time getting to their horses and getting the hell out of Marlonn.

9

Fortunately, it was a clear night because Nate insisted on riding with nothing but light from the stars to guide them. The horses and the mule plodded along at an easy pace, which, combined with the general flatness of Kansas terrain, allowed the small group to get a few miles outside of town where they found a spot to camp.

The words passing between the men were clipped and concise.

Only the most necessary of facts were passed back and forth, half of which were repeated requests for Deaugrey to shut the hell up.

They'd all worked together enough to know better than to waste any opportunity to get a few hours of sleep.

The following morning started off just as quiet as the previous night had ended. All four men slept just past dawn before coming around, building a fire and digging through their saddlebags for fixings to make breakfast. Frank found some salted ham and beans while Nate brewed some chicory coffee. Deaugrey wasn't very fond of mornings in general and sat hunched over with his eyes trained upon the fire, looking every bit the opposite of the man he'd been the night before.

More than half an hour passed before the tranquil silence of a cool, sunny morning was broken.

"What," Nate asked, "the *hell* was all that about?"

More silence.

Finally, Pete looked around as though he'd only just realized someone had spoken. "You talking to me?"

"Yes."

"And you mean what was going on last night in the Three Dog?"

"Yes!" Nate growled.

Pete shrugged and swirled his coffee within his dented cup. "I thought most of it came out before we left."

"Why don't you clear it up for me?"

"I was hired for a job, but the job wasn't nothing but a way to draw attention from what was really goin' on. I was told Cal Worsham was responsible for robbing a string

87

of saloons in these parts, but he didn't do anything of the sort. Nobody must've thought I'd find the real bandit because when I did, I was held at gunpoint until they could figure out what to do with me. More than likely, they were gonna shoot me after saying I cheated them or some other reason they pulled out of thin air. That asshole Jim already robbed me blind," Pete said. "Took every last cent I had on me as well as everything I was paid for that job. Actually had the gall to call my hard-earned pay winnings from that sorry excuse of a game."

"So was the lady bartender sharing a bed with the fellow who came to yell at her before the shooting started?" Deaugrey asked.

"That might explain a few things," Frank said.

"Doesn't matter," Nate said dismissively. "We showed up for the tail end of the affair and now it's over. Let's just —"

"She was getting a cut of the money that was stolen in them robberies," Pete said as if Nate hadn't even spoken. "And since her saloon wasn't getting robbed, all of the paying customers and gamblers were headed there instead of taking their chances of getting caught in a shootout anywhere else."

Deaugrey laughed heartily. "We saw how

that worked out for them!"

"Yeah," Pete replied with a grin. "I guess we did, at that."

"It was fortunate we showed up when we did."

Now it was Frank's turn to laugh, although his wasn't nearly as heartfelt as what had come before. "I would have been more surprised if either of you *hadn't* been in some sort of trouble when Nate and I came along."

"What's that supposed to mean?" Deaugrey asked. "That we're nothing but a bunch of sinners?"

"Man's got a point," Pete grumbled. "Don't know if I'd say I'm a sinner, but we all do see more than our share of trouble."

"And you know what all of us have in common?" Deaugrey asked. He then jabbed a finger at Nate and said, "*Him!* Me, Pete, a preacher and all the other misfits Nate Sathow pulls together got no business being mentioned in the same sentence unless it's to set up a bad joke."

The three of them cut loose with enough genuine laughter to echo in every direction. Frank was caught so off his guard that he spilled a good portion of his coffee on his lap.

Instinctively reveling in the moment,

Deaugrey added, "Nathan even turned a preacher into one of his sinners! I say this man is the devil himself but instead, *I'm* the one who gets locked away!"

Still laughing, Frank glanced over to see how Nate was taking the ribbing. His expression was plenty sour, but there was something beneath it that made it clear he was simply fighting the urge to join in the fun.

"Look at him," Deaugrey continued. "Won't even admit when he's wrong. He seemed more comfortable when bullets were flying on all sides."

"You're right about that," Pete said. "He's always been that way. Ever since I known him."

"You know what I was before I knew him?" Frank asked.

"Free from bullet wounds?" Deaugrey asked.

"Apart from that."

"I can't imagine."

Giving Nate a nudge with his elbow, Frank said, "Bored."

"Well ain't none of us can say that no more," Pete said. "And as for the sinning part, I'd say there's some truth in that as well. I tend to get into a fair amount of trouble with or without the lot of you bein' around to watch. Hey, Nate?"

"Yeah?"

"How'd you know where to find me, anyhow?"

"I make it my business to know where I can find a good sinner when I need one," Nate replied.

Either that made complete sense to the others around the fire or they knew better than to ask the question again because the other three let the matter rest.

"Since we're all in such high spirits," Nate continued, "now seems like a good time for me to tell you why you're all here."

"Good Lord," Deaugrey sighed. "I thought he'd never get around to that."

"The man's a spigot clogged with molasses," Pete said. "Ain't no rushing him."

"I had a more colorful comparison in mind, but I suppose that one works as well."

"You finished?" Nate asked.

Deaugrey shrugged and focused his attention on the task of cutting his ham into more pieces. "Go on and say your piece, spigot."

Nate dug into one of his pockets while asking, "Did any of you men hear about the killings that took place in Gentry County, Missouri?"

"I heard some bit of nasty business happened out that way," Pete replied. "Probably was something in the newspapers, but I don't got no use for reading them things."

"And I never got any papers in Mc-Keag's," Deaugrey said. "Not after one of the patients rolled up a Sunday edition to be used as a club against the orderlies."

"I wonder which patient could have possibly been responsible for that?" Frank mused.

"Why, I am appalled, sir!" Deaugrey said in a voice that seemed to have been pulled straight from the fertile soil of a Virginia plantation.

"Are you idiots gonna listen or not?" Nate bellowed.

The other three quieted down.

"Good," Nate said with exasperation. "Now where was I?"

"Killings," Pete grunted. "Gentry County."

"Right. Have any of you heard mention of a jailbreak in that region of Missouri?"

Frank's head perked up. "I did hear something about that! Very bloody business from what I understand."

"Bloody doesn't begin to do it justice," Nate said. "Three prisoners were tortured and killed. After that, two guards were strung up and whittled down to nothing with knives from the kitchen."

"Good Lord above," Frank said.

Nate nodded. "And that was just meant as a distraction. When the rest of the guards came running, they were ripped to pieces by prisoners who were so riled up they damn near busted the walls down with their bare hands. More prisoners were killed. More guards were killed. Even a few normal folks wound up dead just because they happened to be there visiting family that was locked up."

Pouring himself some more coffee, Deaugrey asked, "If this is what you consider friendly breakfast conversation, I'd rather go back to you being quiet while the rest of us enjoy ourselves."

"I take it these things are connected somehow," Pete said.

Nate nodded. "You got that right. One of the few men to make it out of that bloody jailbreak is the same one who tore through a good portion of the rest of the county to kill those poor souls that were written about in the papers. Casey Pescaterro."

Any bit of remaining frivolity around the campfire dried up and blew away with the mention of that name.

"Casey Pescaterro," Pete said. "The same

Casey Pescaterro who rode with the Youngers?"

"Yep. Rode with them for a short while, anyhow."

"Right. He was booted out of that gang when Cole Younger said he made things too difficult for the rest of 'em. When Cole Younger says somethin' like that about a man . . . let's just say that's no man you wanna meet."

While Pete had been talking, Deaugrey tapped his head in an ever-quickening rhythm. The force with which his finger met his forehead grew until it became loud enough for all of the other men to hear. When it stopped, Deaugrey said, "Wait a second! Casey Pescaterro?"

"That's right," Nate replied with a half grin that showed he knew all of what was going through Deaugrey's mind.

"As in, Casey *'Dog Ear'* Pescaterro?"

"The very same."

"Dog Ear?" Frank asked.

"I've heard of that one," Deaugrey said.

Nate helped himself to some more coffee. "Thought that you might."

Since Frank so rarely lost his patience, it caught everyone's attention when he snapped, "Is someone going to tell me what the 'Dog Ear' is about?"

"I've heard a few different tellings of the story," Deaugrey replied. "All of them start off with him robbing just about any old place he could find. Dressmakers, feed stores, even a schoolhouse."

"What's there to rob at a schoolhouse?"

"Hell if I know!" Deaugrey said with a smile. "Isn't it just perfectly random? One of those stories goes on to say that he was fed up with not being recognized for his crimes like the men who robbed banks and such, so he started marking each of his jobs. Or rather, he started marking the folks he met while on those jobs. Bit some of their ears off. Must've gotten a taste for it because he kept doing it everywhere he went. Left those poor bastards looking like raggedy stray dogs. That's my favorite story."

"I heard another one," Nate said. "Something about him losing his mind while on a stagecoach to Cheyenne. Don't know what set him off, but he tore into everyone in there with him . . . tooth and nail. When he was done, he set the coach on fire from the inside and stayed there until he was through with the last passenger. The only thing that wasn't covered in blood or burnt to ash by the time he managed to get the door open was a dog-eared copy of the Bible."

"Perhaps even a man like him holds favor

with the Lord above," Frank offered.

"You ask me," Nate said, "that don't say much about the Lord's choice of friends. Casey's been locked up a couple of times and every time he escapes, he runs off like a wild dog. Even howls at the moon along the way."

"That could also explain the Dog Ear name," Pete said.

Deaugrey shook his head. "I like my story better."

"Me too, actually."

"I've also heard that he was raised by wolves."

"Is that a fact?" Pete asked.

"Maybe, maybe not," Deaugrey admitted. "It's just one of those things I heard somewhere."

Pete was about to continue with the conversation until he saw Nate glaring at him. "You were saying?"

"Thanks, Pete," Nate replied. To everyone, he said, "Pescaterro needs to be brought in and we're the ones who get the job. The pay is two thousand each."

"Does that include the bounty on any of Dog Ear's associates that we happen to bag along the way?" Pete asked.

"No," Nate replied with a grin. "That's just the pay for bringing in Dog Ear. Anyone else we find who has a price on his head, and there's gonna be more than a few I'd wager, is a bonus."

Deaugrey's narrowed his eyes suspiciously as he asked, "There's an eight thousand dollar bounty on Pescaterro? He's a killer who may also be a cannibal by now, but that's a mighty big bounty for someone who hasn't even bothered to rob a bank. Who's offering that kind of money?"

"It's not a bounty," Nate said. "Not all of it anyhow. Pescaterro is a cold-blooded murderer and a menace, so there is a price on his head. Fifteen hundred, I think. Maybe two thousand. The lion's share of that money isn't being offered to just anyone. This is a special job and we're the only ones who are gonna cash it in."

"That's not an answer to my question," Deaugrey prodded.

"It's a real offer," Nate said. "And we will get paid. That's all we need to know."

"That's not all *you* know, however," Frank said.

Pete looked over to the preacher and said, "I thought you'd know too."

"Do you think I'm always riding by this one's side?" Frank asked while hooking a thumb toward Nate.

Looking between Nate and Frank, Pete

said, "Well . . . yeah."

"If you must know," Nate cut in, "the rest is being offered by a group of men who have a professional interest in seeing Pescaterro brought to justice. Who they are, exactly, isn't important. I'm the one who was called in for this venture and I only met one of these fellows. Discretion is a big part of this deal, you understand?"

"Oh yeah!" Deaugrey said. "I understand all right. It certainly wasn't any bounty hunters offering that sort of money because that just wouldn't make sense. Politicians or anyone in the government like mayors or the like would turn to the law. That means these concerned citizens you're referring to are lawmen! Am I right?"

"Actually . . . you are."

Deaugrey stood up so fast he nearly sent his breakfast plate into the fire. "I knew it! I knew it!"

"I'll be damned," Pete said. "Are you serious?"

Looking as if he barely believed it himself, Nate said, "I'm not supposed to give any names, but the man who approached me with this job is a keeper of the peace and represents others of that sort. As such, these men have a vested interest in hunting down Casey Pescaterro before he does any more damage or causes any further bloodshed."

"As someone who has written his fair share of sermons," Frank said, "that sounds like one well-rehearsed speech."

"And I barely had any practice," Nate said. "The only reason I know it front and back is because the man who hired me must've said it a half dozen times."

Pete scraped up his last few beans and shoveled them into his mouth as he said, "Just a fancy way of sayin' these lawmen don't have the brains or the sand to chase after someone as dangerous and batshit crazy as Dog Ear Pescaterro."

Raising his hands while looking to the sky, Frank said, "Amen and hallelujah, brother!"

This time, Nate didn't try to keep a straight face as everyone started to laugh. When it died down, he said, "I did some checking as I always do and found out there's real money being offered. Due to various business interests and a whole lot of convoluted bullshit of that nature, it truly is in several wealthy people's best interests to put Dog Ear away. He's busted out of too many jails, eluded too many lawmen, and made too many officials look like cowardly fools. And then there's the rest of the Pescaterro bunch."

"Here we go," Pete said. "Ain't no job offered by Nate Sathow is just a simple hunt."

"Of course," Nate scoffed. "Simple hunters are a dime a dozen. If it was an easy job or even just a messy one, the pay wouldn't be so damn good. The big concern after this particular jailbreak is that someone has been putting together a proper gang and they're just waiting for Casey to come along to lead them into . . ."

After a few seconds, Pete asked, "Into what?"

"That's what we're getting paid such good money to find out. Two things I can tell you for certain is it won't be good and we won't see a dime of that money unless we put a stop to it. There's also a real good likelihood that one or all of us will get shot or stabbed —"

"Or bitten," Frank added.

"Right," Nate said. "Or bitten. So if any of you want out, now's the time to say so." When nobody said anything, Nate nodded once. "All right then. Let's ride."

10

The ride back across the state line into Missouri was mostly uneventful. When they stopped at the occasional town or trading post, Pete gathered the supplies he needed while Frank had a word with anyone he could find who might know a thing or two about what Pescaterro had been up to. It came as no surprise to anyone that the few bits of information he did collect were nothing more than wild stories about a wilder man.

As they rode away from a mining camp ensconced in the rolling hills of western Missouri, Nate asked, "Find anything useful this time?"

"Pescaterro passed through these parts not too long ago," Frank replied. "Other than that, no."

"Well that's somethin'," Pete said.

"You know what's something?" Deaugrey asked. "This knife!" With a flourish, he produced a thin blade that had been tucked up into the sleeve of his secondhand coat.

"Where'd you get that?" Nate asked.

"Stole it from one of them miners."

"Can't take you anywhere," Nate said, shaking his head.

Frank looked back and forth between the two as if he couldn't decide which of them deserved more of his disgust. "We're thieves now?"

"After all we've done when riding together, stealing a knife is what ruffles your feathers the most?" Nate asked incredulously.

"Maybe not the most, but —"

"Remember when we were at the saloon where Pete was being held at that poker game?" Deaugrey asked.

"Yes."

"Remember how I managed to deal with a few of those gunmen before they killed you or anyone else?"

"Yes," Frank sighed, obviously regretting he'd opened his mouth on the subject.

"I stole that knife too."

"He's got a collection," Nate said.

"Does he now?" Frank muttered.

"I can think of worse hobbies. Especially for a man who spends so much time in insane asylums."

"Since nobody asked, I'll tell you why this knife is something so special," Deaugrey announced. "It was supposed to have been dropped by Dog Ear himself or one of the men riding with him."

"And when were you going to mention that?" Nate asked.

"Just a few moments ago. Weren't you listening?"

Pete brought his horse up close to Deaugrey's mule and extended his hand. "Give that blade here."

The way Deaugrey flipped the knife to grip it by the blade, he may have wanted to throw it at Pete with the intent of sticking him with it. Although he twitched as if to make that very move, he kept hold of the blade and stretched out his arm to slap the knife's handle into Pete's waiting hand. To his credit, Pete didn't flinch at Deaugrey's posturing. He merely took the knife in hand to examine it closer.

"Pescaterro doesn't have many blood relations," Nate said. "At least, none that will admit to being related to him. When he's been free in the past, he's holed up with a bunch of vagrants and outlaws in the hills northeast of here. They've taken him in as one of their own, so that tells you plenty about their state of mind."

"Meaning they've got no minds at all," Deaugrey said. "I know plenty like that."

"This knife was Pescaterro's, all right," Pete announced.

All three men turned in their saddles to look at him. "You sure about that?" Nate asked.

"The blade is high grade steel and the handle was made by a real craftsman. It'd fetch a real high price in any store."

"In that case, hand it back over," Deaugrey said. He retracted his hand when he saw the scolding look from Frank.

"What makes you think it's connected to Pescaterro?" Nate asked.

"There's a hint of blood smeared on the blade and something caught between it and the guard. Most anyone who would pay whatever price was being asked for this knife wouldn't risk getting it scraped up or chipped by putting it to use like that."

"Mining camps can be tough places," Frank said.

"Sure, but this is just the sort of thing Pescaterro would steal when he storms through some store. Men like him don't rob to get rich. They want the thrill. The things they take are the sort of things that would appeal to a greedy kid. This knife is pretty and would have caught his eye. The fact that he left it behind after using it once or maybe twice seems even more like something he'd do."

"Could have been used for anything," Nate offered. "I'm not doubting you, I just want to make certain we're on the right track."

"We are," Pete told him with absolute certainty. "This knife was used to kill a man. At the very least, it put someone into a whole world of hurt."

"I suppose you can smell death on the sharpened steel?" Deaugrey asked in a voice dripping with sarcasm.

Pete flipped the knife in the air, caught it by the blade and snapped his arm forward as if to throw the knife right into the crazy man's face. The only difference between his motion and the one performed by Deaugrey a minute ago was that his caused its target to flinch. Taking no outward pleasure from his small victory, Pete held the knife so it was within inches of the other man's eyes.

"See what's snagged under that guard?" Pete asked. "That's a piece of clothing. It's also stained with blood. Most likely," he said while flipping the knife again to take it by the handle and tap the tip of the blade against Deaugrey's gut, "it was stuck here. Or here," he added while poking Deaugrey's chest. "And it went in so hard that it took a piece of someone's shirt along with it when it was ripped back out again."

"Could've been a fight between miners," Deaugrey said with much less arrogance than had been in his voice before. "Shouldn't we be certain before we waste time and effort chasing our tails?"

"My gut tells me this was used by Pesca-terro," Pete said as he took the knife back.

"Mine too," Nate said. "Should we turn back around and find the miner Grey stole that knife from?"

Pete shook his head. "Dog Ear's not there anymore. All we'll get from them miners is more stories." He lifted his chin as if he were pulling the fragrant wind all the way into his lungs. "Where was that prison he broke out of?"

"Due south of here, not far from the state line."

"And the hills where he'll be headed?"

"East," Nate replied. "Wish I had more direction to give you than that."

"That's good enough for now," Pete said. He reined his horse to a stop and brought it around to face north. "We head this way. Ride for about . . . ten . . . maybe twenty miles. I'll know more when I get to the trail I'm after."

Deaugrey was about to protest, but Nate kept him quiet with a quickly raised hand and a sharp glare. To Pete, he said, "We're all in this together, Pete. Tell me what's on your mind."

Pete's dark brown eyes shifted in their sockets to fix on Nate. The wind picked up to send his thick mane of hair around his face, making him look like a stallion that was just biding its time before throwing its rider. "Maybe I should wait until we're all sitting around a fire when it suits me better?"

"You know how I do things, Pete," Nate said. "I never offer a job until every man's in the proper frame of mind to know what he's getting in to."

Grudgingly, Pete pointed his fierce gaze in another direction. "Like I said before, this ain't just any knife. It was made by an expert. There's a maker's mark carved into the handle, the way the steel was sharpened, plenty of things most would plumb overlook."

"And I suppose you saw what none of us did?" Deaugrey asked.

Without hesitation, Nate said, "That's why I wanted him along. Unless you've got something to say that's a help, keep your damn mouth shut for a change."

"The way this knife was made," Pete said as he continued to turn the weapon over so he could study it from every angle. "It's distinctive. I think I know where to find the man who put it together."

"Where?"

"He works out of a town called Nagle along the river north of here, but south of the prison where Pescaterro broke out. He would have come to Nagle before getting to that mining camp we found."

"If he went there before the camp," Deaugrey said, "wouldn't the tracks be fresher at the spot where the knife wound up than where it was taken from?"

Nate would have snapped at Deaugrey again if he'd thought Deaugrey hadn't brought up a valid point.

"We can always go back to that camp," Pete said. "But if we know somewhere else that Pescaterro was, there's no reason why we shouldn't check there as well. Someone might have seen what horse he was riding. There could be cleaner tracks to be found. Hell, there could be any number of things that the knife maker saw that could be a help. Any piece I can find will help me find Pescaterro. Tracking is what I do, so let me do it!"

Nate flicked his reins to steer his horse

between Pete and Deaugrey. "Enough!" he said. "I know it's been a while since you two have ridden together, and the pair of you never did see eye to eye."

"Ain't nobody sees eye to eye with that lunatic," Pete snarled.

Before Deaugrey could retort, Nate said, "Be that as it may, I brought you both together because I needed what you've got to offer. And I waited to offer the job until I could get a look at how the two of you reacted when I put you in sight of each other again. I wouldn't have made the offer unless I was certain you could refrain from snapping each other's necks. You both have your talents and I've got mine. Reading dangerous souls is what I do. If you don't trust that, then take your horses and your petty goddamn squabbling, pick a direction and ride it straight outta my sight!"

Rather than stare daggers at each other, Pete and Deaugrey looked over at Nate. His face was impossible to read, whether he was looking over the barrel of his Remington or placing a bet at a card table. Anyone who rode with him more than once knew the futility of trying to guess when he might be bluffing.

"Now that you stopped to take a breath," Nate continued, "perhaps you'll hear me out. I say we split up and cover both the knife maker and that mining camp. Deaugrey, you're coming with me. Show me where to find the fella you pick-pocketed and we'll ask around to see if anyone has anything else to say where Pescaterro is concerned. Pete, you and Frank go to that river town to see what you can see. How's that for a plan?"

"Plans are what you do," Deaugrey said cheerily. "I don't mind going back to that camp. Had my eye on a soiled dove that was working there. At least, I think she was soiled."

Pete merely nodded and flicked his reins to start his ride to that river town.

"Do me a favor, Nate," Frank said. "Try not to kill him while I'm away."

Watching as Deaugrey tapped his heels against his mule's sides to get the animal rushing back along the trail to the mining camp, Nate said, "I'm not about to make promises I can't keep."

11

Nagle, Missouri

Sunlight was fading into shadow by the time Pete and Frank rode into town. The journey was a stark contrast to the one that had brought them across the state line into Kansas, and Frank savored every last moment of it. The air was heavier than it had been on the plains. All of the heat clinging to his sweaty face like slick moss was soothed whenever a breeze came in to brush against his cheek having recently skimmed the top of the Missouri River. Gnats and flies darted past his eyes, only to be swept away by an idle hand.

"This is the place," Pete said while nodding toward a sign nailed to a tree. Written on that weathered plank was the name of the town and the most recent guess as to how many resided there. "Probably too late to have a word with that knife maker, but we should be able to find something to eat."

"I'm starving," Frank said enthusiastically. "Besides, even if the shops were still open, it'd be a better idea to pay your friend a visit tomorrow afternoon or late morning. He'll be more willing to talk then."

Pete looked over at him and asked, "Do you know this man?"

"No, but I've paid plenty of visits to folks at odd hours." Frank tapped the starched collar of his black shirt. "They always start off on their guard because they assume they're getting bad news. More often than not, they're right. When I visited a member of my congregation for supper or to shoot the breeze, it was during the civilized hours of the day. When someone died or had fallen terribly ill, it was usually very late or very early. Let's not start off on the wrong foot with this fellow. Besides, it's not like we were going to talk to him and ride back to meet Nate tonight anyway."

"You could always change into another shirt," Pete offered. "Folks might not be so nervous if they were talking to someone other than a preacher."

"Strangers showing up will only put him on his guard more. What's the matter? You don't want to share a meal with me?"

Pete started to say something but shut his

mouth and faced forward without making a sound.

Frank recognized such mannerisms from plenty of folks who came in to confess to him several times in a row before they got around to admitting any wrongdoing. Perhaps Pete would change his mind or perhaps he wouldn't. For the moment, Frank decided to play along and pretend the conversation hadn't ended with an unanswered question.

Nagle was a town that felt as if it had sprung up as a natural growth along the banks of the river. Instead of straight streets and ordered districts, it followed the flow of the water with a scattering of shops, small houses and a mill. The scent of cooking fires and baked bread still lingered in the air after most of the town had had its supper. Frank couldn't help but tug on his reins when he approached a small restaurant with its doors propped open.

"We're movin' along," Pete said.

"Aren't you hungry?"

"Yep."

"Then let's eat," Frank pleaded.

After moving a few yards past the place, Pete steered his horse to go off the main path and around the inviting building. Before Frank could wonder if he should follow, Pete returned while shaking his head. "Not this place."

"Why not?"

"Because there's no view of the river."

"It'll be too dark to see anything anyway."

But Pete wasn't about to budge. "If you're somewhere close to a river or ocean, always eat somewhere with a view of the water. They'll either have delicious fish on the menu or a specialty that's good enough to make up for the fact that they don't serve fish."

Frank thought about that for a moment. "I suppose that makes some kind of sense."

"Course it does. I spotted another place just down the way. We'll go there and put my theory to the test."

As long as it meant moving closer to a hot meal, Frank wasn't about to protest.

The Miller's Stone was a little place run by a large family. Fortunately for the town's newest arrivals, the mother and daughter of that family were night owls and didn't mind putting together a heaping plate of supper for them. The younger of the two women brought a basket of biscuits and a pitcher of water. She returned soon after with the main course which consisted of shepherd's pie and a bowl of greens.

"It ain't fish," Frank said, "but it sure

beats another night of cool ham and old beans."

Since his mouth was already stuffed full, Pete just nodded.

The cook emerged from the kitchen, untying her apron and using it to wipe her hands. She looked every bit like the pretty, fair-haired girl who'd brought the plates to the table with a few more years behind her. If their similarities persisted, the daughter's future husband would be a very lucky man indeed. "It's been a while since this town has seen the likes of you!" she said.

Frank dabbed at his mouth with a napkin and stood up to greet the woman. "Doesn't a town as fine as this one have a man of the cloth?"

The woman blinked and said, "Of course it does. I meant *him*! Come here, Pietro!"

Pete stood up as well so he could be wrapped up in an exuberant hug. "Hello, Diana."

"Were you going to come along, eat my food and not pay your respects?"

"Didn't want to put you out, is all."

Holding him at arm's length, the woman shook her head and said, "Put me out? Listen to you. Such nonsense. Who's your friend?"

"This here is Frank . . ."

Seeing the vacant look on Pete's face shift slowly toward embarrassment, Frank stretched out his hand and put on a smile that members of his congregation back home got to see every Sunday morning. "Frank Waverly, ma'am. Pleased to meet you."

"My, my," Diana said with a flutter of her eyelashes. "I never would have thought Pete would keep company with a man of the cloth. Especially such a handsome one."

"The good Lord isn't the only one who works in mysterious ways."

She laughed a bit more than the little joke deserved before saying, "It's good to see you, Pete, and very nice to meet you, Frank."

"Likewise," Frank said.

"I'll just tend to your desserts."

"We didn't order no —"

"And you didn't have to, Pietro," she said quickly. "I'll have them ready by the time you're finished with the shepherd's pie."

"I look forward to it." Frank beamed.

As Diana headed for the kitchen, Pete grumbled, "All right, rein it in."

"I wouldn't have pegged you as the sort to be on friendly terms with someone like that," Frank mused.

"Why? You don't think folks like me?"

"It's not that. I just thought you didn't like many folks."

After a moment's hesitation, Pete shrugged. "I suppose you're right about that."

Using his fork to pick at some of the pie's flaky crust and then dip it into a bit of gravy that had spilled out from the middle, Frank asked, "How many times have we ridden together?"

"I dunno. Three. Four, maybe? I worked with Nate plenty of times more than that, but you were off preaching or some such."

"Even so, I would've thought that might have been enough for you to recall my last name."

"I see what I need to see," Pete told him. "There's plenty I need to remember, so I only keep what needs to be kept. You're Frank the Preacher. That's always been good enough for me."

Frank smirked and nodded amicably. "I suppose that seems reasonable. Besides, we've never really spent much time together even when Nate was around."

Looking up from the loaded fork that was poised less than two inches from his mouth, Pete asked, "You're not getting all . . . sentimental on me, are you?"

"A man in my line of work does sometimes

drift toward sentiment, but that's not a bad thing."

Judging by the distasteful expression on Pete's face, he didn't exactly share that opinion.

"How did you and Nate come to work together, anyway?" Frank asked.

"It was some years ago up in the Dakota Territories. He'd been tracking down these killers seeking refuge among the Injuns and came up short for the better part of three weeks. The men who hired him got tired of waiting, so they hired me. I went up there and found those killers in three days. When Nate stepped up to me, I thought he might take a swing on account of me getting paid when he didn't see a cent off'a that job. Instead, he offered me a different job with him. Things worked out and I haven't been able to shake him since."

"Hmmm. A very interesting story."

"If you say so."

In Frank's experience, now would have been the time when someone involved in this conversation would have asked how he'd met their common acquaintance. Instead, Pete kept his head down to create a shorter path between his mouth and the plate in front of him.

After a few more minutes of silence, Diana's pretty daughter walked over to ask, "Are you about ready for dessert?"

"Yes!" both men replied in hasty unison.

12

Mining camp near the Missouri–Kansas state line

Nate hated backtracking. Retreading such familiar ground so soon after the last time he'd ridden over it either meant he was being chased or was lost. There were a few other possibilities, but none of them were any better. This time, however, he'd barely had a chance to think about the trail he was riding. His attention was split between swapping bawdy jokes with Deaugrey and trying to keep the other man from getting so anxious that he jumped out of his own skin. Once they rounded a bend that brought the mining camp into sight, that second job became even more difficult. Every so often, Deaugrey's excitement was passed along to the mule he rode which allowed him to coax enough speed from it to move ahead of Nate.

Overtaking Deaugrey's mule amid the

thunder of hooves, Nate swore under his breath. Part of his frustration came from having to constantly wrangle the other man and the rest was astonishment that Deaugrey had gotten his tired animal to move so fast.

"You're gonna kill that damn mule if you don't ease up a bit," Nate scolded.

"She's doing fine," Deaugrey replied. "Or is it a he? Eh, who cares. We're almost there."

"And if we ride into that camp like our tails are on fire, everyone with eyes in their head would know we've got important business to conduct."

"Damn right I've got important business!"

"I'm not talking about that whore you've been going on about."

Deaugrey blinked as if he'd just woken from a vivid dream. "You're not? Oh yes! The knife. That's not going to take long at all to resolve. After that, it's down to the real business."

Since he didn't seem to be making any headway with words, Nate reached down to snatch the reins from Deaugrey's hands. He managed to wrestle one away from him, which was enough to get the mule to stop and shake its head angrily.

"What the hell's gotten into you?" Nate

asked. "Have you lost even more of your mind? This isn't the first time we've scouted for a job! If you've forgotten everything there is to know about bargaining and negotiations, then you're less than useless to me."

"Say what you want, my friend, but you're not the one who spent the last stretch of time locked away with nothing but filthy men and beastly women to look at."

Since Deaugrey seemed to have lost a bit of his steam, Nate handed his reins back to him. "Beastly?"

"You saw that lady ox at the front desk when you went to McKeag's, didn't you?"

"Yes."

"Well let's just say that the sanitarium was putting their best foot forward when they made her the first one guests would see. Some of the others," Deaugrey added with a shudder, "were the stuff of nightmares. Although . . . there was one young lady who filled out her dressing gown exceptionally well. She tended to be rather gloomy, which made relations with her somewhat less than gratifying."

Even if Deaugrey was prone to exaggeration, Nate saw his point well enough. "This whore you spotted must really be something."

122

"Oh my yes."

"Then why don't you pay her a visit while I have a word with the fella who was in possession of that knife you stole?"

"Sounds fine to me," Deaugrey said as quickly as he could shove the words past his lips.

"We're still not going in like a couple of crazed kids, though."

"Agreed."

"And I think it would be best if we didn't go in together," Nate added.

Staring at the camp ahead of them as if he was already searching for the tent belonging to that soiled dove, Deaugrey said, "Whatever you think is best."

"All right then. Hand over that knife."

Deaugrey tore his eyes away from the camp so he could look at Nate as if he'd just been asked to sign over his soul to the devil himself. "What? Why? Haven't you seen it well enough to describe it?"

"Sure I have, but I'm not exactly a poet. My words won't be as good as having the real thing to show around. And it's not like we've got all the time in the world to . . ." Nate looked over at him with a half smirk. "I know you're touched in the head and all, but even you can't believe we'll get anywhere with this fellow you robbed unless we

123

return his property to him."

"All right, all right," Deaugrey snapped. He pulled the knife from inside his jacket and handed it over. "I'll expect that back as soon as we leave this pit."

Only after he'd tucked the knife beneath his gun belt did Nate say, "That ain't happening."

"But . . . it's mine!"

Just when Nate was sure he was going to have to argue the finer points of possession and theft, he was surprised by Deaugrey's willingness to let it drop.

"Eh, keep it," Deaugrey said. "I can always steal another one. Just don't get in my way before I find that sweet little filly of mine."

Of course, there was no underestimating the attraction of smooth, warm and willing flesh to desperate hands. When Deaugrey broke away from him after telling him all he could remember about the man who'd been in possession of the fancy knife, Nate was more than willing to let him go.

The camp hadn't impressed Nate very much the first time he rode through it and there was nothing to change his opinion now. Ruts in the ground took the place of anything close to roads and, after a few short bouts of rain had rolled through the area, those ruts were filled with muddy water. Unlike most places, rain didn't do a damn thing to break a hot spell in Missouri. Instead, the clouds rolled out to leave watery memories in the air like warm, sticky tendrils that soaked through a man's clothes to pull the sweat from his brow.

From a distance, Nate could see several small groups of workers sifting through the waters of a stream, busting rocks or doing all manners of work that tended to break a miner's back. In front of him lay the main camp which consisted of about a dozen hastily built shacks, tents of varying sizes and several carts lined up to sell various wares. Nate rode to a corral that was just a larger shack with a small patch of ground roped off to keep a few bony horses from getting away. Judging by the sorry condition of those animals, they probably didn't have the strength to jump the low barrier unless a fire was nipping at their rumps. He dismounted and led his horse to a man who sat in a chair with his legs splayed in front of him and his hands clasped over a belly that poked out from beneath his ill-fitting shirt.

"Howdy," Nate said as he came to a stop in front of him. "Is this a good spot to put up my horse for a short stay?"

"I don't know," the fat man grunted. "Is it?"

Nate reached into his pocket for a silver dollar and flipped it into the air. The fat man took notice of the sound of a thumb meeting the edge of the coin and was sitting up by the time the dollar slapped against Nate's palm.

"Is this what passes for a stable in this shit hole or isn't it?" Nate growled.

The fat man couldn't get up fast enough. "Sure it is! Sorry about before. We get plenty of undesirables through here that don't have a penny to their name. Didn't I see you come through here not too long ago? Maybe you were riding with a group of other fellas?"

"I got a real common face," Nate told him.

Dismissing his own question, the fat man said, "I'll watch over your horse, feed him and even toss in a good brushing. Best bargain in camp!"

"I doubt that, but here," Nate said while tossing the coin to the fat man. "If I come back to an unhappy horse, I'll come looking, and a man like yourself," he added while eyeing the other fellow's ample belly, "will be mighty hard to miss."

"Take a look at these horses right here. There ain't an unhappy one in the bunch."

Although none of the animals in the corral looked healthy enough to pull a cart,
Nate doubted that was the fat man's fault.
"Just be sure to feed and water him. I don't
intend on being here long."

"You here looking for work or just passing
through?"

"I'm looking to have a word with someone
who's supposed to be working here. Name's
Dan or . . . maybe Jesse."

"Which one? Dan or Jesse?"

Silently cursing Deaugrey for not paying
closer attention to the men he robbed, Nate
said, "Maybe . . . both?"

Instead of looking at Nate like the fool he
felt he was, the fat man nodded and said,
"Oh! I bet you mean Stan Jessowitz!"

Nate mimicked the other man's expression. "That's him. Any notion of where I
can find him?"

"See that big tent right over yonder?" the
fat man asked while using a pudgy finger to
point deeper into the camp.

Nate looked in that direction, past a
cluster of fur traders sitting behind their
stacked pelts toward what amounted to the
center of camp. "You mean the one with
the red scarves tied to the top of its posts?"

"No. That's the whores' tent."

If he'd looked just a bit harder, Nate

would have been able to see as much for himself since Deaugrey's mule was already tied off in front of that place.

"Plenty of nice ladies in there, though," the fat man said through a lecherous smile. "And they're open to negotiation, if you know what I mean."

"That ain't what I'm here for."

"Right. The place I meant to show you is the tent just past that first one you spotted. That next tent is where you go for a drink or a game of cards. Whenever Stan ain't working, he can be found in there. Tell the bartender I sent you, and your first drink is free."

"Much obliged," Nate said. After all the help he'd been given, he felt a little bad for being so harsh with the fat man earlier. If the information panned out, and if his horse still looked better than the poor specimens in that corral, Nate decided to toss a bit more money into the other man's hands. If things went a different way, the fat man would get something much different for his troubles.

"How long will you be staying, if you don't mind my asking?"

"Shouldn't be long," Nate replied. "Tell me, this is a mining camp, right?"

"That's right," the fat man grunted as he

waddled over to a spot where the rope was looped over a post to act as a kind of gate to the corral.

"What is it that's mined?"

"Some silver. Some copper. A bit of zinc. I ain't never been a miner. I just go where the money is and when there ain't enough of it to keep food in my mouth, I move along to the next place."

Nate could read most men just by talking to them for a few minutes. Some took a bit more time. Others, like the man in front of him now, took a whole lot less. Since he would have bet everything he had that the fat man would sell him out for the price of a steak, Nate took that option away by saying, "If Jessowitz or any of his friends come around, let them know I'm looking for him. No trouble. Just a friendly conversation."

"Will do, boss."

13

When Deaugrey got close enough to see the tent with the red scarves flying from the top of its posts, he swore he could smell the sweet scents of what awaited him inside. He climbed down from his mule, snapped the reins around a hitching post without bothering to check how sturdy it was and marched inside through an open flap. Inside was a small room sectioned off by cheap partitions containing a small folding table bearing a ledger, pen and inkwell. A tall woman with dark blond hair stepped up to meet him with her hands on her hips and her chest thrust forward.

"My, my!" she said. "Aren't you in a hurry! Been out working on your own for a while, cowboy?"

"I'm looking for a woman," Deaugrey said.

"We have plenty of those. What's your preference?"

"She was here a few days ago when I last visited this camp. A might bit taller than me, but not quite as tall as you, slender, pale skin, short, dark, curly hair. At the time, she was wearing a dark red ribbon with a bow near her left ear."

"You have quite the eye for detail," she told him with a smile.

When Deaugrey smiled back, he leaned in to whisper, "Actually, I've got two of 'em. And," he added while allowing his gaze to wander down the front of her dress, "speaking of good things coming in twos . . ."

"Why don't I find you your lady?" she said. "It seems you're fit to be tied."

"You're not the first to point that out, my dear."

She went to the table, picked up the pen and started writing in her ledger. "The girl you're after is named Kaylee."

"I do hope she's available."

"Why don't you first let me know if I've got the name right after your colorful description." After setting down her pen, she pulled aside another flap behind her which led to a narrow walkway formed by curtains sewn to the roof that went all the way down to the tent's canvas floor. "Kaylee!" she called out. "You have a visitor."

Along the walkway on either side were

doors consisting of narrow wooden frames used to support thick velvet curtains. One of those curtains, about halfway down the walkway on the left side, parted so a young woman could step out. She fit Deaugrey's description to the letter, right down to the ribbon in her dark curls.

"Have we met, sir?" she asked while extending her hand to him.

Deaugrey took it, stooped in a cordial bow and kissed her gently between her first two knuckles. "Oh, I'd say we're about to get real acquainted."

The tent next to the camp's patched-together cathouse was slightly wider in front and just a bit taller. Its structure was maintained by a wooden frame that was meant to be as close to permanent as something with canvas walls could be. Those walls did nothing to keep sound from escaping, however, and Nate's ears were soon flooded with the cacophony of rattling glasses and impatient fists slamming down onto tables. A banner stitched to the wall next to the front entrance bore nothing but a crudely drawn poker hand: a straight to the eight.

There was no door for him to open. Judging by the ravaged state of the frame, there had been a door attached to it at one time or another that had probably been used for kindling after being smashed down by drunkards one too many times. Nate ducked his head slightly to step inside.

The bar was to his right and was built from spare lumber laid flat over stacks of old crates. One of those pieces of lumber could very well have been the door that had once hung in the frame at the front of the place. Nate stepped up to the bar and knocked on it.

"Help yerself to a beer," shouted a muscular fellow standing behind the bar at the opposite end.

Nate leaned over, found a mug and filled it from a tap. The brew was cloudy and smelled vaguely of orange peels. His first sip wasn't easy to get down, but the beer was potent enough to make him want to come back for seconds. After a few more gulps, the bitter citrus taste started to grow on him.

"What brings you to the Straight, friend?" the bartender asked as he made his way over to stand in front of Nate. "Hopefully it ain't a lack of funds because you owe me for that beer you're drinking."

"The fellow at the corral sent me," Nate told him.

"Who? Fatty?"

"Sounds about right."

"Then your beer's on the house. At least," the barkeep added, "the first one. The second one's double the price."

"I'm here looking for a man named Stan Jessowitz. You know him?"

"Perhaps."

"And perhaps," Nate said as he shifted aside his coat to reveal the Remington holstered over his midsection, "I'm getting awfully tired of arguing what should be some pretty damn simple points."

The barkeep smiled nervously. "I was only joking about charging you double for the second beer."

"All right. Now what about this Jessowitz fellow?"

"That'd be him right over yonder," the barkeep replied while nodding toward the rest of the room.

Nate turned to glance in that direction without taking his eyes fully off of the bartender. "Could you be a bit more specific?"

"You ain't no bounty hunter. Or a lawman, for that matter. Them sorts are usually able to spot their man when they're pointed in the right direction."

"Is Jessowitz the sort who'd have a lawman or bounty hunter coming after him?"

"Not as such."

"Then don't worry about who I am," Nate said. "I'm not out to start any trouble and if I do, you've got my permission to toss me out on my ear."

That brought a smirk to the barkeep's face. "Don't think I won't take you up on that," he said before turning away from Nate and finding another customer with an empty glass. "Hey, Stan!" he shouted. "Someone here wants to buy you a beer!"

One of the gamblers perked up like a groundhog sticking its head from its hole. "Make it a whiskey and we're in business!" he said.

Nate nodded at the man who'd tipped his hand for him and waited for him to pour the liquor. When the barkeep walked the glass over, Nate said, "There was a payment in it for you if you would've kept your mouth shut."

"Oh, really? You didn't specify."

When Nate thought about what he would have liked to do to that barkeep right then, a few very specific things came to mind. Instead of airing his grievances, he took the whiskey and headed over to the table where Jessowitz was sitting.

Bartenders were a strange sort. Part

busybodies and part mercenaries, they were always on the lookout for scraps of information that could be put to use. Nate had come to rely on them while also being wary not to take his eyes off of them for too long. Like unfaithful women, if they were willing to do the dance with you, they'd just as surely do it to you.

Jessowitz was probably within a few years of Nate's age, but had weathered enough hard times to make him seem much older. A scraggly beard covered the bottom portion of his long face and when he smiled, he showed a set of crooked teeth that had been stained by years of chewing cheap tobacco. There was an empty seat at his table, so Nate sat down and placed the glass of whiskey amid a scattering of clay chips and small coins.

Grabbing the drink before it could be taken by anyone else, the man with the tobacco-stained teeth asked, "What'd I do to earn this here drink?"

"You're Stan Jessowitz?"

"Sure enough."

"Then think of it as an advance," Nate said.

"For what?"

As Jessowitz slurped his free whiskey, Nate drew the finely crafted blade from its scabbard and drove it into the table directly in front of him. "For telling me everything you can about this here knife," Nate said.

Jessowitz's eyes turned wide as saucers, and he set down the glass in his hand so quickly that a good portion of whiskey wound up dribbling into his beard. "Son of a bitch!" he roared as he got to his feet. "That's my damn knife!"

Having surely practiced the move several times in the past, the other miners and drunks scooted away from the table so as not to be knocked over if it was tossed onto its side. Nate, however, grinned widely as he stood up and plucked the blade from where he'd stuck it. "All right, then," he said. "Let's take this outside."

Perhaps Jessowitz had been expecting more of an uproar after his display. By the time he reached for the gun at his side, Nate had already come around the table to charge straight at him. Driving his shoulder into Jessowitz's gut, Nate wrapped his arms around the other man's midsection and shoved him back into the wall behind him. If that wall had been made of wood, the impact might have driven the wind from Jessowitz's lungs. Since it was only a piece of stretched canvas however, the wall gave way to allow both men to stampede outside like a pair of proverbial bulls making their way through a china shop.

Once the two men had left the tent, one of the gamblers tugged the canvas back in place while another pair straightened the table so their game could commence.

"All right, everyone!" the bartender announced. "Show's over. Anyone else makes a mess and they're cut off."

Half of the gamblers weren't about to go against the bartender's decree and the rest didn't seem to give a damn that he'd spoken in the first place. None of them missed Nate or Jessowitz one bit.

14

Jessowitz landed on his backside, bounced, skidded a few inches and used both feet to push himself a little farther. "You stole my damn knife!" he wailed. "You're a thief! Thief!"

"If you're expecting help to come swarming in from all sides, I think you'll be waiting awhile," Nate mused. "This doesn't strike me as that sort of place."

Darting his eyes back and forth, Jessowitz looked for any source of backup but didn't find anything. He then stared at the knife in Nate's hand and opened his mouth in stark terror as Nate reached out for him.

Nate grabbed Jessowitz's collar and hauled him to his feet. "First of all," he said while dragging Jessowitz to a lot behind the saloon tent, "I'm no thief. Second, I know for a fact that you didn't exactly walk into a store, lay down your hard-earned money and purchase this fine blade."

"Yeah? I won it! So what?"

"Who'd you win it from?"

"Some rough-looking bastard on his way to some train depot outside of Joplin."

"He's going to Joplin?"

"That's what he told me," Jessowitz replied shakily. "But he was drunk as a skunk. Who the hell knows if it was true? We was all saying plenty of things to each other while playing cards."

"Was he traveling alone?"

"How the hell should I know?"

Nate bared his teeth as if he were about to use them to tear the face off of Jessowitz's skull and snarled, "You sat with him. You must've seen something. Tell me, or I swear to Christ . . ."

Very rarely did Nate ever have to finish that threat, and this time was no exception.

"He wasn't traveling alone," Jessowitz sputtered. "I didn't see who he was with, but I recall him mentioning someone."

"Just one?"

"He might've talked about a few here and there, but you gotta believe me that I ain't gonna remember every name he might have mentioned. We was playing cards and that's all I cared about. Also, I was drinkin' and . . ."

Nate nodded quickly just to shut the other

man up. He didn't have any problem believing that, but now that the gears in Jessowitz's memory seemed to be turning again, he pressed onward. "What's your best guess about the number of men that were with him?"

Jessowitz thought for a moment since Nate had let him go and backed up a step. It helped Nate's cause even more that the men who glanced at them as they passed by were more interested in catching sight of something interesting than they were of lending a fellow miner a hand.

"I suppose he could've been riding with a small group," Jessowitz said. "Or could have been a larger one."

"All right then. Tell me about the man himself."

Kaylee's room was sectioned off, but not private by any means. The walls were still canvas and they didn't even stretch as far up as the tent's ceiling. None of that mattered to Deaugrey as he was led into the room, however. It had taken every bit of restraint he'd had to keep from dropping his britches before she'd closed the flap behind them. As soon as he'd pulled some money from his pockets, those pants were down around his ankles and a beaming smile was plastered onto his face.

"You're an anxious one," Kaylee mused as she took his money.

"More than you know."

Having counted up her pay, she secreted it into a small pocket in her skirt and gazed down at what Deaugrey had to offer. Kaylee raised an eyebrow and said, "Let's get started then."

"God, yes."

She lowered herself to her knees and cupped him in one hand while reaching around to grab his backside with the other. Her soft, painted lips parted and she took him into her mouth. As she slid all the way down his length, she used her tongue to trace a line along the base of his shaft.

Deaugrey let out a breath and eased his fingers through her thick, curly hair. Although she responded expertly to even the slightest touch, he didn't need to direct her. She knew exactly what she was doing, and Deaugrey wasn't about to mess with perfection.

After a minute or so, however, he eased her head back and said, "Just a moment, just a moment."

Licking the corner of her mouth, she asked, "Was I doing something wrong?"

"Not in the slightest, my dear. In fact, you

were doing it better than right. I just need to catch my breath so you can get my money's worth."

Before she could correct him on his choice of words, Kaylee was helped to her feet and wrapped up in his wiry arms.

"You catch your breath yet?" she asked.

Deaugrey's hands wandered freely over her body. First, they went around to feel the tight curve of her hips and then moved up along her back. Next, they spun her to face the other direction so he could wrap his arms around and cup her breasts. "How much time did my money pay for?" he asked in a hungry whisper spoken directly into her ear.

Squirming at his desperate touch as well as the closeness of his voice, she replied, "For you, as long as you want."

He smiled like a wolf that had finally cornered the biggest hen in the coop. Keeping one hand firmly on her breast, he hiked her skirts up to find she wasn't wearing any undergarments beneath her slip. Pressing against her, Deaugrey savored the way their bodies came together. She leaned forward to grab the frame of her cot while moving her legs into a wider stance. Looking over her shoulder at him, she asked, "Is this what you had in mind?"

"A thousand times over, darlin'," he said while guiding himself into her.

There were always noises coming from the rest of the tent, but a few of them became sharp enough to catch his ear. Since Deaugrey was finally indulging in what he'd been thinking about for way too long, it wasn't difficult to ignore them.

Kaylee let out a satisfied grunt as she took him inside of her, but was more easily distracted from their dance than a man who'd been locked away for months at a stretch. "What's that sound?" she asked.

Grabbing her hips in both hands, Deaugrey closed his eyes and committed himself to his task. "Don't hear a thing. Just . . ."

"I think something's wrong."

"Things couldn't be better."

Jessowitz had stopped fighting. Like any other man who'd let go of the hopes he'd been entertaining before, his entire body deflated and he couldn't come up with a good reason to struggle against the tide any longer. "The man who lost that knife," he said, "was a cold son of a bitch. Best bluffer I ever did see." He closed his eyes as if he were seeing him at that very instant. "Come to think of it, I do recall someone else being with him."

"Yeah?" Nate asked. He'd backed up to give the other man some room to breathe but was close enough to grab him if Jessowitz got the sudden urge to run. "Go on."

"I was hoping *that* one would've sat down at the table, but he didn't. I could've won a fortune off'a someone like that."

It was Nate's experience to allow men like this to stray a little when they started reminiscing. It meant they were more comfortable with their company and oftentimes getting ready to let go of something really good. For that reason, Nate fought the urge to nudge Jessowitz along with a swift boot to the ribs and instead grunted, "Uh-huh."

Jessowitz wasn't aware that his audience was barely tolerating his reflections. "Yeah, that other fella wouldn't have been able to bluff for shit. The ones with the crazy eyes never can."

Suddenly, Nate perked up. "What was that about crazy eyes?"

Despite the fact that most of the blood had run to the lower portion of Deaugrey's body, even he could now hear the sounds that had caught Kaylee's attention. That didn't mean he was going to stop what he was doing, however. Still thrusting his hips back and forth, he took one hand off of her rump so he could reach for the door flap. It was just a bit too far for him to open without moving away from the cot.

"Damn it," he grunted.

"I know," Kaylee replied. "It — it sounds —"

"Yeah — I think —"

Suddenly, their bodies forced them to pay attention to only one thing. Both of them were rewarded by a flood of sensation that caused Kaylee's toes to curl in her boots. In just a few more crucial seconds, Deaugrey would be next to feel the surge of pleasure.

A second before that surge happened, the sounds from the front of the tent became too loud to ignore.

"That sounded like trouble," Kaylee said.

As much as Deaugrey wanted to ignore what he heard he couldn't help but agree. A man's gruff voice said something to a woman who now shrieked at him to leave. Her demand was cut short by the unmistakable smack of a fist against flesh.

"Just a little more . . ." Deaugrey pleaded.

Kaylee was looking toward the door, fidgeting on her feet, but not pulling away from him just yet.

The voices at the front of the tent were quieter, but Deaugrey was paying enough attention to hear them.

"I won't let you hurt her," said the woman that he recognized as the one who'd greeted him at the front door.

The man's words were indiscernible but filled with enough anger for Deaugrey to get their meaning.

There was going to be more noise soon that would put the previous commotion to shame.

Deaugrey stepped back and pulled up his pants. He was buckling his gun belt around his waist when Kaylee turned around to face him.

"What are you doing?" she asked.

"Just cover yourself up and be ready for me when I get back."

"That other fella," Jessowitz said, "had crazy eyes."

"What did he look like . . . apart from the eyes?" Nate asked.

"Taller than you. Big bull of a dude."

Brushing his hand along one part of his chin, Nate said, "Were there burns on this part of his face?"

"Not as I recall. He did have half a beard, though. I thought that was mighty strange. Could be it was burnt. I don't know."

"And this fellow with the crazy eyes, he

wasn't the one playing poker with you?"

"Nah."

Nate's stomach twisted into a knot. Mostly, he was angry at himself for committing one of the worst and most common sins for a man in his line of work. He'd gone into a situation thinking he already knew the answers and hadn't given anyone a chance to prove him wrong. He'd been so convinced that he knew who'd played cards with Jessowitz that Nate hadn't asked what should have been the first question as soon as they got outside.

"This man you played cards with," Nate finally asked, "what was his name?"

"Abraham Keyes. I remember because of Lincoln's name and . . . well . . . keys."

"Awww hell."

Deaugrey stomped out of his room with gun in hand, fully expecting to put the scare into some drunk who'd stepped out of line by hitting a woman.

"I don't give a damn what you want," the man at the front of the tent said in a voice that was as steady as a stone slab.

The woman who ran the cathouse stood with her back to the opening that led to the small room at the front of the place. "You won't hurt my girls!" she said.

148

Before Deaugrey could make it all the way to the front of the tent, the woman's head was snapped back by another blow to the face. She reeled from the impact, spinning all the way around while dropping to one knee. Now facing Deaugrey, she started shaking her head but was too afraid to do much more than that.

When he motioned for her to step away, Deaugrey smirked in anticipation of putting that rowdy drunk in his place. He took a few more steps and, now that his path was no longer impeded by the fallen woman, could see a tall man dressed in a black suit and a knee-length brown coat standing with fresh blood still dripping from his knuckles. He stared at Deaugrey with the cold, dead eyes of a killer and kept his other hand resting on the grip of his holstered gun. That pistol cleared leather before Deaugrey could even think about taking aim with his own weapon.

"Deaugrey Scott," the man with the cold eyes declared. "There's some important people looking for you."

"Awww, hell," Deaugrey sighed.

15

"There he is," the madam said as she swept a hand back at Deaugrey. "That's the man you were after, right? The one that just arrived?"

The man with the cold eyes nodded once. It was a barely perceptible motion that struck anyone who saw it like a jab to the kidney. "He is," the man said.

"Then take him and go!"

"Hey, now!" Deaugrey said. "A moment ago, you were trying to keep me alive."

"Not you, you damned fool," the man growled. "Her girls. She was just trying to make sure her girls stayed alive long enough to pick another man's pockets." Shifting his eyes to her, he added, "And they will."

Wilting like a flower that had been tossed into a fire, the madam lowered her head and sought shelter behind the table where her ledger and ink pen were kept.

"Seems I picked the wrong time to leave

my room," Deaugrey said. "I've always insisted that being a coward was severely underrated."

"You are definitely Mr. Scott," the man said. "I've heard a lot of stories about you and every last one of them mentions that big mouth of yours."

"Who the hell are you?"

"Don't matter. Shut your fucking hole and drop that pistol."

Deaugrey prided himself on being able to know more than one way out of any situation. Even more valuable was being able to quickly decide which of those ways to take. He made his choice this time by diving to one side with the most powerful jump he could convince his legs to give him. A shot blazed through the air, tearing through the canvas near Deaugrey's head and causing one of the girls inside the tent to scream frantically.

As soon as he hit the ground on his chest, Deaugrey scrambled to get his feet beneath him and plow into the next wall. His plan had been to charge straight through one flimsy barrier after another until he was outside. Unfortunately, his gall was more powerful than his sense of direction and Deaugrey wound up stampeding into yet another girl's room. He caught a glimpse of

151

long red hair and fair skin before his feet knocked against something solid that had been on the ground directly in front of him. Whoever had been huddled there grunted in pain after taking a boot to the ribs. The grunt sounded too deep to be feminine, but Deaugrey wasn't overly concerned with that since he was already tripping through the next canvas wall.

The next room he came to was much bigger than the first. Instead of the cot that had been in Kaylee's space, there was an actual bed as well as a dented bathtub filled with cloudy water. What caught Deaugrey's eye most, however, was the large post next to the tub that ran from floor to ceiling to prop up that section of the tent. Knowing the other man wasn't far behind him, Deaugrey lowered his shoulder and charged at the post. The wooden support cracked and buckled, but didn't give way on his first attempt.

Cringing with pain, Deaugrey spotted a wet, naked man and a woman wearing only filmy silk robes. "Why is there always someone nearby to witness my bad ideas?" Deaugrey grumbled. Since he'd come this far, he charged the post again. This time, the damaged support snapped all the way and brought a good portion of the tent down along with it. Deaugrey may have had an aching shoulder, but he'd gotten his bearings well enough to know which way to run this time around.

He exploded from the tent and into the narrow space between the cathouse and the neighboring saloon. Looking around in a daze, Deaugrey smirked when he saw the partially collapsed section of the cathouse tent. There was movement inside and Deaugrey reminded himself that there were several others in there apart from the one man he was worried about. Even as he thought about the women and their paying customers, Deaugrey contemplated firing a few shots into the tent just to tip the scales in his favor.

Whatever part of his ethics that had remained intact over the years kept him from shooting blindly into the tent. He gripped the .38 and thumbed back its hammer. His eyes sighted along the top of the barrel, waiting for even the slightest glimpse of the gunman's cold eyes or dark clothes.

The saloon behind him had plenty of activity inside of it, but no sign of panic with regard to the dust he'd just kicked up. Yet another thing Deaugrey liked about this camp.

"Grey!" a familiar voice shouted from

behind the saloon.

Deaugrey turned to look in that direction to find Nate circling around the back of the saloon while holding his Remington with a steady, straight arm. There was sharp authority in Nate's tone when he barked, "Down!"

Every reflex in Deaugrey's body told him to drop, which is precisely what he did. Before his chest could slam against the ground, two quick shots were fired. The first came from Nate and the second came from the front end of the cathouse. Deaugrey clamped his teeth together and gripped the earth with his free hand as if he were in danger of being cast off its surface and thrown into the sky.

More shots exploded back and forth, sending pieces of lead hissing over him. Suddenly, Deaugrey lost his reservations about firing blind and swung his arm back to point the .38 vaguely in the direction of the cathouse while pulling his trigger. The borrowed pistol bucked against his palm, adding an irregular voice to the staccato cracking of shots that came in more precise rhythms.

"Grey, get up, damn you!"

Deaugrey had never been happier to hear Nate's voice. As soon as he propped himself up, he felt a callused hand grab his free arm and drag him along. Deaugrey allowed himself to be pulled up until he could stand on his own. Just as he got his bearings, he caught a glimpse of Nate's angry face.

"Don't stop shooting, you fool!" Sathow shouted.

That was the last thing Deaugrey heard for a while because Nate's next shot was fired a might too close to his ears. In a strange way, the muffled quagmire of sound that filled Deaugrey's head was comforting in comparison to what had come before. The gunshots sounded like distant thunder; soothing to him in the same way his own breaths had soothed him in the sanitariums when he'd defiantly starved himself to the point of passing out.

Soon, a ringing blared through his skull to replace the soothing roar. Deaugrey shouted something at Nate that neither man could understand. He extended his arm, pointed the .38 at the dead-eyed gunman who'd stepped into view and pulled his trigger repeatedly. One of their shots must have come close, because the gunman stepped out of sight once again.

Deaugrey pulled his trigger again, but the pistol no longer jerked within his grasp. He'd run out of ammunition somewhere along the way and hadn't been able to hear when his shots had stopped coming.

Nate's voice was just another dull roar amid the ringing and other roars. Rather than try to speak to him, Nate shoved Deaugrey aside while reloading his Remington. Nodding as if that would make all the difference, Deaugrey fumbled for the bullets fitted within the loops on the thin belt Frank had given him. The roar was fading away in his ears, which unfortunately made the ringing that much clearer.

Even though Deaugrey's hands were becoming steadier with every passing second, he hadn't completely reloaded the .38 by the time Nate walked far enough to see the front entrance of the cathouse. From where he stood, Deaugrey could only watch Nate shift into a sideways stance while raising his pistol to take careful aim. Nate's voice made it through the ringing in Deaugrey's ears somewhat, but not enough for him to understand why he lowered his arm and allowed the Remington to slip from his fingers.

"What are you doing?" Deaugrey shouted.

Nate scowled and clasped his fingers behind his head. He put up no resistance when the pair of scruffy miners carrying shotguns stepped up to him and kicked the pistol away. As Nate was saying something to one of the men, the other one cracked him in the back of the head with the shotgun's stock.

By the time the men looked between the saloon and cathouse, Deaugrey was nowhere to be found.

16

Nagle, Missouri

Frank slept well that night. His rented room was tiny but its window allowed a cool breeze to drift through and fill it with the scent of the river. The fee for the room included breakfast, which wound up being griddle cakes, bacon and coffee. Pete didn't poke his nose from his room until Frank had made his way through half of his stack of cakes. When the tracker saw him sitting at the breakfast table, he looked to the window, which was bright with the deep orange glow of morning, and then back to the table.

"It's early," Pete said.

"A man in my line of work gets into the habit of waking up early," Frank replied cheerily.

"And enjoys it as well," Pete grunted as he made his way over to the table and sat down. When the woman who owned the place greeted him, he responded with, "I'll take what he's having, with some more bacon."

"Certainly," she said. "Be right there."

After Pete had filled a cup of coffee from the pot that had been left on the table, Frank said, "You weren't expecting to find me down here yet."

"Nope."

"We've ridden together a few times, Pete. We should be able to trust each other."

Pete stirred a cube of sugar into his coffee and stared quietly down into it. Eventually, he said, "It ain't a matter of trust. It's just . . . he ain't only a knife maker."

Frank smiled and got back to work on his breakfast. "I've pretty much gathered that on my own. Is this man is a good friend of yours?"

"No, but I've known him awhile," Pete said.

The cook returned with Pete's breakfast and set it down. Once she was happy that her work was done, she went back to the kitchen.

"I've got plenty of patience," Frank said, "but my supply is running short. Tell me who this knife maker is so we can get on with what we're here to do."

"His name is Caster Grunwaldt. He . . ."

Lowering his voice until it almost couldn't be heard at all, Pete said, "He's done some things he ain't so proud of. Caster has been getting soft in his old age and he's the sort who might just decide to repent once he gets a look at a preacher."

"So . . . what's the problem with that?"

"I was thinkin' maybe you could just show yourself, but not be close enough to let him talk to you. Sort of . . . grease the wheels."

"Why didn't you just come out and ask that before?" Frank said.

Pete shrugged and cut a portion of griddle cakes that looked almost too large to fit inside a human mouth. "Thought you might find such a thing disagreeable."

Frank waved that off and chewed on his last strip of bacon. "I've had to do many disagreeable things in my time, and not all of them are because of Nate. If seeing me will rattle this Caster person enough to talk a bit more, then so be it. I think I could do even more good if I was close enough to put a few words in myself, though."

"Guess I underestimated you."

"You're not the first to do that, my friend. Tell me some more about this man we're going to meet."

"He's made weapons of all sorts," Pete explained. "If you needed something that

160

could kill a man in the best possible way, you went to Caster. If he didn't have any in stock or know where to get them, he'd make the weapon for you himself."

"Sounds like someone Nate would like to meet."

The fork Pete pointed at Frank still had a bit of bacon on it when he said, "That's another reason I was treading carefully on that matter. Caster's trying to make good. He ain't another one of us who's just given in to what we are."

"We do good work, Pete. You're no criminal."

A shadow fell over Pete's face as he lowered his fork. "Caster ain't cut out to work with Nate Sathow. He's a might shaky in the head. Not as shaky as some men we both know, but he's . . ."

"Haunted?" Frank offered.

"Yeah. Haunted by what he's done. That being said, I don't think he's through doing it, either. Truth is, I don't know quite what to think. That's why I thought you'd be a good partner to have along when we talked to him. Perhaps we can shake something loose."

"If there's anything to come loose."

"There is," Pete said. "It ain't just some coincidence that a killer like Pescaterro gets ahold of a knife made by someone as fluent in death as Caster."

"What else is there, Pete? I know when someone is holding back from saying something important. Also, I've never seen you so uncomfortable."

Pete stabbed a few more chunks of griddle cake, used them to sop up some syrup and chewed them down. Finally, he said, "I don't know if we can trust him. He's dangerous."

And there it was. The hesitance in Pete's tone, the sudden pensiveness, even the way he shifted his eyes away came from a little flame of guilt within Pete's core. If anyone could spot that flame from a mile away, it was a preacher. "A man who makes the best guns would naturally be a fairly good shot," Frank said. "For a man with the talents of your friend . . . I imagine his skills extend into some pretty exotic directions."

"That's right. I know Nate trusts you, but I ain't never been right with him letting a man of the Lord ride along with us when we're getting shot at. But on these jobs, Nate calls the shots. Now that it's me callin' a shot or two . . ."

"First of all," Frank interrupted, "Nate doesn't *let* me do anything. He's damn lucky I offer my services, as are the rest of

162

you. Second, we can't do what we do by holding back. We work together or not at all. If we, as a people, could take anything beneficial from the War Between the States, that lesson is it."

"All right then," Pete said as he sat up straight and wiped his face with his napkin. "For this to go the way we want it to, I need to be certain you'll go along with the plan and not step on my toes when I'm goin' to work."

"That sounds . . . ominous. I thought he was a friend of yours."

"You're the one that's been callin' him my friend," Pete said. "I only mentioned that I know him."

"Fair enough."

"I've worked with Caster enough to know when he's lying," Pete said through a mouthful of breakfast. "I also know what it'll take to push him into helping if he's feeling uncooperative. What I need from you is —"

"Is to make my presence known as a man of God so I can appeal to this man's sense of guilt for his past, but not assert myself so much that I get in the way of you breaking his spirit and possibly parts of his body," Frank said. "Does that sound about right?"

Pete nodded. "It would also help if you

didn't try to do nothing like confuse him with spiritual talk or discuss ways he can repent and such."

"I see how a preacher trying to save a lost soul might inconvenience our need to beat information out of somebody."

"When you say it that way, it sounds downright savage."

"Well then," Frank said through a warmer smile, "at least we're both finally seeing eye to eye. Let's get this over with."

17

Caster's shop was a simple one, located near a sawmill and an easy walk to any raw materials a man of his profession might need. There was a blacksmith within sight of his shop, but not so close as to be considered a proper neighbor. Nagle itself was a small community filled with people who were mostly uninterested in meeting the gaze of two strangers walking through it, which suited Frank and Pete's needs just fine.

On their way to the shop, Pete and Frank discussed how they would approach this weapon smith. It was fairly straightforward, but Pete was a stickler for sorting through any eventualities his fertile mind could produce. By the time Pete was ready to knock on the shop's door, Frank felt like he'd already met with its owner three or four times in a row.

The shop was locked up tight. Every

window was covered and, if he were alone that day, Frank might very well have been convinced the place was empty. He certainly wouldn't have switched from knocking to kicking the door hard enough to rattle it within its frame. That was the path Pete decided to take, so Frank stood by and watched him go.

After a minute or two, the door's latches were worked from the other side. Amid the rattle and clatter of the metal posts being pulled back, a grumbling voice could be heard. Frank recognized the language as German. Having a basic understanding of a language didn't help him decipher the steady torrent of it that was accentuated by colorful gestures and what must have been some nasty requests.

When the door was finally opened, a short man with beady eyes peered out at them. Almost all of his hair was sprouting in a thick curtain covering his upper lip. Whatever grew from his scalp had been cut so short that it wouldn't have made a serviceable brush. "What do you want?" he asked in an accent that reeked of dark beer and heavy breads.

"Hello, Caster. It's Pete Meyer. Remember me?"

"Of course I do," Caster replied in short,

chopped words. "What do you want?"

"I need to talk to you about a knife."

"There's a general store in town."

Pete grinned. "Not just a regular blade. One of your special orders. I got the money to pay for the job to be done right."

Caster squinted past Pete to where Frank was standing. "Who's he?"

"A friend. Can we come in or should I start laying out the details on your front porch?"

The door swung open, and Caster stepped aside. He was dressed in simple clothes that were clean, functional and not much else. The black trousers he wore had obviously been mended several times and went along nicely with the rumpled white shirt and dark gray vest that was buttoned most of the way up.

Pete led the way into a shop that was anything but what Frank had expected. Where the front of the store was tightly shut to any intrusion from the outside world, the back was open and embraced its natural surroundings with true vigor. Windows larger than doors lined the far wall, allowing every possible bit of sunlight to flood the wide-open workspace. The floors were immaculately clean. Both work benches had such a high degree of polish that they

167

looked freshly made. Even the collection of tools hanging on the side wall and arranged on a long table had been assembled like a jigsaw puzzle. Each and every piece came together in the most efficient way to make one glorious whole.

"What is this knife you need me to make?" Caster asked. "Probably one of my custom throwing blades?"

"I don't know if it's supposed to be thrown, tossed, dropped or used to butter a biscuit," Pete said. "But yeah. It's one of your fancy custom models."

As he listened to Pete talk, Caster cringed at every word. Frank couldn't help but notice that Pete was stringing more words together in an unusually messy way and now he saw why. Just listening to the prolonged patter of unnecessary syllables clearly raked Caster's nerves.

"You are working for Nathan Sathow again, yes?"

"Yes indeed. What makes you pose that question?"

"Because you are still prattling on about nothing instead of buying something," Caster snapped. "Ask your question and then be on your way."

"Don't get snippy with me," Pete said.

"Why does that one keep staring at me?"

Caster asked while staring pensively at the third man in the workshop.

Frank stepped forward with his hands clasped and a tranquil expression on his face, which was the pose he struck whenever he was with someone who expected to talk to a more traditional preacher. "Patience is a virtue, my friend."

"Sathow has sunk to new lows," Caster said, "if he has taken to recruiting priests to do his bidding."

"I only answer to one call, I assure you," Frank said in a good-natured manner. He then held his hands about a foot apart. "The knife in question is about this long and was purchased by —"

"I haven't sold a custom blade in years."

"Then it could have been stolen," Pete said. "It had your mark on it, so I know it's yours."

"You don't know anything," Caster said.

Storming over to one of the workbenches, Pete grabbed the trigger guard of a rifle that was laying in pieces. He turned it around and quickly grinned while pointing to a small design of two sideways *V*s pointed in opposite directions overlaying each other that had been stamped into the iron. "This mark right here!" Pete said. "You're the only one who stamps such a thing into his

169

weapons. Not only that, but this man would've passed through here on his way south from up north of here where he broke out of prison."

Although he was still riled up, Caster didn't quite know what to make of Frank. He didn't have that problem when he looked back over to Pete, though. "I want you to leave. Both of you."

Pete now stood at a long table where an array of drills was displayed beneath several saws hanging from pegs on the wall. Letting his fingers drift from one drill to another, he appeared to be seriously contemplating which was best for a job before he selected one and threw it through the closest window. The move was so swift and so catastrophic to the pane of glass he'd targeted that both Frank and Caster nearly jumped out of their skins when the crash filled the formerly immaculate shop.

"What is the meaning of this?" Caster fumed.

"It's about that damn knife!" Pete roared. "You may not have a problem lying in front of this here priest, but I'm not gonna stand here and take it from you! I just came across that knife and it was from someone who sure as hell hasn't been holding on to it for years!"

In all the times that Frank had worked with Pete, he'd never seen him move as quickly as he did on this day. Pete grabbed another one of those drills and was poised to bore a hole into some random part of Caster's anatomy when he was stopped by a frantic voice.

"No!" the weapon smith shrieked. "Listen to me! Please!"

"Go on and talk," Pete said.

"I was telling the truth before. I haven't sold one of those blades for some time." Turning to Frank with what seemed to be very genuine sincerity in his eyes, Caster added, "After so many lives were ended with those blades, I swore to my God above that I would not sell another one. You must believe me, Father."

Frank rarely let himself be addressed on such formal terms, but Caster spoke the title with such reverence that refusing him would have been a sin in itself. Nodding quietly, Frank let Pete's strategy unfold.

"I've kept those knives here," Caster continued. "I can show you."

"Not all of 'em are here," Pete said. "I've seen it and there's no mistaking one of them blades. Just tell me about the one that's missing before I get agitated."

"It was stolen from me."

Pete allowed himself to ease back into his normal speaking voice as he said, "Now we're getting somewhere."

When Caster looked his way, Frank gave him another nod and said, "Go ahead. It's all right."

Those words often had a soothing effect on folks. For Caster, they were more. They were a balm that alleviated whatever pain he'd been feeling from a wound that so clearly festered within his soul.

"A man came through town," Caster said. "He arrived at night, more than a week or two ago now. To be honest, I have tried to forget him since he left. He was a large man. Muscular. Unruly hair. His face was scarred. Burnt, I think. His whiskers only grew in irregular patches."

Pete nodded. "Sounds like the man we're after. He have crazy eyes?"

"No."

Now it was Pete who glanced over to Frank. Quickly recovering his commanding demeanor, the tracker asked, "Are you sure about that? His eyes are what most folks remember about him."

"He wasn't a normal killer," Caster told him. "I have seen more than my share throughout the years. But he didn't strike me as crazy. He spoke calmly and knew exactly what he wanted."

"Which was one of those fine knives?"

"No, no! He was poking around in my stock when he found those knives. He took a liking to one of them and took it from me. It would have been more trouble than it was worth to try and stop him so I let him walk off with it. That's all there is to it. I swear to God."

"So what else did he talk about?"

"You asked about the knife," Caster said. "I told you about the knife."

Pete started nodding again. "I did, Caster. And now I'm asking you about the rest."

Turning toward Frank, Caster reached out with one hand as if he'd suddenly found himself sinking in a pool of black water. "I can't. Just . . ."

"Don't talk to him!" Pete roared. "You'll talk to *me*! Because no preacher and no Lord above," he said while selecting one of the smaller gauge drills and holding it up for all to see, "can help you if you don't."

Now that Pete's demeanor had changed, so did Caster's. "The two of you can't tell me what to do in my own shop," he said through gritted teeth while reaching for a pistol stashed beneath the flap of his dark gray vest. "Not even Sathow's own priest!"

Without pause and without sparing a mo-

173

ment to try and convince the man in front of him of his wrongdoing, Frank drew his own weapon and steeled himself to end that man's life.

Like any other predator, this one knew when he'd awakened the wrong prey. "Easy, Father," Caster said.

"Don't call me that."

"All right." Looking to Pete, Caster asked, "Can't you tell him I won't shoot?"

Pete stepped up to Caster, turned him around and took the pistol from him. The drill was still in his other hand and he jabbed its tip against Caster's belly while saying, "If I gotta tell you one more time not to talk to him . . ."

Snapping his eyes to Pete, Caster disregarded Frank altogether. He was shaken and confused when he said, "I don't know everything Casey had planned. He just came to me to ask some advice."

"So you know who was paying you the visit?"

"Yes. I've met Casey Pescaterro once before, and I've dealt with some of his men over the years. All of those men are either dead or locked away. This most recent time, Casey only came to me with one other man that I've never seen before."

"Who was this other man?"

"I don't know." Feeling the drill twist against his gut, Caster squirmed and rose to his tiptoes in an attempt to put any sort of distance between himself and the tool he knew so very well. "I swear on my eyes, he never gave me his name. He was an older gentleman, though. Tall. Lean."

"And he was in Pescaterro's gang?"

"Actually, I got the impression that Pescaterro was in *his* gang."

Frank didn't like the sound of that one bit and knew Pete was feeling the same cold discomfort in the pit of his stomach at the notion of someone being able to rein in Dog Ear enough to give him orders.

"So the knife was just stolen on a lark," Pete continued. "What business brought them here in the first place?"

"They had an order to pick up. They were headed south from here. I don't know where."

"And here I thought you were retired."

"I was," Caster insisted. "But the money for this was too much for me to resist. After something like this, I could maybe retire for certain very soon."

"Very soon, huh?" Pete mused. "Isn't that what you were sayin' about a year or three ago?"

Knowing there was no way to talk himself

out of that one, Caster stopped trying to plead his case. "If I tell you everything, these men will find out. This fellow who placed the order knows a great many things. It is how he has gotten as far as he is."

"You don't even know the man's name," Frank pointed out.

"He will kill anyone who crosses him," Caster said. "That is all I need to know."

Tossing away the drill, Pete grabbed Caster with both hands and dragged him over to a shorter, rectangular workbench. "Well it ain't enough for me," he said fiercely. He lifted the German up onto the table, slammed his shoulders against the clean surface and grabbed a saw hanging from a peg on the table's edge and lowered the jagged teeth of the saw across Caster's neck. "You came this far," he said. "Might as well finish the story. Otherwise I'm gonna have to cut you short."

That was one of the few jokes Frank had ever heard Pete tell. It was also one of the best.

Caster didn't find it nearly as amusing. Sweat poured down his face, which had suddenly gone fish-belly white. "The order was for mounted Gatling guns and a specially modified cannon."

"Are you serious?" Frank asked as he

176

moved over to the table so he could look directly down into Caster's eyes.

The weapon smith pressed himself against the table as if he thought he could shove all the way down to the floor. He seemed to be looking at his Maker when he said, "I'm telling the truth."

"Go on with it then."

"He also wanted mounted armor plates."

"Mounted onto what?" Pete asked.

More than happy to look away from Frank, Caster said, "The armor is essentially made from steel plates attached to hooks that can be hung from railings, the side of a wagon or even windowsills."

"What about the rest of the order?"

Caster nodded. "He wanted one of my special order safes and a few crates of rifles and such."

"Men don't come to you just for rifles. What was the safe for?"

"What's any safe for?"

Not knowing much about safes, Pete went back to more familiar territory. "How was the cannon supposed to be modified?"

"He wanted something that could inflict as much damage as possible. I had already been working on something along those lines. I call it a flame spout."

"What the hell is that?" Pete asked

through a perplexed scowl.

"Well," Caster said uncomfortably, "I've been putting it together as something of a curiosity and the stranger seemed very interested in it. Quite simple really. It's similar in design to hand pumps used by fire departments in New York City and Europe. Instead of water being pumped, kerosene is used. There are some other precautions to take when dealing with a combustible like that. Once you make those considerations, all that's needed is an ignition source that will not set fire to the kerosene tanks. It was an unusual project, but I managed to fill it in time for delivery."

"Which is when?" Since Pete only got a bewildered grimace from Caster, he placed the saw across Caster's chest and started dragging it just hard enough to rip his vest and shirt.

"It's already happened!" Caster yelped. "That's why those men stopped by and were here for so long. Pescaterro and that stranger I told you about came with a wagon to collect the order."

"How long ago was the order placed?"

"A few months. I needed time to figure out how I would complete my flame spout and then build it along with the armor plates."

Frank surprised both of the other men by pressing the barrel of his .38 beneath the German's left eye. "Why?" he snarled. "Why would you make weapons like this?"

"I just do what I'm asked!" Caster insisted.

"If you were asked to execute a family or burn a schoolhouse full of children, would you?"

"I — That's not the same."

"Isn't it? You must know those weapons will be used to inflict pain, death and suffering!"

"I wouldn't take part in killing anyone. I'm just a craftsman. I make tools. I don't use them. Please forgive me, Father. I'm trying to be a better man. I would never —"

"Shut your mouth," Frank said in a strained voice. Holstering the pistol as if he'd forgotten that he'd drawn it in the first place, he whispered, "Just . . . be quiet."

Frank pulled in a long breath and let it out. Keeping his hand on the grip of the .38 to push it as far down into its holster as possible, he put his back to the sunny side of the workshop and headed for the door.

Once outside, it took a few moments for the scent of the air or the sound of the nearby water to register on his weary senses.

All of the natural wonders were still there, but it took Frank a bit longer to recognize them. He walked around the building until he could see the river as well as hear it. The wind had calmed somewhat but with some concentration, Frank was able to feel its touch on his cheek.

Birds sang lazily to each other from the branches of slowly swaying trees.

Horses tied nearby let out a few huffing breaths and stomped their feet to fret at something or other.

A door swung open and a set of boots crunched against the ground. When Frank felt a pair of eyes burning into his back, he turned around to check if anyone was staring at him. Although Pete was approaching, he was looking toward the street. Frank checked the door and saw the nervous weapons maker holding it open while staring at him. A second later, the door was quickly shut.

"You doing all right, Preacher?" Pete asked.

"Yeah. Did he have anything else to say?"

"It started as a bunch of rattling on about Dog Ear and that stranger he was with. He thinks the two of them pulled together a small amount of men. Less than a dozen in all. You squeezed all the really good stuff out of him before you left. That was damn impressive, if I do say so myself."

"I lost my temper. That shouldn't happen. Not anymore."

"You're still a man, ain't ya?"

"Very much so," Frank replied.

"Then you got nothing to be sorry about. You didn't let him walk all over you or try to preach to him. And, when you surprised both of us at the end there, you didn't do any real damage. There might be some damage to Caster's trousers, but it ain't nothing a good wash can't fix. Did that stranger Caster described sound familiar at all?"

Grateful for something else to think about, Frank pondered that and then shook his head. "Not as such. I don't know anyone who would —"

"Who would what?" Pete asked. "Want to kill so many men in as quick a time as possible?"

"No," Frank said with a tired laugh. "I've known more men like that than I've known good souls who want nothing more than to tend to their field or bring their children up right. I'm talking about someone who would want to have something built that can spray fire and cause not just pain and death but . . . screaming agony. Have you ever seen someone burn?"

"Yeah," Pete replied. "Two men who went into a burning stable to try and pull out a couple of panicked horses. They made it to the door and then dropped. The flames were so bad . . ." He closed his eyes and quickly opened them again to focus on the slowly rippling river. "Me and the others trying to douse the blaze couldn't get close enough to do anything. We just had to stand there holding those heavy, useless goddamn buckets of water and watch those men and horses melt down like candles."

"And not only did someone think up a way to spread that kind of misery," Frank said, "but another man actually built it for him."

Pete put a hand on Frank's shoulder. "If it makes you feel any better, we're all workin' to find those killers and they're all bound for the noose when we do."

"How many more killers must be dealt with after that?" Frank wondered.

"We'll just chip away wherever we can. The way I see it, if enough folks do their part, this filthy stink hole of a world may have a chance after all."

Frank nodded, but not enthusiastically. For now, it was the best he could manage.

18

Frank and Pete left later that same day. Because Nagle was such a small, tight-knit community, it didn't take much for them to be convinced that there was a gang of killers lurking about somewhere. After eating a quick lunch and stocking up on supplies, they put Nagle behind them.

There was a trading post which was roughly halfway between Nagle and the mining camp where they were supposed to meet up with Nate and Deaugrey. Having arrived slightly ahead of schedule, Frank found some other folks in need of a good conversation. Apart from the trading post, there was also a small platform and ticketing office used by several local stagecoach companies. Waiting on the platform were a family of four on their way to Nebraska and a man traveling on his own who was headed all the way to San Francisco. It did Frank a world of good to speak with them and, when

Pete sauntered up to the platform, he went unnoticed for several minutes. Finally, Frank excused himself so he could stand by the burly tracker.

"You seem to be in better spirits," Pete said.

Frank smiled and clasped the lapels of his black jacket. "I do, indeed! It feels nice to be among people who regard a man in my profession as a comfort instead of as a threat to their tainted souls. No offense meant, of course."

"You think I got a tainted soul?"

After a short but uncomfortable silence, Frank asked, "Did you find anything in regards to Nate or Deaugrey?"

"Not a damn thing." Pete's words carried just far enough to catch the attention of a mother traveling with her two young boys. She was a pleasant woman with curly blond hair and a round face who quickly escorted her sons away from the source of the foul language to which they'd just been subjected. Pete tipped his hat to them and shrugged apologetically to the tall bespectacled man who walked over to accompany the woman and children.

"Did you check for a message?" Frank asked. "There's a telegraph desk. That's why Nate chose this spot to meet."

"I know there's a damn telegraph desk," Pete snarled in a quieter voice. "I saw the damn wires. There ain't no message waiting there, no telegrams and none of the folks working in this place have seen anyone that looks like Nate or Grey."

Now worry began to show on Frank's face. "It's possible they might forget about seeing Nate. But Deaugrey . . . he's memorable if nothing else."

"That's one way of putting it. How much longer do you reckon we should wait here?"

"We've got plenty of sunlight left. If we head out now, we should make it all the way to that mining camp by this time tomorrow."

"Earlier, I'd say," Pete told him. "I know some shortcuts we can take that may be a bit tougher of a ride, but will shave a good amount of time off the trip."

"We can't stray too far from the original trail," Frank insisted as he and Pete walked to where their horses were tied. "There's always the chance Nate and Deaugrey were merely delayed and are on their way to meet us. They'll be taking the same route as we did but if we take another one, we might pass each other without knowing."

Pete approached his horse to check the saddle's buckles and reins to make certain all the essentials were securely in place. "I could always look for high ground every so often to check for anyone using that other trail."

"Could you do that well enough to see that trail without losing any of the time we'd gain by taking the other route in the first place?"

It didn't take long for Pete to arrive at his conclusion. "No."

"Then we'll do the most obvious thing," Frank said. "You ride ahead on your shorter route and get to that mining town as quickly as you can while I ride the original trail back so I can meet up with Nate and Deaugrey if they're headed that way."

"I don't know if I like that idea too much," Pete said.

"Why? You think a preacher wouldn't be able to handle himself if things got rough along the way?"

Pete grinned. "After what I seen over the last couple'a days, there ain't no doubt in my mind you can handle yourself. Still, if you run into Dog Ear or any of his boys, that could be the sort of trouble that no man can handle on his own."

"It's not a very long ride. Both of us will move quickly and silently, avoiding trouble wherever possible. Besides," Frank added, "if we ran into Dog Ear or his men, having one or two of us wouldn't make a big enough difference to worry about. From what we've heard of the ordnance they're packing, all four of us are going to have our hands full on the day we cross paths with them."

"Yeah. I see your point. Can't say as I like it any better, but you're right. So we split up, and if you do happen to find Nate or Grey, the lot of you turn back around and head for that mining camp. No matter what, that's where we pick up the next leg of Dog Ear's trail."

"Agreed." Frank was about to snap his reins when he saw Pete reach one hand straight out to him.

When Frank shook the hand that was offered, Pete said, "My apologies for before."

"No need for that," the other man assured him.

"That's where you're mistaken. I wasn't thinking too highly of you. To be honest, I never did quite warm up to the notion of Nate riding with a preacher. You always struck me as a burden that wasn't good for much apart from steering a bit of suspicion away from us."

Frank shrugged. "I doubt I'm really good for that, to be honest."

"Right, which just makes you a burden." Smiling, Pete surveyed his surroundings with the scrutiny of someone who had the skills to truly see everything there was to be found. "I was wrong about that, and I was wrong about you."

"Lord, I hope so."

"I can see why Nate has you as a partner. You did a hell of a job. I can't speak for any of the others on Nate's list, but I'm someone who'll be more than willing to put his life into yer hands."

"Thanks," Frank said. "I hope it doesn't come to that, but thanks."

The two men parted ways. Frank retraced his steps down the trail they'd originally taken to get to Nagle at a brisk, steady pace. Unencumbered by worry about anyone else keeping up with him, Pete snapped his reins to coax his horse to a gallop as quickly as possible. When he disappeared into the Missouri woods, they swallowed him up like a ghost.

19

As far as Pete was concerned, being in the company of his fellow human beings wasn't nearly as beneficial as everyone else seemed to think. If he had things his way, his days would all rush past him in a furious gust of wind and the thunder of a horse's hooves beating against the ground. When he didn't have to concern himself with things like another person's well-being or the letter of the law, everything just became clearer.

Not all folks were cut out for living in the hills or forging new paths across an untamed land. Those were the folks who needed to keep to their towns and lock themselves away behind their walls. As he rode over the rough terrain, watching for any flaw in the ground before him that could send him flying from his saddle, Pete wore a cruel grin at the notion of tenderfeet trying to survive in his world.

Out there, miles from civilized niceties,

was most definitely Pete Meyer's world. Anyone who couldn't read every last sign given by the grain of the earth or the creatures dwelling there was headed for a swift and painful end. For those folks, there was no practical way to find a bloodthirsty animal like Dog Ear Pescaterro until he showed himself in his own terrible way. All Pete had to do was keep his nose to the wind and his eyes open wide. Sooner or later, even the deadliest predators stepped where they shouldn't. Bear, wolf or man, it made no difference. They all made mistakes.

For the next day's ride, Pete reveled in his element and tore through Missouri like the last plate of Nate Sathow's cooking had ripped through his innards. With nobody else to guide through the mess of Missouri's backwoods, he traversed a route that barely qualified as a trail. Since Pescaterro would have needed to be a miracle worker to bring a wagon through there, Pete didn't even need to concern himself with tracking the outlaw. His only task was to move swiftly, and he fulfilled that purpose with true tenacity. By late morning of the following day, he'd made even more progress than he could have hoped.

A simple breakfast of cold oatmeal and jerked venison kept him going for the rest of the ride. Before he could even think about supper, he caught sight of a small cluster of men huddled around a crook in a stream. Pete skirted the men's position, getting close enough to tell they were panning in the water. Not much farther along, Pete met up with the proper trail leading toward the mining camp. He was so far ahead of schedule that he didn't bother looking to see if Frank was there or not. If the preacher had beat him to that camp, Pete would gladly pick up a shovel and join the miners in a new line of work.

The camp was less than a mile away. Once his horse slowed to a walk and the wind in his face had dwindled down to a hot, sticky breeze, Pete wished he could look over to Frank and nod for the preacher to take over from there. But Frank was still somewhere in the dust behind him, and Pete needed to do some scouting of a different sort, which involved talking to folks and getting a few answers. It wasn't anything new to him and neither was the sour expression that settled onto his face as he climbed down from his saddle to lead his horse through camp.

The first place he went was the corral where he, Nate and the others had put up their horses during their last stop there. He handed over his reins to the same man who'd been there before and gave him enough money to pay for a feed bag and some clean water. Holding out a bit more cash, Pete asked, "You seen the other men that were with me the last time?"

"Oh yeah," the stableman replied. "There was another one, sure enough. Had a scar, I believe."

"When did they leave?" Pete asked.

"Leave?"

"Yeah," he said. "You've only got one horse here and I ain't never seen it before. The loud one and the one with the scar probably left in the last few days. If you could narrow it down for me, I'd be obliged."

Once a bit more money was dangled in front of him, the stableman asked, "What horses were they riding?"

Pete looked in the corral roped off in front of him. "I don't see them. One should be a spotted gelding and the other's a mule."

"Right. They're still here. I got 'em inside."

"Inside?"

The stableman nodded over to a long tent set up nearby. All this time, Pete had written it off as a bath house or laundry because of all the puddles around it.

"I own that place as well," the stableman said. "Use it to wash the horses and clean half the clothes in this camp."

"At least I was half right," Pete grumbled.

"Huh?"

"Forget it. You were paid to give my friends' horses baths?"

"Nah. I also use that place for anyone who wants to rent a space for extended periods. That don't happen very often since most folks who stay are workin' here, and they can keep their own horses themselves."

Now more than ever, Pete longed for the solitude of an open trail. "You're not making this very easy on me," he grumbled as he walked over to the long tent.

"What do you mean?" the stableman asked. "Where are you going? Hey! You ain't allowed to just poke your nose in wherever you like!" Although he was more than willing to grouse about what Pete was doing, the stableman wasn't about to get off his wide ass to do anything about it himself.

As the man outside continued to holler at him, Pete stepped into the long tent to have a look. The interior was divided into spaces the size of stalls for the horses, two of which were occupied. He was relieved to find the spotted gelding and mule he'd been after and was even happier that he didn't have to continue talking in circles with the stableman. Unfortunately, there was just one more question that needed to be asked.

Once Pete had walked away from the tent that reeked of wet animals, he made his way back to the stableman. Obviously pleased with himself for some reason, the fat man folded his hands across his belly and looked up at Pete. "Sorry to speak so roughly to you," he said. "A man's got to protect his interests."

"I understand," Pete replied. "How long have the two men who own those animals been in camp?"

"Awhile."

"Have they ever left?"

"No, but I expect they won't be leaving anytime soon. Ever since Dale got ahold of one of 'em, that fella ain't seen the light of day."

Keeping his face an unreadable mask, Pete asked, "Who's Dale?"

"Dale Chester. Him and Adam Ross act as regulators in this camp. Closest thing to law there is around here."

"Where can I find them?"

"Dale only got one of your friends. The other one was fit to be tied when he came around to try and get the horses from me. Didn't have any money on him, though. He was the one with the big mouth, so I guess that other fella with the scar you mentioned is the one in lockup. Ross keeps drunks and vagrants in the old smokehouse on the western edge of camp. There was some sort of commotion outside the Straight to the Eight, shooting and all. I imagine your friends were wrapped up in that somehow."

"Much obliged," Pete said with a tip of his hat.

"Hey!"

Turning around again, Pete expected any number of threats or boasts from the fat man who seemed to have grown roots into his chair. Instead, the stableman nodded up at him and asked, "You need a spot to put your horse up for the night?"

"Don't think so."

"Suit yourself." With that, the stableman settled back into his blissful state of apathy.

On his way through camp, Pete went through the thick of the settlement, which included a saloon and some other large tent marked with red scarves fluttering from atop two of its posts. Having spotted the bar through the saloon's wide front entrance, he went inside and rapped on the warped wooden surface.

"What can I get you?" the bartender asked.

"I hear there was some sort of commotion here not too long ago," Pete said as he placed enough money on the bar to cover a drink and then some.

"Sure was," the barkeep replied while scooping up the money. "What can I get you?"

"You can get me a beer and keep the change if you let me know what happened."

"The two who were in that shooting. They friends of yours?"

Pete nodded once.

"Then you'll be willing to pay a bit more to hear about what terrible bit of business befell them."

"Or," Pete offered, "I can consider it a kindness if you'd let me know what happened. In exchange, I'll do you the kindness of not putting a match to this pile of kindling you call a bar."

The barkeep was quick to offer a wide smile. "Kindness is a reward in itself, right? There was a fight or some such at the cathouse next door. Scared the hell out of the girls working there and part of the tent was knocked down. Dale got to him before anyone was hurt."

Pete patted the bar and said, "Keep the beer and all the money," even though the barkeep hadn't made a move toward the tap. "What about the other one? My friend that wasn't caught and dragged away."

"The one with the big mouth?"

"That's him."

"Over yonder," the barkeep replied while nodding toward the card tables.

When Deaugrey wasn't acting like a fool, he didn't stand out nearly as much. Still, it didn't take long for Pete to spot him leaning over one of the tables with his back to the bar. Pete approached him, grabbed one of Deaugrey's shoulders and gave him a shake as he leaned down to whisper, "You shouldn't keep your back to the door like that, Grey."

"I like surprises," Deaugrey said.

"Where's Nate?"

"Oh, that's a hell of a story."

"I already got most of it," Pete said.

"Then why come and bother me?"

Tightening his grip on Deaugrey's shoulder, Pete started to lift him from his chair. This wasn't the first time Deaugrey was forcibly taken from one place to another, which meant he'd had plenty of practice in shaking himself loose. After a few quick twists of his body, he pulled free of Pete's grip and turned to face him.

"Can't you see I'm busy?" Deaugrey snapped.

Pete gave a stern look to the rest of the players before they could object to the inter-

197

ruption of the game. "We got plenty to keep us busy so come along with me, crazy man, before I embarrass you in front of all your new friends."

"If you've truly heard about our predicament, then you should be able to guess that we're in need of as much money as we can get as quickly as we can get it."

Admittedly, Deaugrey had a point. His case gained even more strength when Pete took into consideration the impressive stack of chips and cash in front of Deaugrey. Add that to the hopeful expressions that were starting to appear on the faces of the other players and Pete was certain Deaugrey's luck was showing no hint of running out soon.

"How much longer?" Pete asked.

Settling into his seat and straightening his clothes, Deaugrey said, "It's a game of ebbs and flows." In a quick whisper, he added, "Two hours."

Pete excused himself and headed for the bar. "What's he been drinking?" he asked the tender.

"Whiskey. The cheap stuff."

"Keep them coming," Pete said as he placed some more cash onto the bar. "But start watering them down, you hear?"

In his experience, that was never a request

a barkeep was unwilling to fulfill. So as not to disappoint him, this bartender smiled and reached for a bottle on the shelf behind him. It was one of the largest and least dusty in the entire place.

In the short amount of time that he'd been in the camp, Pete had gotten most of the answers he needed. He could get the remaining ones by simply doing what he did best. After leaving the Straight to the Eight, he went to the tent marked with red scarves and took a moment to have a gander. In a matter of seconds, a pretty young thing wrapped in nothing but a slip sauntered over to him and asked, "You look lonely, handsome. I can help with that."

"I hear there was some trouble here recently."

"Yes, but don't worry about that," the young woman replied with a dismissive wave. "Let me take care of you."

"What's your name?"

"Sadie."

"Tell you what, Sadie. When I come back after collecting some money I'm owed, I'll ask for you special."

She winked and walked away to let him get to it.

Pete hadn't asked where the trouble had been exactly because she'd told him enough by the direction she'd waved and glanced when he'd mentioned the commotion. Wandering outside to circle around to the side of the tent, Pete studied the ground carefully and blocked out everything else around him. It felt mighty good to get back to what he did best.

20

Nate had been sitting in the same position for hours. Shoulders against a wall, knees tucked in close to his chest, head back, eyes closed. Considering he was locked up inside a box that fell somewhere between the size of a toolshed and a coffin, he didn't have many other choices. The walls were thick, charred black and smelled of burnt meat. There was only one window that looked to have been cut out by someone who barely knew how to work a saw, but the iron bars fitted into it had been crafted by a master. The only door in or out was so short that even a child would need to duck in order to get through and, when it came open, Nate didn't bother moving from his spot.

"You here to ask for another handout?" he grunted. "Because I ain't earned much money since the last time you came looking."

"You got a visitor," said the man in his

early thirties who was one of two keeping watch over him. When Nate had been tossed into the makeshift jail, the man had introduced himself as Adam Ross.

Nate opened his eyes to find the skinny fellow stooping down to gaze in at him with the same melancholy expression he always wore. "A visitor?" he asked.

"Yes. He says he's the preacher from back where you call home."

Nate jumped to his feet and almost knocked himself out cold by slamming his head against one of the thick wooden beams above him. Rubbing the sore spot on top of his skull, he shuffled forward. "About time!"

"You expecting a visit from a preacher?"

"Yes, sir. Are you gonna deny me my chance to pray in a time of need?"

"I suppose not," Ross said. "It's about time for you to have a stretch and relieve yourself anyway. You've got a few minutes to do all of that, including talking to your friend. Make any moves I don't like and —" Ross finished his statement by showing Nate the shotgun with which he'd already become very familiar.

"Got it," Nate said. "Can I step out now?"

Ross took a few steps back, held his shotgun at hip level so he could point it inside the little structure and shouted,

"Come on out. Make it slow and keep your hands where I can see them!"

Nate followed the directions to the letter until he got a look at who else was out there waiting for him. "Pete?" he said while dropping his hands and taking a few quick steps toward the tracker.

"Easy!" Ross warned. "Is this your preacher or not?"

"Sure he is," Nate replied. "I'm just surprised he took the time to pay me a visit."

"Anything to tend to my flock and all of that," Pete replied.

The skinny man with the shotgun backed away. "You've got another couple of minutes. I'll let you know when your time is about up. Once it's over, there ain't no more to be had and you'll go back inside. Otherwise . . ."

"I know, I know," Nate said. "You'll cut me in half with that shotgun or some such thing."

"Well . . . right." Without any more threats in his arsenal, Ross stepped even farther back where he could hold a quiet conference with another fellow who was a squat, younger man with a thick head of black hair.

"I thought Frank would be out here," Nate said in a hushed voice.

"I've seen the way the waves part for him

203

when he tells folks who he is," Pete told him. "Worked for me just as well even without the starched shirt. All I had to do was carry myself like Frank, mention I was a man of the cloth and I got a chance to see you even quicker than by showing those old tin stars you carry with you. Speaking of them, I suppose those two idiots over there didn't have much respect for whatever badge you were carrying?"

"It wasn't one they recognized. Besides, they were paid to lock me up no matter who the hell I was. How much money did you bring? Those two aren't exactly beholden to anyone other than whoever paid them most recently."

"Deaugrey is working on passing the collection plate around."

Nate sighed and shook his head. "You didn't have to say you were a priest. Mentioning you wanted to visit me probably would have been enough."

"Just thought I'd give it a try," Pete said offhandedly. "Call it an experiment."

"Maybe your next experiment could be tracking down a man named Abraham Keyes. Ever hear of him?"

"No."

"About eighteen months back, Keyes shot a marshal in Wyoming named Russ Cav-

204

anaugh."

Pete nodded. "I remember hearing about Cavanaugh. Just never knew he was a lawman. Nobody had much good to say about him as I recall."

"I was tending to some business down in New Mexico at the time and when I came back, Cavanaugh was in the ground and Keyes was locked up for putting him there. He had a date with the hangman and my only regret was that I couldn't get to town quick enough to watch him swing."

"So you knew Cavanaugh?"

"Yes," Nate said with a solemn nod. "He was a good man. More importantly, he was a good lawman."

That raised Pete's eyebrows as he said, "Mighty high praise coming from you. I've never heard so many disparaging remarks about lawmen from someone who owns so many damn badges."

"That's because I was given most of them badges while serving in some official capacity or other. I've been a deputy, a sheriff and the servant of a few state courts. More often than not, my job ended on account of me refusing to go along with an order given by some crooked son of a bitch who sells justice to whoever's got the most coin in their pockets. In the time we've known each other, how many of the killers or backstabbing cocksuckers we hunt down wind up being lawmen?"

"Quite a few," Pete admitted.

"Not all lawmen are bad, which means the good ones deserve a hell of a lot better than Russ Cavanaugh got."

"Plenty of good folks get killed, Nate. If they don't get what they deserve from the law, we take it to them. That's why I sign on to work with you so much."

"It would have been fine if Keyes got what he deserved, but that's not what happened," Nate continued. "Keyes has pulled together a small fortune from corrupting lawmen. He finds any crooked son of a bitch wearing a badge and sends work his way. Sheltering fugitives, helping prisoners escape, lining up robberies . . ."

Pete let out a slow whistle. "I'll be damned," he said. "Forget about the small fortune, he could stand to make a large one. Probably a few. I can think of about a half dozen more uses for some lawman who's willing to ride in and do what I asked."

"Keyes thought of plenty of uses for them. He even arranged to have honest lawmen killed in particular towns or counties so he could have one of his snakes take over the position in preparation for some larger job put together by any number of outlaws who'd paid for the privilege."

"Hot damn."

"I only found out about this later." Nate glanced over to where the two guards were standing. Ross and the shorter fellow were keeping an eye on him from a distance but didn't seem anxious to move him back into the repurposed smokehouse. "When I got back from that job in New Mex back then and heard about Keyes being tossed into a jail cell for gunning down Cavanaugh, I thought that was the end of it. A friend of mine sent word to me of what happened with the trial, but her telegrams stopped coming."

"Did something happen to her?"

"I looked into it and never did find out what the hell happened where she was concerned, but news on the trial wasn't hard to come by. Russ Cavanaugh's name was being dragged through the mud in every newspaper there was."

"That's where I heard it," Pete said.

Tensing as so much past anger flooded back into him, Nate said, "You ain't the only one. Cavanaugh was a good man. He was one of the few lawmen who I was proud to serve as a deputy. After I handed in my badge, he brought me in again whenever he needed help hunting down some outlaw that had gotten by him. And there weren't many of those."

"More high praise coming from you."

"Damn right it is. Everyone talking about his murder was suddenly calling him every filthy name in the book. Shootings were pinned on him, even a rape for Christ's sake. Cavanaugh was a family man in his sixties when he was killed. I knew him well enough to know for certain there was no way in hell he could have done those things!"

"Just a bit longer!" Ross shouted. "Then it's back in the box for you."

Nate nodded to him impatiently before turning back to Pete. "I jumped onto a train the first chance I got to do what I could to clear Cavanaugh's name. By the time I got there, it was already over. Cavanaugh was branded a murdering liar who threatened to kill Abraham Keyes in cold blood. Keyes was found guilty of killing him, but the shooting was written off as self-defense. I took it upon myself to find out what happened and it barely took any digging at all to figure out Keyes was behind it."

"How many men did he have working for him?" Pete asked.

"Enough to get the job done. As for exact

numbers, nobody but Keyes himself knows that. What I do know is that Keyes pulled every string he could to try and get himself free and when that didn't work, he pulled more strings to make Cavanaugh look like a demon straight out of hell."

"That's a long way to go to spite a dead man's name," Pete mused.

"But worth it considering his sentence went from what was sure to be a hanging to three years in jail."

"Three years?" Pete said in a voice that was loud enough to catch the attention of the two armed men nearby. Noticing the curious looks he was drawing, Pete lowered his voice and asked, "That's all he got for killing a lawman?"

"For killing a crooked lawman who was painted as something worse than most of the men he'd locked away, yes."

Pete squinted before saying, "I thought you said this was a year and a half ago."

"I did."

"And Keyes is already out?"

"Yeah. I've seen him," Nate replied. "He busted in on Grey when he was about to bed that whore he was talking about during the ride here. That crazy bastard barely got away long enough for me to come pull his fat from the fire."

"Oh, the crazy bastard you mean is Grey?" Pete asked with half a chuckle.

But Nate wasn't laughing. "Keyes is plenty of things, but he ain't crazy. After all the searching I did to try and set things right after Cavanaugh's trial, I never did find anything that could be used as real evidence to put a noose around his neck or at least get him transferred to some hole in the desert where scum like him goes to rot for the rest of their goddamn lives. No matter how many dead ends I found, I always thought I had more time to keep looking.

"If things got too close to the time when he was to be let out, I could look that much harder. And if it got down to the time that Keyes was to be released, I could be there when he stuck his nose out in the open and hound him until he made a mistake. Hell, I could even be there if he got sick of looking at my face and decided to try and kill me," Nate said as if he were yearning to find a melon-sized gold nugget at the bottom of a river. "Instead, the son of a bitch gets out free as a bird — ahead of schedule!"

"All right," Ross said as he approached with his shotgun held at hip level. "Time to get back in there."

"Just give me another minute," Nate said. Before he got permission from either of the armed men, he looked back to Pete and spoke in a rush. "More than likely, these two assholes right here are crooked and were fairly cheap to buy off," he said while nodding over to his guards. "Keyes used them to cover his escape and stick me in here for as long as possible. I've heard them bickering with one another when I was brought in, and I'm just being held until someone else comes to pick me up. If that someone is a lawman, he's probably gonna get a story similar to the one that smeared Cavanaugh's memory and I'll be hauled off as some sort of outlaw. If he's one of the lawmen in Keyes's pocket, I'll be dead in less than an hour."

"I said that's enough, damn it!" Ross said. "Now get into that box or you'll be dead in less than a minute!"

Both Pete and Nate took a good, long look at the armed men. Having seen plenty of killers and twisted souls in his day, Nate was able to take stock of Ross and have absolute confidence in his conclusion. The younger man would defend himself, but he wasn't about to pull his trigger just to make a point or enforce his demand. The other one, though, had the look of someone who would go along with any order he was given.

"Get me out of this damn smokehouse,"

Nate said. "Do it before Keyes's men get here or things will get even worse."

"I'll do what I can," Pete said.

Those words were barely out of Pete's mouth before he was shoved away by the shorter guard. Ross pushed Nate at the end of his shotgun until he was once again surrounded by the stench of smoke and the sweat of every prisoner who had been locked up in that squalid little box before him.

21

After taking a bit more time to scout the vicinity of the smokehouse while also watching the men who were guarding it, Pete made his way back to the Straight to the Eight. Deaugrey was at the same table and barely looked up to acknowledge Pete was there after being tapped on the shoulder.

"Just another hour or two," was all Deaugrey said before shifting his intense gaze back to his cards.

Normally, Pete didn't take kindly to being brushed off in such a casual manner. When dealing with Deaugrey Scott, however, it helped to set one's expectations somewhat south of normal. Pete stepped up to the bar and waited for the tender to come to him.

"You get what you needed, friend?" the barkeep asked.

"Mostly. How's he doing?" Pete asked while nodding over to Deaugrey's table.

The barkeep looked over there as well.

Shrugging, he said, "Seems to be doing well enough. The other players don't seem too happy when they take a stretch or come over for drinks, so I guess that bodes well for your friend."

"Speaking of drinks . . ."

"Your friend hasn't had one that wasn't at least half water since you left. I was about to start tapering it off even more in a few minutes."

Pete watched Deaugrey for a few seconds, taking careful note of his manner and posture. Deaugrey seemed relaxed, but not overly so. When he spoke, his voice still boomed to its normal, aggravating bluster. "He's fine the way he is," Pete told the barkeep. Placing some money on the bar, he added, "This should cover the rest until the game is over. You're doing a fine job."

"Happy to be of service. Anything else you need? Something that'll hit you harder than liquor? Maybe some company for the night?"

"I'll let you know. You got any rum?"

"Part of a bottle. Don't know how well it's held up, though. There's not much call for that particular poison around here. Only reason I have any was because one of the former —"

"I'll have a glass," Pete said sharply.

Knowing how to take a hint, the barkeep searched the bottles behind him without another word. When he found it, he pulled out the stopper, took a sniff, winced and poured some into a glass.

Pete reached for his drink and had a sip. He'd tasted better, but he'd certainly had a whole lot worse. After finding a comfortable spot where he could watch Deaugrey's table without being jostled by too many other customers, the tracker settled in for a while.

Surprisingly enough, Deaugrey actually did realize Pete was sitting there the entire time. He came over to stand beside the tracker before Pete could finish his second glass of rum.

"How you holding up?" Pete asked.

Deaugrey let out a snorting laugh. "I was about to ask you the same thing. It's not too often that you indulge in that piss water you like so much, but when you do it usually means a wild night."

"That remains to be seen. I've gone to visit Nate."

"Still just those same two morons standing watch over him?"

"Yeah," Pete said. "But they're armed morons."

"Most morons tend to be armed," Deaugrey said while slapping the bar to get the tender's attention. "Answer me one thing. Do I have to stab you or him for bringing me the watered-down drinks?"

Pete looked at the barkeep who was squarely in Deaugrey's sights before admitting, "That'd be me. I figured you'd want to stay sober for a while."

Standing so he faced Pete head-on, Deaugrey held out both arms as if to embrace him and asked, "Do I look like a man who's doing badly for himself?"

"No more than usual," Pete said, which was part truth and part jab. Every time Deaugrey took a fall, whether it was being tossed into a cell or getting knocked onto his ass, he managed to pull himself together and rebuild. When Pete had met up with him this time around, Deaugrey had been dressed in something close to rags and riding a slope-backed mule. Now, not only was he wearing better clothes than before, but he'd somehow managed to get a new pair of boots as well.

"You're supposed to be collecting money to buy Nate's freedom, am I right?" Pete asked.

"Yes."

"Then why are you spending so much on new clothes?"

Deaugrey daintily grabbed the lapels of a

gray waistcoat and peeled it open to reveal a battered double rig holster strapped around his waist. Along with the .38 that Frank had lent him, he also carried what looked like a .44 Colt. "You mean these old things? These were kindly donated by some patrons of this establishment who have since seen fit to seek their pleasures elsewhere."

"You mean you cleaned them out for everything they had."

"Every dime, as well as some choice pieces of clothing, a pistol, these boots and a very nice pocket watch."

"What about cash? How are you doing in that regard?"

"I think I've collected enough to take a good run at getting Nate out of that jail," Deaugrey replied. "That is, unless you've already broken him out yourself?"

"Not quite, although I don't think it would be too difficult. Has Frank shown up while I was away?"

"No. What have you two been up to while the rest of us were working so diligently?"

Pete ran through the broad strokes of what had happened while they were in Nagle. Although Deaugrey listened, it was difficult to tell whether he was truly paying attention or if some other kind of nonsense was running through his head.

"Sounds like Dog Ear has been busy since his most recent liberation," Deaugrey said.

"Yeah, but it seems Nate has all but forgotten about him. He's hung up on the notion of finding this Keyes person."

"Ahh, yes. The prolific Abraham Keyes. Quite the sordid history with that one."

"You knew about him already?" Pete asked.

"I read a good deal about his trial in the papers. It happened around the time I was tucked away in a hospital in Colorado. There wasn't much to do there apart from read. Oh," Deaugrey tossed in as if it was the punch line of a dirty joke, "and getting healed."

"Nate thinks the two men watching that jail were bought and paid for by Keyes," Pete said.

"Oh, most definitely they were. Seems many men in this very saloon have had run-ins with them two regulators. They're for sale but don't do much to earn their money. The man who donated his watch to my wardrobe mentioned there's a third who is still out somewhere working a silver mine. He's the killer of the three and, if that's what Keyes paid for, he'll get it as soon as that one returns."

"Then we've got to get Nate out as quickly

as possible."

"I thought that was the plan all along."

"Yer damn right it is."

"What's this for?" Ross asked.

The sun had become a memory in the time since Pete had paid his last visit, and there wasn't much light shining on the regulator's face. The torch a few yards from the old smokehouse was burning bright enough for Pete to see an expression of genuine bewilderment. Pete's grip tightened on the wad of cash as he held it closer to Ross's face and asked, "What the hell do you think it's for? Ain't this enough to pay my friend's fine?"

"What fine?"

"Whatever it is I need to pay to get him out of there! This has got to be enough."

"There isn't a fine," Ross said. "He's staying in there for another day at least."

"Why?"

Ross's eyes darted back and forth, but found nothing to fix upon. "Because," he reluctantly said, "that's our orders."

Pete's hand tightened into a fist around the dollars he was holding, which he thumped against the other man's chest. "Take this goddamn money and open that goddamn smokehouse."

Shaking his head, Ross stepped back. "You're gonna have to leave."

"Yeah?" Shoving the money back into his pocket, Pete slapped that hand against the gun holstered at his side. "You wanna tell me one more time what I gotta do?"

"I thought you were a priest!"

"You're gonna need a priest if you don't —"

Since it was clear that things weren't going to get any better from there, Deaugrey patted Pete on the shoulder and stepped in. "Obviously, you were paid to keep that man locked up. Am I right?"

"That, uh, doesn't matter," Ross stammered.

"I can see I'm dealing with someone who knows their job well and isn't to be trifled with," Deaugrey said in a voice that didn't betray the first hint of sarcasm. "For that reason, we're willing to hand over some additional compensation." He reached into his jacket's inner pocket, which also allowed him to show the guns he kept on his person. Flashing an additional hundred dollars, he said, "This is more than the job is worth, but you drive a hard bargain."

Without hesitation, Ross shook his head. "I can't. We, uhh, we can't take that."

"Then how about this?" Deaugrey asked

as he dug out another twenty.

Ross looked around as if he had an audience surrounding him. All that could be seen at that late hour was the usual assortment of drunks, vagrants and tired miners shuffling to whichever tent contained their bed for the night. "Tell you what," he said in a voice that could barely be heard. "Bring that back in two days. We'll open the door and your friend can go."

Smiling, Deaugrey stashed his money away and said, "There now. I imagine that was some of the easiest money you'll ever make. We'll be seeing you and your associate real soon."

Several paces behind them, Ross's stout partner glanced about a few times before realizing he was the associate that had just been mentioned.

When Deaugrey walked over to where Pete was waiting, the tracker was gnashing his teeth like a horse chewing on a bit. Still smiling, Deaugrey looked over his shoulder at the regulators who were holding a nervous conference about twenty yards away.

"What did they tell you?" Pete asked.

"He told me to come back in two days," Deaugrey replied. "If we do that, Nate will be dead. I say we give it an hour, wait for them to get nice and tired, stroll back over there, knock them over the head, take their keys and escort Nate to freedom. After that, we have a nice plate of breakfast."

"We can't do that."

"Why? I'm starving!"

"We gotta think about getting out of this camp as well as just getting Nate out of that box," Pete told him. "These miners take care of their own. Them regulators may be idiots, but they gotta have some friends in this camp who'll back their play. You see all these men standing and lying about?"

Deaugrey looked around to see the same drunks, vagrants and miners he'd seen before. The men's dirty faces were every bit a part of the landscape as the rocks, tents and rich Missouri soil. "Yeah, I see them."

"They've been glaring at us every time we so much as look at that smokehouse or them two who are guarding it. We make a move on those regulators and we'll have trouble coming at us from all sides."

"These aren't bad men," Deaugrey scoffed. "They're tin panners."

"They all got guns," Pete said. "And if they all start shooting, at least one of them's bound to hit something. We'll only get one shot at getting all of us out of here before things get too messy, so we need to make it a good one."

When Deaugrey looked around this time, he took special notice of all the dirty faces pointed back at him. They were in doorways, tent flaps, windows and shadows and they didn't turn away until the pair had put some distance between themselves and the camp's makeshift jail. "Even if we did get Nate out of there, we don't have much of an idea of what Keyes has got brewing or what sort of meat grinder we'd be going into if we did find him."

"I wouldn't be so sure about that."

"So we go it alone?"

Pete grinned. "I wouldn't be so sure about that, either."

22

Nate woke up covered in sweat, stinking of stale smoke and aching in every joint in his body. He'd slept as he had the night before: curled into a half ball with his legs tucked in close to his chest and his head cocked at an awkward angle. A beam of sunlight pierced through a split in the smokehouse wall. It was the same split he'd been digging his fingers into all night long in the hopes of widening the crack enough for him to be able to break open a hole in the wall. All he'd gotten for his trouble were bloody fingers.

It was no easy task to get back to his feet. The effort involved a whole lot of grunting and groaning, pushing and struggling before he was finally standing inside the cramped space. "What the hell kind of idiot savages use a thing like this as a goddamned jail?" he grunted to himself while rubbing the aching kink in his neck.

His hand balled into a fist and he started pounding on the door. Every thump against the wooden boards was a reminder of how infuriatingly solid the door was. Pounding on it even harder, he shouted, "Where's my damn breakfast?"

So far, Nate had only been given food twice and, even if combined, it wouldn't have been enough to call a meal. Even though he could gladly go hungry rather than eat that trash, he still liked to make a fuss about getting it, if only to make his jailers regret the fact that he was there. It wasn't a surprise when nobody responded to him. After a few more loud reminders of his presence, he gave his throat a rest and pressed an ear against the door.

Listening for information on his captors had yielded even fewer results than banging on the door. Everything he'd needed to know had been gleaned in the first minute or two after he'd seen Ross and the other one the very first time. The fact that they'd barely blinked when shown the badge he'd been carrying told him there was no reasoning with them. Even though the badge didn't represent any genuine authority, most folks at least gave it a moment's consideration. But these regulators were already bought and paid for by someone who was an expert in buying the loyalties of petty men.

Nate peeled his ear away from the filthy door and immediately put it back again. Just before he'd moved it, the sound of voices drifted through the air outside. After a few moments, he found the voices again and concentrated on making out what was being said.

He couldn't hear them clearly enough to piece any words together, but Nate swore he recognized one of the voices as Deaugrey's. After a short scrap of conversation, the squat regulator groused angrily about something as the familiar voice hurried to defend himself in a steady string of syllables. That was Deaugrey, all right.

Grinning, Nate pushed his ear even harder against the door to listen for anything at all that might tell him what Deaugrey had up his sleeve. The conversation quickly tipped in the regulator's favor as he snarled, "Now git the hell outta my sight!"

Nate strained to hear past the door, hoping to hear a signal from Deaugrey or something to let him know that the crazy man was doing more than just annoying someone out there. Instead, what he heard was the scrape of something against the smokehouse itself. Nate recoiled and looked around, certain that some piece of the wall had fallen off or possibly come loose after all the beatings he'd given it. The interior was still intact, however, even as something else scraped against the sides of the cramped little structure.

"Who's out there?" Nate asked in a voice that he hoped didn't carry too far. There were more scrapes, this time followed by the rattle of wagon wheels approaching the smokehouse.

"Hey!" the squat regulator shouted. "Get away from there!"

While Nate may have finally been able to hear the outside voices clearly, he was in no position to celebrate. His entire world was quickly turned on its ear as several scrapes came from all four corners of the smokehouse at once and the entire thing began to tilt. The more of them he heard, the more familiar the scrapes sounded. When they took on a more taut sound, Nate realized what they were.

Ropes.

There were ropes being tied around the smokehouse that were now cinching in tight to —

Completing Nate's thought for him, the smokehouse tilted once again before tipping all the way over so the door was now angled toward the sky. It was all Nate could do to brace himself using all four limbs against whatever surface he could reach. The smokehouse didn't tip all the way over, but it did tremble as the edge that was digging into the earth dug a rut as the structure was pulled from the spot where it had been rooted.

"What in the . . . ?" Nate hollered as he was jostled around inside that box like a single bean in a jar.

"Hang on!" someone shouted from above and behind the smokehouse. Since the ropes must have been tied to the wagon that Nate had heard, the man speaking now must have been its driver. The voice was vaguely familiar, but was getting washed away by the wagon wheels, the grinding of the smokehouse against the ground and the growing number of men shouting on all sides.

Just when Nate thought things couldn't get any more chaotic, a shot cracked through the air to knock a hole through the top edge of the smokehouse. Sunlight stabbed through the bullet hole and wood splinters rained upon his face. "Shit!" he cried out as that single shot grew into a volley.

For the most part, the gunshots were

behind the smokehouse. Every so often, however, some would come from up high and send a bullet to drill into Nate's cell. After the second round had been driven through one side of the smokehouse and out the other, Nate tucked himself into a tight ball and covered his head with both arms. From there, all he could do was shout obscenities into his sleeves and absorb the impact of his body against the jostling back wall of the smokehouse.

After a minute or so, the gunshots became distant enough for Nate to move his arms and take a look at the walls around him. There were a few more holes, but most of them were at the edges of the smokehouse that would have been the top front corner if it were standing upright. The jostling slowed to a stop as a brake was hastily set to keep the wagon from rolling another inch.

"Who's out there?" Nate shouted. "What the hell's goin' on?"

"Do me a favor and lean against the front of that outhouse instead of flapping your gums so much."

"That you, Pete?"

"Yeah. Now would you like to keep talking or can you help me set this thing upright?"

Nate didn't have to think for long about

that one. Digging his heels into the floor, he threw himself at the door as he'd done so many times since it had been shut on him for the first time.

"One more time," Pete grunted in a strained voice. "On three. One . . . two . . . *three!*"

Nate charged the door as best he could. This time, the wooden box shifted forward to set itself back into the position for which it had been built. Now that he was standing, Nate only had to stoop a bit to look through one of the fresh holes that had been shot through the door. A second later, the light coming through that hole was eclipsed by a body stepping directly in front of it.

"Get this door open, Pete!" Nate said.

"Stand back."

He may not have had very far to go, but Nate shuffled backward until he hit the rear wall and then pressed himself into a corner. The next gunshot that he heard was a lot closer than the rest, but he greeted it with a wide, expectant smile.

"Damn," Pete grunted.

"What is it?"

"This is one solid door."

Nate used both arms to push himself up. "Shoot it again!" he said.

"Stand b— Shit!"

Before Nate could ask what was keeping Pete from taking another shot, he heard another volley of gunfire erupt from not too far away. Bullets whipped through the air so close to the smokehouse that Nate could hear them through the thick walls. This time, however, he didn't care. Instead, he propped himself in place as best he could while driving the bottom of one boot into the door. It rattled slightly in its frame, but was nowhere close to opening. Nate could even see a spot where one or both of Pete's rounds must have landed but kicking there didn't help his cause one bit. Staring at the unmoving barrier directly in front of him, Nate sighed. "Good Lord. Who built this damn thing?"

The gunshots grew into a storm that closed in once more on all sides. Pete returned fire, but was forced to do so at a slower, more calculated rate. "Grey!" he shouted. "Hurry up and get your ass over here!" Slamming against the outside of the smokehouse, Pete said, "We were afraid of this, Nate. That outhouse looked pretty damn sturdy. It's been reinforced and won't come open easy."

"Keep shooting it," Nate demanded. "Kick it! Find a hammer! *Anything!*"

"No time for that. But don't worry, we'll

get you out of here."

"You gonna drag me all the way out of camp?"

"Wouldn't be fast enough. We got another — Ah! Here it comes now. Just hang on and get ready for some more jostling."

"I don't care if you turn this thing upside down!" Nate said. "Just crack it open!"

Amid the thunder of shots being fired as quickly as triggers could be pulled, Deaugrey let out a holler that sounded like a cross between a wild Apache and a rabid coyote. A good amount of gunfire was still being sent toward the smokehouse, blasting holes through the walls every now and then. Only now did Nate realize that not every hit put a hole into the smokehouse. And even the spots that had a few holes in them wouldn't give way to Nate's pounding fists. As he shifted his furious efforts from the wall to the door, he could feel a difference in the thickness of lumber used to build them. The true curse was the iron lock that kept the door shut. Nate had gotten a few quick glances at it on his way in and out of the jail, which was enough to tell him the lock was a formidable mechanism.

Another set of wheels rolled past the smokehouse to come to a stop behind it. By the sound of them, they were attached to something larger than whatever had dragged Nate this far. He could hear latches being opened and a wooden gate swinging down amid the squeal of old hinges. Footsteps scrambled around the smokehouse, followed by a few hasty slaps against the door.

"Ready?" Pete asked. "Here comes!"

Without counting to three, Pete shoved against the front of the smokehouse as the ropes that were still wrapped around it strained taut. It tipped back to fall farther than it had before and landed upright with a jarring slam that Nate felt through every last bone in his body. Now laying almost completely horizontal, Nate struggled to get up. His efforts were hindered by the impact, which felt like being kicked by three mules at once to knock all the breath from his lungs.

The gunshots kept coming.

The smokehouse was now starting to sway back and forth, up and down.

So many sounds washed through Nate's ears. Too many. The snap of leather. A woman screaming. Horses whinnying. Something hissed in Nate's ear like a hornet flying past. He rolled onto his side and knocked his head against both walls of the corner into which he'd landed.

Nate's stomach felt like it was sloshing

around inside of him, not attached to much of anything. His throat was raw from so much swearing and shouting. His head was splitting, and his body felt as if it had been run over by a wagon instead of being dragged behind one.

When the gunshots started to fade, Nate wasn't sure if they were getting farther away or if he was simply losing consciousness. Whichever it was, he just lay where he was and let it happen.

Before he could get too comfortable, the wheels that were moving him along hit a rut that was so deep it sent Nate an inch or two in the air before dropping him straight down again. So much for laying back and enjoying the ride.

The gunshots had all but faded away. Before much longer, the ride became smoother and the team pulling the wagon was given some extra incentive. Nate could feel speed building up, and he could hear the rumble of another horse's hooves thundering to catch up to the wagon. A few seconds later, a second horse raced to catch up to them.

"He in there?" Deaugrey shouted.

Pete responded from somewhere nearby. "Of course he's in there. Where the hell is he gonna git to?"

"Is he . . . alive?"

After drawing a breath that hurt his ribs worse than a solid punch, Nate said, "I'm alive."

"You are?" Deaugrey said. "After the beating this outhouse took and all the shooting, I thought — what I mean is — glad to hear it."

The light streaming into the box was blocked by someone standing close to the side wall. "You hurt?" Pete asked.

Looking toward the sound of Pete's voice, Nate told him, "I've had better days, that's for certain."

"It looks like them regulators and the rest of the folks that were shooting at us have given up on trying to bring you back, so we've got some time to try and get that door open. Shouldn't take long."

Strictly speaking, Pete was correct. Even so, the couple of minutes required to bust that lock and pry open that door felt like an eternity to the man who'd been tossed around within those four wooden walls for far too long. Every so often, the sound of their efforts to break the lock was interrupted by the crack of a rifle and the metallic rattle of a fresh round being levered into place. By the time the lock finally gave way and the door was pulled open, Nate was too tired to get up and greet his rescuers.

The light flooding into the cramped space caused Nate to pinch his eyes shut and lift a hand to shade them. Even that hurt.

"Rise and shine, Sathow!" Deaugrey said.

"You . . . crazy son of . . . a bitch!" Nate said as he struggled to lift himself up so he could grab the hand that was being offered to him.

"I may be crazy," Deaugrey replied while pulling Nate out of the battered jail. "But at least I never got locked in an outhouse for so long that it caused all of this ruckus."

"It's not an outhouse! It's a . . . *smoke*-house." Nate wheezed.

"That explains the smell," Frank said from the driver's seat of the wagon, "and my powerful hankering for peppered strip steak!"

23

The remains of the smokehouse were miles behind them when Pete called for the small group to come to a stop. He climbed down from his saddle, tied his horse off near a stream and headed through a patch of trees so he could climb a small hill and get a look at the trail behind them. Deaugrey followed suit and tied his reins off next to Pete's horse by the stream.

"What happened to the mule?" Frank asked.

"I gave it away."

"How generous of you. Who'd you give it to?"

"I left it for the fella who used to own this horse," Deaugrey replied while patting the side of the sleek new animal he'd been riding.

Frank climbed over the driver's seat of the flatbed wagon that had been used to carry the smokehouse away from the mining camp. "And somehow you managed to say that proudly. I am constantly in awe of your ability to justify anything at all to yourself."

Nodding, Deaugrey replied, "Everyone's in awe of me for some reason or other. How's our patient?"

"I'll be fine," Nate said while peeling away a ripped section of his shirt sleeve that was soaked through with blood. "Must've caught a bullet while I was trapped in that goddamned box. It's a wonder I wasn't killed in there. Couldn't you try bribing one of those regulators to get me out?"

"We did," Deaugrey said. "Neither one would bite."

"What about stealing their keys?"

"They weren't carrying them on their persons. Can you believe that? I've heard of locking someone up and throwing away the key, but I'd always assumed that was just an expression."

"So the next thing you came up with was dragging the whole damn smokehouse out of town?" Nate asked. "Now I see why I'm the one who comes up with most of the plans to carry out our jobs."

"Actually," Frank said, "our little escape route was *my* idea. And you should know better than to say you cook up all of the plans for getting our jobs done."

Nate slowly turned toward the driver's seat of the wagon. Having spent most of the ride sitting in the back like a bale of hay, he didn't have far to turn. That was fortunate since his entire body still ached. "Your idea?" he mused. "Maybe you should stick to spouting Bible verses."

"Would you have rather sat and rotted inside that little wooden box like a ham hock or bide your time in the middle of a crossfire while we tried to chip away at that reinforced door?"

"What about picking the lock?" Nate asked while looking over to Deaugrey. "Isn't that the sort of skill you bring to the table?"

"That antiquated contraption was so rusty that it barely qualified as a lock," Deaugrey said. "I think one of those tin panners found it at the bottom of a river."

While Deaugrey talked, Nate rolled up the sleeve that was stained with blood and torn to shreds. Once he got a look at the wound beneath the ripped cotton, he reached for a canteen and started pouring water over it to clean off some of the blood. "I suppose I should be grateful you three came back for me."

"Yes," Frank said as he sat down beside him. "I suppose you should be grateful. Now let me take a look at that."

"I already handed myself over to your reckless ministry," Nate snapped. "I'm not about to gamble on your doctoring skills."

"Shut up and let me see." Before Nate could protest any further, Frank grabbed his arm and pulled it toward him.

"Jesus Christ!" Nate grunted. "Take it — *Ow!*"

When Frank tugged on that arm a second time, he was looking Nate straight in the eyes to see his reaction. Having gotten what he was hoping for, he said, "That's for your poor choice of words. Hold still or you'll get another."

Nate may have held still, but he didn't hold his tongue. As Frank poked and prodded the messy gash on his upper arm, Nate spewed a steady torrent of foul language. He didn't, however, take the Lord's name in vain.

"Lucky man," Frank eventually said. "Looks like this little scratch was put here by some flying chunks of broken wood. You've got a nasty splinter, but there's no bullet lodged in there."

"Yeah," Nate grunted. "Real lucky."

"The really lucky part is that I happen to have some damn fine whiskey to help ease the pain a bit."

"Really?"

"Nope," Frank said as he mercilessly tore the jagged piece of wood from where it had been lodged.

Nate clenched his jaw, refusing to give his partner the pleasure of seeing him wince. After Frank plucked out the splinter, he held it out to show Nate before tossing it over the side of the wagon.

"Sorry about that," Frank said. "Had to distract you."

"You ain't sorry."

"Got me there. Here's something you can use to dress that wound," the preacher said, handing over an old blue bandanna.

Now that the splinter was gone, Nate could finally draw a full breath. He still hurt in a dozen different ways, but at least one of them had been taken away. Sometimes, a man just had to savor what little bits of goodness were tossed his way. He sopped up some of the fresher blood and started wrapping the bandanna over the cut.

"Where the hell have you been, anyway?" Nate asked.

Frank sorted through the gear that had been hastily tossed into the back of the wagon. "I was in Nagle with Pete. He just took a faster way back to the camp on the crazy notion that you might be in trouble. I barely got back before I heard about you getting yourself tossed into that box. You'll be happy to know that your regulator friend — Ross, I believe his name was — also took work running food and supplies out to miners who were out working their claims."

"Why would I give a damn about that?"

"Because," Frank said, "this is his wagon."

"You're stealing now too, Preacher?" Nate asked through a smirk.

"Guess you're a worse influence than I thought."

Nate winced as he tightened the bandanna around his wounded arm. "Did the two of you at least manage to find anything worthwhile in regards to that knife maker?"

"He makes a whole lot more than just knives, for one thing. Seems Dog Ear himself came to visit him to pick up an order of some specialty items."

"Pescaterro, huh?" Nate said. "Almost forgot about him."

"No you didn't," Frank said. "Once you're put onto someone's scent, you don't let loose of them until the job's through. Pescaterro wasn't alone, though. Seems he had a friend along. The man who made that knife didn't know the stranger's name, but he was certain he was even more of a handful than Dog Ear."

Now that he was bandaged up, Nate took

a swig from the canteen and drained it dry. "That other man . . . I know his name. Abraham Keyes."

"Keyes?" Frank asked cautiously. "Isn't he the one who was locked away after killing Marshal Cavanaugh?"

"The same. It seems his short sentence was cut even shorter."

"Son of a bitch."

"Hooo boy!" Deaugrey exclaimed as he returned from the little stream where the horses were tied. "Things must've really taken a turn for the worse if our holy father is spouting obscenities. I take it you've been told about our meeting with Mr. Keyes?"

"You met him?" Frank asked. "Here?"

Nate nodded. "I'll tell you all about it once we're riding again."

"I wish I could help more in that regard," Frank sighed. "All Pete's knife maker friend could tell us on that account was that Pescaterro and his friend were headed south. That's all he knew. Trust me."

"They're headed to Joplin. What did you mean when you said that knife maker put together a special order for Keyes?"

A shadow seemed to fall over Frank's face as he thought about the answer to that question. Finally, he said, "Weapons and fortifications. Gatling guns, armor plating, even some sort of kerosene pump to spread wild-fires."

"Holy shit," Nate groaned. "Sorry about that."

"No need to apologize," Frank told him. "I don't approve of that sort of language, but every so often, it's justified."

"Is this a sign of the end of days?" Deaugrey chided.

Frank didn't respond to that, but Nate said, "Only for Pescaterro and the piece of shit riding with him. How many weapons were made?"

"Not enough for an army," Frank replied, "but more than enough to spill a whole lot of blood. According to the weapons maker, Pescaterro and Keyes weren't riding with a large group."

"Less than a dozen, I'd say," Pete added as he strode toward the wagon. "Of course, the tracks were far from fresh. There was also mention of a safe."

A grin flickered across Nate's face.

"Thought you might like the sound of that," Pete said.

"What was the safe for?" Nate asked.

"What's any safe for? I'd imagine we'll be needing to get it open and, unless we know for certain we can get the combination, there ain't none of us here that are suited for the job. Do you know where to find Corday?"

Nate nodded. "It may take a day or two, but I should be able to get her here."

"Finally," Deaugrey said as he rubbed his hands together. "One of Sathow's sinners that isn't a trial to be around."

"I'll do my best to find her. I've got a notion of where to look, but even if I can't bring her to Joplin, I'd say we've got plenty to go on already," Nate said confidently.

"Oh yes," Deaugrey said. "We've got this bull by the horns. Should be a walk through a field of daisies to finish the rest of this job."

"It very well may be," Nate said. "At least until we get closer to Joplin. I'd bet everything I have that none of those men were along with Keyes when he came through these parts and met up with me. In fact, I could venture so far as to say that he was in a rush to get back to Joplin."

"Would you now?" Deaugrey asked.

"Yeah. Otherwise, he would have stuck around to put a bullet between my eyes rather than leave the job to a pair of incompetents like them regulators."

"That would mean he isn't overly concerned about being followed back to Joplin," Frank pointed out.

"If you had the sort of armaments you mentioned waiting for you down there, would you be concerned about a small group of men like us?" Nate asked.

After a very short bit of consideration, Frank shrugged and admitted, "I suppose not."

"I think you two are forgetting one key bit of information," Deaugrey said.

The other men looked at him. They didn't bother asking for more because they knew it would be forthcoming whether it was requested or not.

"The infamous Mr. Keyes," Deaugrey announced, "came straight after *me.*"

"Is that so?" Frank asked.

Still looking at Deaugrey, Nate replied, "Yeah. It is."

"Why?"

"I don't know. Why don't you tell us, Grey?"

Clearly enjoying the discontent he'd sown, Deaugrey smirked and told them, "I haven't the faintest idea. He marched straight into that cathouse, though, and requested me by name."

Nate got to his feet and worked his arm to make sure the bandanna would stay in place. He climbed down from the wagon, grateful for the chance to walk more than a half step without running into a wall. "This wagon looks like it's in rough shape," he said while giving it a look from front to back.

"That smokehouse may have been pretty small, but it couldn't exactly be considered normal cargo," Frank said. "Every axle was rattling something awful during the last stretch of our ride away from that camp. I doubt it'll make it much more than a few more miles before something vital gives way."

"Then we're in luck," Nate said. "Because it won't need to roll another couple of feet. It served its purpose, so we're safe to move on. That right, Pete?"

"More or less," the tracker said. "There's some small camps scattered about and what looks to be a few claims in the area, but they ain't no concern. They either didn't hear what happened back in the main camp or don't care because they ain't taking their noses out of their work."

"Good." Nate placed his hands on the edge of the cart and took a look inside. Whatever gear wasn't already loaded into the saddlebags being carried by the other horses was in the wagon being pulled by Frank's mare and Nate's gelding.

Pointing to a bundle in the wagon, Nate asked, "Is that my pistol and belt?"

"Sure is," Deaugrey replied. "Getting to you wasn't exactly easy, but stealing your gear from those regulators was child's play. I don't see why you insist on using that model Remington, though. It's not nearly as well balanced as a Colt."

"I'm sentimental. Because of that, I'd hate for Keyes to miss out on the rest of the fight he started after he went through so much trouble to get to you. How'd you like to pick up where you left off?"

Deaugrey's smirk was a wicked sight to behold. "I believe that would only be proper."

24

The next four days weren't easy by any stretch of the imagination, but after being locked up in a repurposed smokehouse, even a hard ride through rugged territory was a welcome change. Nate Sathow's thoughts churned through several possibilities of what they might find in Joplin, adding new bits of information he'd learned from Frank and Pete to the mix of what he already knew regarding Casey Pescaterro and Abraham Keyes. For every path to victory he dreamt up, Nate came up with two others that led straight to doomsday. The effort of sifting through so many different outcomes put a contemplative scowl onto his face. Such an expression wasn't unusual for him. In fact, it was so common that the lines scratched into his forehead and near his eyes had become permanent fixtures.

Little was seen of Pete during that ride. In the morning, he woke up, filled himself with chicory coffee and bacon, and rode ahead to scout the trail that lay in front of them. When the sun set, he made his way back to the spot where the others had made camp, stuffed his belly full of whatever Frank cooked for dinner, relayed whatever he'd learned that day to Nate and fell asleep. For him, that was more than just a common expression. Pete was usually so tired after he returned that he would literally fall back against a tree or rock and be snoring a few seconds later. Despite the long days, Pete was in his element. He scoured the hills for any possible dangers whether hostile Indians or bridges that had been washed away by floods. He didn't need to be told what to do. He simply . . . was.

Deaugrey was kept busy as well. Since his particular talents didn't lend themselves to life in the saddle, he perked up whenever he caught sight of a town, homestead or any other spot where he might be able to scrounge for supplies. While the rest of the group rode on, he would divert himself to any settlement he'd spotted and return stinking of liquor with his hair tousled by whatever woman he'd sweet-talked and his pockets filled with enough money to fund the ride for another day. Although some of Deaugrey's offerings had surely been plucked from their unsuspecting owners, Nate knew that most had either been bartered or won. A swindle all the same, perhaps, but a legal swindle. Mostly legal, anyway.

As for Frank, he kept to himself. He stayed busy tending to the normal duties required along the way such as making and breaking camp, cooking, tending to the horses and anything else that needed doing. Nate had once heard the preacher mention something about the simple purity of putting things in order. For Frank, the notion applied to any and all things. When he set things right, he was just as happy springing an innocent man from jail as he was in making sure there was enough wood in the pile to keep a fire going. He did both tasks with the same amount of vigor and enthusiasm.

It was their fourth night of the ride, and Frank was contentedly stirring a pot that bubbled with a pungent odor. "What's in there?" Pete asked after a quizzical sniff. "Don't smell like squirrel."

"We finished off the last of the squirrel for breakfast," Frank replied. "This is rabbit."

"Don't smell like rabbit."

"It had plenty of meat on its bones, so it'll do just fine."

Deaugrey shifted in the rut he'd dug for

himself using his restless backside. "Plenty of fat is more like it. That rabbit was the slowest of the lot that we flushed out of those bushes. That means it was the fattest."

"It's what we have," Frank said with an easy smile. "And it'll be just fine."

"Makes me nervous when he gets so quiet," Pete said while staring at Frank. "Usually only happens right before things go from bad to worse."

"When the bunch of us are gathered up by Nate Sathow," Deaugrey said, "things don't usually go any other way."

"You can leave if you want," Nate pointed out.

Deaugrey shrugged and dipped a spoon into the stew-pot. "I'm not complaining. This beats the hell out of being trussed up and tossed into a locked room."

It wasn't often that Nate knew exactly where Deaugrey was coming from and it was even rarer for him to not be frightened by that prospect.

After taking his sample of the stew, Deaugrey raised his eyebrows and nodded in appreciation. "Not that I don't enjoy all of this time beneath the majesty of the stars and enough cold air to make me pucker in places I'd rather not mention, but are we anywhere close to having a bed to sleep in for a change?"

"Joplin ain't far from here," Pete reported.

"Then why don't we ride the rest of the way into town?" Deaugrey asked as he sat bolt upright. "We could make it!"

"Sure we could."

"Excellent! Then —"

Stopping Deaugrey with a backhanded swat, Nate said, "There's a good reason why we don't just ride into town without breaking stride."

"You're all gluttons for punishment," Deaugrey muttered. "That's the reason."

Speaking in a tone that was just as merry as if he were talking about a recipe for pumpkin pie, Frank said, "We're close to whatever Dog Ear and Keyes have built up. Whatever it is, they surely want to protect it. Keeping watch on the town would be a standard precaution, so we won't ride in like a parade. We'll trickle into town throughout the day like normal folk. Do you think this stew needs more salt?"

"Pepper," Deaugrey said grudgingly.

"We don't have pepper."

"Of course you don't. Gluttons, I tell you."

"The preacher's right," Pete said. "I been to Joplin, and there's men keeping watch on the trails coming into town as well as at the train station and stagecoach office."

"Were they armed?" Nate asked.

"No. They was just scouts."

Deaugrey let out a breath. "There," he sighed. "You see? They weren't even armed. That's a good thing."

"No," Nate said sternly. "If they were armed, they'd probably be posted there to meet anyone looking to intrude on Keyes's business. If they're scouts, their job is to take any news back to their employer and bring back however many gun hands are necessary to deal with a problem. Are you certain they were Keyes's men, Pete?"

"I recognized a few of them as having run with Dog Ear Pescaterro," Pete replied. "From what I hear lately, that means they're most likely taking orders from Keyes as well. I didn't recognize every last one of them scouts, but my gut tells me they're all keeping watch for the likes of us."

"And that's good enough for me," Frank said.

Nate nodded and helped himself to some stew. "Me too. According to that miner I spoke to, Keyes and Dog Ear were headed for a train depot outside of Joplin. Did you happen to see anything like that while you were out and about?"

Pete laughed so hard that he dribbled some of his stew into his bushy beard. Using the back of his hand to wipe it away, he said, "If you know one man who could scout ahead for the best path to ride while also visiting train stations and picking out which men lingering on the outskirts of town are vagrants and which are scouts *and* still have the time to look around for train depots . . . I'd like to shake his hand."

"Just checking," Nate said. "You and me can have a look tomorrow. Frank, see what you can do to figure out which of those men Pete found really *are* working for Keyes and how many of them we need to worry about."

"What about me?" asked Deaugrey anxiously.

"You can keep your head down, your mouth shut and stay out of trouble for once."

Deaugrey made a sour face and said, "You can't be serious."

"A man can hope, can't he? If that's too much to handle," Nate told him, "then you can go into Joplin and put your ear to the ground. See if anyone knows much about Keyes. If he's planning on putting those weapons he bought to use, he'll need more men and that means recruiting. As for Pescaterro . . ."

"Right," Deaugrey said sharply. "I know just where to go for word on Dog Ear.

255

There's a few stops he'll want to make after being locked away and then spending so much time on the trail. In fact, I might wanna join him in a few of those ventures. Not join *him* per se, but —"

"I know what you mean, Grey," Nate cut in. "Just get the job done. We'll all head out after first light tomorrow. Got that?"

There were nods all around.

"Sathow is back on a schedule," Deaugrey mused. "Once again, all is right with the world."

With that, the conversation disbanded. Pete looked for a comfortable spot away from the glow of the fire, Deaugrey sat so close to the flames that he nearly set his sleeves alight, and Nate stepped away to stare into a southern sky colored by the distant glow of Joplin, Missouri. He rolled a cigarette using a pouch of tobacco purchased from one of the merchants that Deaugrey had swindled and by the time he was lighting it, he was no longer alone.

"You're not planning on riding off on your own, are you?" Frank asked.

"Too dark," Nate replied.

"I mean once you learn where Keyes is holed up. Don't forget, the job was to track down Pescaterro."

"I know what the damn job is."

"You tend to take things personally sometimes. If I didn't know any better, I might think you were sending Grey out knowing he'll draw too much attention to himself as a way to force a fight with Keyes and the others before we're ready."

Nate looked over to him, only to get an unwavering stare in return. The tip of the cigarette glowed as he inhaled, casting a deep red light on the bottom portion of his face. "You don't have to ride along if you don't want to."

"See? You're high-strung at the moment. Perhaps it would be better if —"

"Grey will be fine," Nate said. "I've worked with him more than you have and trust me, he'll be much easier to handle after he's blown off some steam. Besides, he's good at his job."

"All right. Then you should know I'm good at my job also."

"Your job is to watch our backs."

"It's also to make certain the lot of you don't step too far out of line," Frank pointed out. "Considering your history with Keyes, recent and otherwise, someone might think you're overly anxious to face him again."

"Whether we're just after Pescaterro or not, we're gonna have to face Keyes."

"Yes. Just watch yourself. He's not only

loaded for bear, he's ready for a small war."

Nate drew a deep, smoky breath and let it out in a stream of fragrant smoke. "Consider me warned. Thanks, Shep."

"Tell me something," Frank said. "You were planning on riding into whatever fortifications Keyes has, burning down his men and worrying about those weapons and fortifications later. Am I right?"

The next breath he took caused the cigarette to flare up even brighter. After holding its smoke in him for a spell, Nate let it out while savoring the acrid taste that was left behind. Eventually, he said, "Not anymore."

"Good," Frank said as he gave Nate's shoulder a friendly pat. "I knew there wasn't anything to be concerned about."

After Frank had wandered off for some solitude, Nate made his way back to the fire. Deaugrey was still sitting there and looked over to ask, "Who's Shep?"

"Pardon me?"

"I've heard you call Frank 'Shep' once or twice. What's that about?"

Nate shrugged. "The Lord is his shepherd and on more than one occasion, Frank has been mine."

"Does that make you a sheep?" Deaugrey asked.

"Shut up and get to sleep."

"Baaaaaa!!"

25

Late the following afternoon, Nate found
an answer to his telegram waiting for him in
Joplin's wire office. It read:

LEAVING NEBRASKA NOW STOP
WILL SEND WORD BEFORE TRAIN
ARRIVES STOP

                                        AC

He told Pete about it when the tracker
returned from his most recent scouting run.

"More people on the job?" Pete grumbled.
"That gonna take a bite out of our pay?"

"If things go right, there'll be plenty of
pay to go around. Now tell me what you've
been doing to earn your share."

The first thing Pete mentioned was a small
train depot just south of town. It was fed by
a rail line switching off of the main one that
stretched all the way to St. Louis. Almost
immediately, Nate climbed into his saddle

and followed the tracker out for a closer look.

The depot Pete showed him consisted of two buildings: one small shed and a longer structure about twice the size of a modest ticketing office nestled at the bottom of a wide gulch with hills on one side and woods on the other. At the moment, the only movement to be seen came from a few horses drinking water outside the shed and a trio of men sitting on the porch of the larger building with their feet propped up on the front rail.

Nate and Pete had left their horses about a quarter mile back on the slope of the hills facing away from the depot. After a round-about walk, they eventually picked a spot where they could lay on their bellies and look down at the depot through a set of field glasses which they passed back and forth.

"Doesn't look like much," Nate said as he examined the larger building. "But it sure isn't a depot used by any railroad line. At least, not anymore. There's a bigger one about three miles from here and another on the western outskirts of Joplin. Both of those would be much easier to supply than this one here."

"That's why I brought you here instead of any of them other depots. I doubt anyone with illegal intentions would choose to run their business out of a train station or depot that's still bein' used by the railroads."

"Looks like this place was used by one of the companies at some point," Nate said while studying the old signs that were now warped by rain and gathering dust from the damp Missouri winds.

Pete's eyes were so sharp that he rarely needed anything like field glasses. He squinted and stared at roughly the same spot as Nate while probably seeing close to the same amount of detail. "Most likely, that was a supply station used during the construction of these tracks. Could have also been used for some large venture related to the town itself. Joplin was built on all the jack that was pulled up from these hills."

"Jack?" Nate asked.

"Zinc."

"Doesn't look very busy."

"It sure was when I first found it," Pete said. "There were twice as many horses tied out front and at least three more armed men standing guard near that smaller building."

"Looks close to deserted now," Nate said while lowering the field glasses so he could shoot a sideways glance toward Pete.

The tracker nodded once. "Sure does."

"Maybe now'd be a good time to take a

closer look?"

"My thoughts exactly," Pete replied.

The two of them worked their way slowly and steadily toward the depot. Since the slope of the hill facing the two structures was mostly bare and fairly steep, they circled around and into the woods on the opposite side. Once they had the thick cover of trees for protection, they could move a bit faster. Their progress was slowed, however, by the constant need to stop and wait to see if anyone had spotted them or heard their movements. As near as they could tell, nobody had.

Fortune smiled on them when two of the men who'd been guarding the place walked over to their horses, climbed into their saddles and rode toward Joplin. Although that was encouraging, Nate and Pete knew better than to take that as a signal to hurry up and march straight toward the depot.

After several more minutes of cautious progress, they arrived at the edge of the woods and gazed out at the back end of the depot's largest building.

"I doubt we'll get a better chance than this if we're gonna get a close look at that place," Nate whispered.

"There could still be guards lurking about."

"That's why I'm the only one that'll break from cover. If anyone comes after me, I'll lead them off in another direction and you can take a look."

"And if there are even more guards who see me?" Pete asked.

"Then this just wasn't our lucky day, now was it? We didn't come all this way to turn back now, so stay put, keep your head down and keep those eagle eyes open for anything that might pose a threat." Without another word, Nate drew his Remington and moved into the clearing that marked the outer perimeter of the lot where the depot had been built.

Setting his sights on a door atop a set of three stairs next to a wide window, Nate hurried across the stretch of open ground without once looking back. He didn't need to check to make certain Pete was covering him. Whether the tracker liked the plan or not, Pete wouldn't leave a partner high and dry. He made it to within five or six paces of the building when Nate heard the crunch of boots against gravel and dirt. Someone was walking along the closest side of the building directly in front of him and would round the corner within seconds.

Nate shifted his weight to the balls of his feet and lowered his stance while holding the Remington so he could easily fire a shot at anyone who stepped into view. A half second later, something rustled in the trees. It was either a mighty big animal or a tracker of Nate's acquaintance making as much noise as possible. Either way, the sound caught the attention of whoever was approaching the corner.

The footsteps halted. Someone grumbled to himself in a rough voice. When the footsteps started up again, they moved slightly faster.

Even though there wasn't much of anywhere to hide, Nate hunkered down to lean against the railing of the short set of stairs leading up to the door. The man who came around the corner would have spotted him easily if he hadn't already been looking at the trees several yards away. He carried a rifle, which was also pointed at the woods. Nate took advantage of the opportunity he'd been given by holstering his pistol and rushing over to the rifleman.

His distraction bought Nate enough time to get to the rifleman, but just barely. Nate was about to take the rifle away from him when the man pivoted and drove the rifle's stock into Nate's midsection. Nate twisted to the side, allowing the rifle to glance off of him rather than land flush. From there, he grabbed the rifle with both hands and used his momentum as well as his muscle to try and pull it away from its owner. While the rifleman was surprised, he wasn't about to be disarmed so easily.

"Anstel's got some set of balls sending just one of you bastards," the rifleman snarled.

"One's all it takes," Nate replied.

That put an angry sneer on the rifleman's face as he tried even harder to reclaim his weapon from Nate's grasp. Nate resisted for a second or two and then shifted his efforts into the opposite direction. When he snapped the rifle around toward its owner, Nate met no resistance whatsoever. In fact, the rifleman was taken off his guard to such a degree that he pulled the contested weapon straight into a blow ending with the rifle's barrel cracking him in the jaw. Nate followed up by twisting the rifle around to thump its stock solidly against the other man's stomach. When the rifleman doubled over, Nate slammed the side of the rifle against the other man's temple to drop him into a heap on the ground.

Turning toward the source of the distraction that had made his attack possible in the first place, Nate found Pete waving at him. Once he had his attention, Pete pointed toward the smaller building. Nate didn't see anyone over there, but trusted that Pete had and concentrated on getting into the larger building.

His first stop was the large window, which turned out to be mostly painted over. The only spot that wasn't blacked out was a wide strip along the top which was too high for Nate to reach. Next, he tried the door. To his surprise, it was unlocked. Unfortunately, the iron-reinforced door just past the first one wasn't.

Nate still hadn't seen the other guard that Pete had spotted, but every instinct he had was screaming at him that his time had run out. There was just enough space between the two doors for the outer one to swing about halfway inward. Stepping inside and pulling the outer door shut, Nate side-stepped along the interior wall while bringing the rifle he'd taken up to his shoulder.

"Eddie?" someone outside hollered.

Apparently, Eddie was the man that was lying on the ground because there was no response to the call.

Nate's mind raced with all the different possibilities for what might come next. Given the current set of circumstances, his hopes started low and only sank with each passing moment.

"Eddie? Goddamn! You all right?"

Nate's grip tightened on the rifle, certain that the new arrival was now close enough to check on Eddie's well-being.

"Come on out, asshole!" the man outside said.

It wouldn't be long before that man came to the door, opened it and found Nate standing there in the dusty shadows.

"I see you, you bastard!"

Steeling himself, Nate sighted along the top of the rifle and aimed at the window. Just because he hadn't found a spot to look in didn't mean there wasn't one to be found.

"Come out or I'll shoot!" the man outside shouted.

Nate wasn't about to show himself so he prepared for the shooting to start. He only hoped he could pin down where the other man was before getting picked off like a stupid fish in a large barrel.

"Bastard!" the man outside shouted as he took his first shot.

Unlike the last time he'd been shot at, Nate didn't see any holes get blown through the wall in front of him. No glass shattered. So far, he still couldn't even see any movement. The shots kept coming, though. Fortunately, whoever was pulling the trigger was also moving away from the building.

Nate was all too anxious to open the

exterior door and take a look outside. He saw another man with a rifle firing round after round into the woods. Standing among the trees, Pete returned fire without sending a bullet anywhere close to its mark. That way, the rifleman had no qualms about standing his ground. Keeping his steps quick and quiet, Nate hurried away from the building at an angle that took him into the woods without catching the rifleman's eye.

The shooting went on for a short while, ending when Nate was about three strides away from getting himself behind solid cover. He made it into the woods safely since the rifleman hadn't yet lost interest in shooting at Pete.

"Go on, you coward!" the rifleman shouted. "And tell Anstel that it'll take a hell of a lot more than the likes of you to gain any favor with us!"

Nate worked his way straight back into the woods, slowly circling around toward the path that he and Pete had taken to get to the depot. Once he'd put a fair amount of trees between himself and the rifleman who was still screaming at thin air, Nate began heading for the hill. By the time he'd gotten to the other side of the hill and spotted his horse calmly grazing, he was damn near out of breath.

"What's the matter, Sathow?" Pete said as he stepped forward. "Getting old?" He must have been crouched somewhere preparing to put a bullet into any person who found the horses because he eased his pistol into its holster even as he made his joke.

"Too old to put up with the likes of you, that's for certain," Nate said while doing his best to keep from panting like a mangy dog. "Did you take care of that other guard?"

Pete let out half a chuckle. "All I needed to do was toss a few rocks over near that shed to get him headed in that direction. He'll probably be cussing and yelling at them rocks for at least an hour. What about you? I saw you got inside that depot."

"Partway inside," Nate corrected. "And just barely, at that. There's a whole other wall and door behind the one you can see. The first is barely a shell. The second felt like a damned fortress. Iron-reinforced door was locked so tight it wouldn't have budged if you took a run at it using that thick head of yours as a battering ram."

"Did you at least get a look inside through a window or something?"

Nate untied his reins and climbed into his saddle. "Nope."

"Well that's just great. All this way for

nothin'."

"I wouldn't say that. We found out that we can't just storm the place."

"Was that option really on the table?" Pete asked.

"Not anymore. We also got a feel for the sort of men being used to watch over this place and how many we might expect."

"I'd add a few more to that expectation after you left one lying in the dirt."

"Even so, we know this is the depot we need to watch. At least that's something."

"Sure it is," Pete said as he mounted his horse and flicked his reins. "Fat lot of good it'll do us. You pulled together the three of us to track one man. That man may be Dog Ear Pescaterro, but he ain't no gang holed up with a batch of heavy weaponry."

"Don't be so grim," Nate said. "If these jobs always went smoothly and according to plan, nobody would need the likes of us to do 'em. Besides, when I sit down to any game, there's always an ace up my sleeve. We just gotta find it."

26

"You've got an ace?" Deaugrey asked. "Well that's a coincidence. I've got two of 'em myself." He placed his cards on the table in front of him and spread them out for all to see. "And three sixes to go along for the ride."

The place was the House of Lords, and it was one of the rowdiest saloons in Joplin. Plenty of money flowed through its doors thanks mostly to the gambling taking place within its walls at any time day or night. Food was served, liquor flowed like water and there was a cathouse on the third floor, all of which were for the benefit of the miners, who stopped in before tunneling underground, and the cardsharps, who came along to fleece them. Even though Deaugrey had been playing there for the better part of two days straight, the other men at his table were having a tough time figuring him out. The man directly across the table from him, however, thought he had a firm grasp on the situation.

"You're a goddamned cheat!" the man said.

"You'll need to prove an accusation like that," Deaugrey said. "Otherwise, you're just one of many sore losers in this world."

"Son of a bitch!" the man roared. He shoved away from the table, got to his feet and slapped his hand against the gun on his hip.

"It's your deal, sir," Deaugrey said.

"You don't think I'll shoot you?"

"Quite frankly, I don't care if you do or don't."

The man drew his pistol while glaring into Deaugrey's eyes. He even went so far as to start thumbing the hammer back, but stopped short when he realized he wasn't getting any reaction at all from the other man. In fact, Deaugrey had picked up his cup and taken a drink as if he were sitting on a breezy porch all by his lonesome.

"Just sit down, Ed," one of the other players said. "You weren't cheated."

Ed jammed the pistol back into its holster and sat down so heavily, it was a wonder the chair didn't collapse beneath him. "Gimme that deck," he grunted as he took the cards and started to shuffle them.

"Actually," Deaugrey said, "I believe I'll sit this one out."

"Sit your ass down and ante," Ed said.

Deaugrey let out a dramatic sigh while picking up his cup. "I wish you'd make up your mind. Last time I checked, you wanted to shoot me."

"I'll just have to settle for taking my money back the hard way."

"That's the spirit! Oh, and just so you all know, I do know how to count. Very well, in fact. If any of these are missing when I return," Deaugrey said while waving a hand over his stacks of chips, "the man responsible will be gutted and emptied onto the floor. Next round of drinks is on me."

It took a few moments for the other players to collect themselves after Deaugrey delivered his icy threat. Eventually, Ed dealt the next hand and conversation sparked up again.

Deaugrey wound between the tables, patting complete strangers on the back and nodding to anyone who met his gaze. His destination was a small table in the corner where a solitary figure sat hunched over a cheap cut of beef. "There's more fat on that steak than there was on Hildy Bevins back in Reno," Deaugrey said. "Remember Hildy?"

"She was a fine woman," Nate replied while gnawing on his supper.

"She punched me in the jaw. Twice!"

"Probably on account of you calling her fat. I'm surprised she didn't knock you around any more than that. Have you been cheating at cards again?"

"Everybody cheats," Deaugrey said. "But this time, no. I've been ingratiating myself to the locals and being a perfect gentleman."

"You hungry?" Nate asked.

Looking down at what Nate had ordered, Deaugrey sneered and said, "Not for steak. I'll just have some soup."

"I thought you hated soup."

"Why would you think that?"

"Because when I found you at McKeag's Sanitarium you were screaming to high heaven about being forced to eat soup." Nate finally managed to saw off a portion of his steak and popped it into his mouth. "You were trying to stab the orderlies with a fork, if I recall."

"Funny. You'd think I'd remember something like that."

Knowing when it was time to switch to a different tack, Nate asked, "Did you do anything in here apart from piss off the locals?"

"Actually, yes." When a slender redhead

275

in a low-cut dress walked by, Deaugrey reached out to snake an arm around her waist and reel her in. She smiled warmly and brushed a hand along the side of his face.

"You ready for seconds, honey?" she asked.

"Not quite," Deaugrey replied. "I'd like some soup instead."

The woman was obviously an expert in disentangling herself from men's arms because she got away from Deaugrey with minimum effort. Her smile was still intact when she told him, "I'll be right back with that," and walked away.

"Found the depot," Nate said.

Deaugrey had yet to take his eyes off of the redhead's backside. "How exciting."

"Frank's stumbled upon some interesting bits of information as well. Seems Pescaterro has signed on with the Western Cartage Company. You hear mention of that from anyone around here?" When he didn't get a response, Nate took his dirty fork and tapped it against Deaugrey's forehead.

"*Now* I remember what I did with the cutlery at McKeag's," he said. "What you saw then was child's play. Hit me again like that, and you'll see what I can really do with a fork."

"You've got me quaking," Nate said flatly. "Answer the fucking question."

Deaugrey picked up a napkin and dabbed at the mess left on his head from Nate's fork. "The Western Cartage Company has been hiring on plenty of men around here. They're paying well, too."

"Is that so?"

"Well enough for a good number of their workers to find themselves in here with money burning holes in their pockets. The only ones pulling in as much money as them, excluding the miners who get lucky of course, are the men working for Anstel and Joyner."

Nate looked up from his steak. "I've heard mention of that company as well. What have you heard about them?"

"Anstel and Joyner?"

"Yeah. What have you heard?"

"From what I've been able to gather, they're just another big company looking to cash in on business brought in by the rail-roads."

"The railroad already runs through Joplin," Nate pointed out.

"But it's set to grow and grow big. I've only been here for a short time, and I'm already tired of hearing about it."

Now, more than ever, Nate had to focus

on maintaining his poker face. He felt a smirk bubbling to the surface, simply because he was watching Deaugrey perform like a racehorse that had just found its stride. If he showed any of that admiration, however, he would have to spend the next several minutes listening to Deaugrey sing his own praises.

"What are these companies involved in?" Nate asked.

"I've sat across from miners, merchants and a few men who drive spikes into the ground."

"You've been here two days."

"And I haven't left this room," Deaugrey replied. "In that time, I've sat across from —"

"Point taken," Nate cut in. "Get on with it."

"What I was trying to say is that damn near all of those different folks I mentioned have had some ties to one or both of those companies."

As a bowl of soup was placed in front of Deaugrey, Nate asked, "You're sure about that?"

"Isn't that why you brought me along?" Deaugrey asked.

"Yes, now get on with it."

Grinning as if he'd received the highest

praise imaginable, Deaugrey took a few spoonfuls of his soup. When he was good and ready, he said, "Both Anstel and Joyner as well as the Western Cartage Company are vying for any rights they can get their hands on. Between the mining claims and interest shown by the railroads, Joplin stands to see some very nice profits in the years to come."

"The railroads are always looking to expand," Nate said. "Have you been able to get these men talking about anything that'll help us?"

"The workers I've been socializing with around here aren't exactly interested in talking about work. They do, however, have plenty of wind in their sails when it comes to grousing about their employers."

"One of the true constants in this world," Nate said. It was also one of the most welcome since it provided him with an endless supply of information. It didn't take much to get just about any man to insult his employer. Workers for more reputable men were less likely to talk, but Nate Sathow was rarely hired to go after reputable men.

Deaugrey leaned over his soup with both elbows resting on the table. "It seems there is no shortage of gossip surrounding both of these companies. The short of it is that they are in a nasty struggle to lock up all of the interests within Joplin."

"How nasty?"

"Nasty enough for both sides to have killers on their payrolls. Word is that the hired guns have already earned their more-than-generous wages."

"I take it that's where Pescaterro comes in," Nate said.

"Oh yes. The Western Cartage Company approached Dog Ear to tip the scales back in their favor since they are the smaller of the two companies. None of the men at my games knew him by name, but they described a bloodthirsty maniac who cut a man open, bathed in his blood and howled at the moon. That same man had a nasty encounter with a poor fellow on a particularly bad streak of luck. He was left with one ear fewer than he'd had when he'd first crossed this man's path. I doubt these stories should be taken at face value, but . . ."

"Sounds like our man, all right," Nate said. "And here I thought this bad streak of luck you mentioned was just this fellow being cleaned out at the card table."

"Oh, I cleaned him out also."

"Nobody's ever accused you of having a heart."

"The only hearts that belong in a poker game are drawn onto the cards. Besides," Deaugrey added, "this fellow was playing so badly that he would have suspected something if he didn't lose."

Knowing better than to question logic that sprang from a mind that had more twists than a Gordian knot, Nate said, "I imagine this fellow who was attacked works for Anstel and Joyner."

"That's right, but I also found out more than that," Deaugrey replied proudly. "That fellow may not have known the name of the lunatic who cut his ear off, but he was fairly insistent that he was attacked because he refused to talk about what tactics would be taken to secure the next contracts that are about to be offered. There was also some mention of mining rights, but I couldn't learn anything more specific than that."

"The business specifics don't matter," Nate said. "Not to me, anyway. We're not here to make sense of contracts or politics. What does matter is that we put an end to whatever havoc Pescaterro is causing." Squinting across the table at the other man, he asked, "What is it? You've got that smug grin on your face. A different one than usual, I should say."

"A few of that poor, unlucky fellow's compatriots joined him at the game. I bought a round of drinks, which wound up being one of several that greased the wheels of conversation."

"I'll add more to your cut of this job if you sift through everything you plan on saying and just tell me the important parts," Nate snapped.

To that, Deaugrey quickly replied, "Several men from both companies share the opinion that Western Cartage somehow arranged for their most vicious new worker to be liberated from his former accommodations."

Nate leaned in so he could talk without the possibility of being overheard by anyone but his partner. "The Western Cartage Company broke Dog Ear out of jail?"

"That's the rumor."

"And they're putting him to work terrorizing their competitor's men?"

"Mostly," Deaugrey said. "I've heard rumblings of some particularly ugly robberies and a few bodies that have surfaced that seemed to have Pescaterro's stamp on them."

"How so?" Nate asked.

"Bodies were found recently that have

been the topic of more than a few conversations. Mutilated bodies. One whore was cut apart and chopped to pieces. A few more men from Anstel and Joyner were found with their throats slit and various other pieces missing."

"You think those were all done by Pescaterro?"

Deaugrey took a moment to think and didn't seem to like what he found. "I've been locked up with plenty of savages. Men who deserve to be tossed into the deepest pit that's ever been dug. There's a certain . . . special kind of brutality that's inflicted for no reason apart from the sheer joy some get from pain. While I can't tell you that every terrible crime of late was committed by our man or wasn't just the subject of some tall tale spouted by a drunk gambler, I guarantee some of them were very real. Also, I've discovered that rumors such as these come from somewhere. A few of these killings were real enough, and they weren't connected to the feuding companies. They were local news. Pescaterro is one of those brutal, savage sorts I've encountered in various institutions who likes what he does and would want to get back to it as quickly as possible. No matter who he's working for or what he's getting paid,

Dog Ear will eventually be the cause of news stories like those."

"Agreed. Have you heard anything in regard to Abraham Keyes?"

"Just that he's climbed the ranks of the Anstel and Joyner Company."

"You have learned quite a lot by sitting here playing cards."

"I'm a good listener and know how to keep people talking," Deaugrey said. "Those simple talents have served me more good than an entire arsenal of firearms while I've been locked away. Granted, I've drawn some conclusions of my own, but I know for certain that both of these men we're after have been keeping very busy through-out their short stay in Joplin."

Nate nodded. "Makes sense. We already know Keyes and Pescaterro were working together."

"Now it's you who needs to listen. Dog Ear is aligned with Western Cartage."

Nate rubbed his chin, creating a scraping sound from the friction of his fingers against coarse stubble. "They must be working some angle. What did you hear about those specialty weapons?"

"You want more? That's gratitude for you," Deaugrey scoffed. "I'll have you know I'd still have a hell of a lot more of my winnings if I hadn't spent them in getting some of those men I mentioned to part with their colorful stories."

Hearing that put some of Nate's mind at ease. It wasn't unusual for Deaugrey to embellish when it came to the rumors he'd overheard. A few wisely placed bribes were not only within Deaugrey's bag of tricks but explained how he'd come across some of the information he'd just relayed. Even a man with Deaugrey's talents could only overhear so much.

"I've done the job of three men," Deaugrey announced. "How have you been passing your time?"

"Pete and I found that depot. We were discovered, but . . ."

"We?" Deaugrey asked. "As in . . . both you and Pete were discovered?"

"Fine," Nate grunted. "*I* was discovered."

"That sounds much more plausible."

"One of the men who took a shot at me thought I was with Anstel and Joyner. Stands to reason that the depot and whatever is in it is owned by Western Cartage."

Deaugrey's eyes widened. "That's quite a find. I'm guessing you already have some diabolical way to put it to use."

"Not yet," Nate replied.

"Won't be long, though," Deaugrey said.

"The wheels are turning inside that head of yours. I can smell the smoke."

"Finish your soup and get back to work."

After draining the rest of his soup by tipping the bowl straight to his lips, Deaugrey stood and reached into one of his pockets. When his jacket opened, Nate could see not only a new shoulder holster but two more watch chains that crossed his belly and that had not been there the last time Nate had spoken to him. Deaugrey removed a small bundle of cash and placed it on the table. "Here are some funds for this little venture," he said. "If you need more, I can play to win instead of stringing along the men with the most stories to tell."

"How about you mention Pescaterro's and Keyes's names more often?" Nate suggested. "That might get some more people talking."

"Could be dangerous."

"Then forget it," Nate said as he scooped up the money and tucked it away. "I can do it myself."

"What's next? You insult my backbone?"

"Actually, I was saving that for a bit later."

"I'll kick over a few more rocks," Deaugrey said with a rare show of trepidation. "See what scurries out. I'll have to wait, though. At least until some fresh faces come in.

Some of these miners are getting a bit suspicious of me."

"Do what you can," Nate told him. "Join a game in another saloon if you like. Once the well's run dry, see if you can find out what the hell Keyes wanted with you back at that mining camp. Leave word for me at a hotel called the Joplin Grand. I'm staying there now."

"I won't leave this room," Deaugrey told him. "The House of Lords is the center of this town as far as I'm concerned." With that, he left the table. Nate didn't hear Deaugrey's voice again until an entire table of drunken gamblers started hollering to each other about winning back what they'd lost. Seeing how completely the local gamblers had taken Deaugrey in as one of their own, Nate had even less trouble believing how much information had been wrung out of them.

After paying what he owed for the meal and drinks, Nate left the House of Lords and headed down the street toward the Joplin Grand. Despite the regal name, the hotel was a fairly small structure wedged in between an assayer's office and a bakery. About halfway through his walk, Nate heard another set of footsteps fall in beside him.

"Did Deaugrey perform to his usual

standards?" Frank asked.

"I swear I don't know how he does it," Nate replied.

"We don't need to know. Just be glad that he does."

"Have faith?" Nate asked with a smirk.

"Something like that. What's next on the agenda?"

"It seems there are two competing companies trading blows over money rights from property to mining claims here in Joplin. Pescaterro is working for one and Keyes the other."

Frank let out a tired sigh. "Both ends against the middle. That never turns out well, especially when we barely know either side."

"We've dealt with enough men like these to know them well enough. Let's start by scouting out both companies' offices here in town. Perhaps if we play this one right, we can take Pescaterro and Keyes out of the picture before it gets any bloodier than it already is."

"One can always hope," Frank said rather unconvincingly.

If there was one thing that tied Nate's stomach into a knot worse than anything else, it was when Frank was the one who was short on optimism.

27

The next two days were mostly uneventful. Nate, Frank and Pete did their share of scouting in the town to get a feel for the balance of power between the two companies vying for their share of it. Anstel & Joyner had their sights set on the tracks being built from St. Louis heading west and the Western Cartage Company was primarily interested in the line coming into Missouri through Kansas. Once the two lines met, the task remained of deciding which company would carry on from there.

Nate was no businessman, which was something he never wanted to change. While he didn't know the specifics of all the deals involved with railroad expansion, he'd seen enough with his own eyes to know that plenty of business opportunities came along with it besides ticket sales. There were labor contracts, entertainment and food to be provided near the stations, even whole towns to be built along the way to keep the railroad moving and its paying customers satisfied. All he'd needed to do to hear about such things was visit a few local stores and mention the railroad. After that, he'd simply kept his ears open to hear one local after another spout their praises or condemnations.

Now that he'd done some digging in the obvious places, Nate decided to go to a source that rarely let him down. While Deaugrey hit the saloons and wheedled information from drunks, Nate scouted a few locations of his own, and one of them paid off nicely.

"So, Mr. Keenan," said a rotund fellow in a white jacket who towered over the chair that dominated the center of his shop, "are you still interested in investment opportunities here in town?"

Nate leaned back beneath the towel that was draped over his chest and lifted his chin so the straight razor could be placed to his throat. The tall fellow in white had already trimmed Nate's hair and was about to do the same to his chin and cheeks. The sign at the front of the barbershop advertised a special that included a bath, but Nate was saving that for another day. "An investor is always interested, Jerry," he said. "I hear there's going to be some mighty fine opportunities coming along."

"Depends on what sort of thing you're after."

Opening one eye, Nate said, "When it comes to making money, it doesn't pay to be picky. Am I right?"

Fancying himself a shrewd expert on just about everything, Jerry nodded and started shaving Nate's chin. "Indeed you are. I've dabbled in a few investments, but I don't really have the funds for that sort of thing."

"Do you know what a finder's fee is?"

"I believe I got one of those when Mrs. Lannerly left her handbag here after she came along to buy some rosewater. I found it and returned it without stealing anything from inside and I got a nice little something for my trouble."

"Actually, no."

"Then I don't know, Mr. Keenan."

"A finder's fee is something a man is paid for pointing someone in the right direction. For example, I asked about any business opportunities and if you knew of any that panned out, I'd pay you for your help."

"Oh," Jerry said happily. "Then I wasn't too far off after all. I can't say as I'd know any way to point you, though."

"Have you heard about anything regarding the railroad being built up near here? Perhaps you might have heard something from one of your customers who maybe works for a company that would be working with the railroad in some regard?"

"You mean like someone from Western Cartage?"

Nate turned toward Jerry ever so slightly, which was enough to put a fresh nick on his cheek. While the barber hurried to dab the blood trickling from the cut, Nate said, "That is exactly the sort of thing I mean! Do you know the name of anyone I should talk to over there?"

"Not as such."

"It's a large company. I'm sure you know someone."

"Sorry, but no," Jerry told him, even though the twitch in the corner of his eye and the slight tremble in his hand told a much different story.

"You've never even met anyone who might work there?"

"I'm not certain. I don't know where all my customers work."

"What about one named Casey Pescaterro?" Nate asked.

Jerry's hand lingered in one spot, but remained steady enough to keep from cutting Nate's face again. "Pesca . . . what?"

Nate kept still as well. His eyes remained fixed upon the barber's face as he said, "Pescaterro. Big fellow. Some burns on his face. You'd remember that, I'm sure, since he's seemed mighty interested in keeping what's left of his beard in good shape. Well, as good as it could be I suppose. Any of that striking you as familiar?"

Having finished with most of Nate's shave, Jerry quickly tended to the remaining patch of whiskers and started wiping away the remaining lather with a towel. "I'm sure I would remember something like that."

"Tell me, how many others do you have working here for you?"

"Just me, sir. Why?"

"Because I've been tracking this fellow for a short while," Nate said. "I've also heard a thing or two about him before I was put onto his trail, and one of the things I've pieced together is that he's started taking pride in his appearance. Since he's been in Joplin, Pescaterro's been making enough money to see a barber every other day."

Jerry stood behind Nate's chair and was noisily fidgeting with combs in a small drawer. Nate could keep an eye on him thanks to the large mirror on the wall directly in front of him. "Is that a fact?" the barber asked.

"You know it is. Several of your neighbors on this street told me so. And before you tell me they're full of beans, I should add that I caught sight of Pescaterro here two days ago. The two of you seemed to be on awfully friendly terms for someone you don't even seem to recall meeting."

Jerry suddenly became very still. Although Nate had never gotten the impression that the barber might turn on him wielding one of his razors or some other weapon, he watched the larger man very carefully. Beneath the towel covering the front of his body, Nate's hand snaked toward the Remington in his cross-draw holster.

"What do you want me to tell you?" Jerry asked nervously.

"You and Pescaterro must talk about things while he's here and I know he ain't exactly the sort who gossips. For that matter, he must have struck you as unusual. You've probably even heard a thing or two about him from other folks since he's been in town."

"He . . . hasn't been coming to me for very long."

"That's a start," Nate said, grateful that Jerry wasn't trying to feed him another lie.

"I know he works for Western Cartage."

"You know he's a killer, right?"

Jerry turned to look down at Nate and then looked up so he could face him indirectly using the mirror. "I've heard some things," Jerry admitted. "There's been plenty of unflattering rumors going around about all of these new hands hired on by Western Cartage as well as Mr. Anstel's company. There's no telling how many of those things are true."

Easing a hand up from beneath the towel, Nate showed the barber one of the smaller badges from his collection. This one simply said MARSHAL. "Whatever you've heard is likely true," he said. "And there's plenty more that I'm certain you haven't heard."

Jerry didn't even bother trying to hide his nervousness. In fact, he seemed relieved at not having to maintain his charade. "All I do is shave the faces in front of me and cut hair. I swear. Whatever that man's done, I didn't have no part of it."

Even though Nate had been hoping to elicit a reaction along those lines, he couldn't help but feel a touch of guilt at having his efforts work well enough to turn the poor barber into a jellyfish. "I never thought you had anything to do with the sort of thing Pescaterro is doing," Nate assured him. "I just need a couple of favors."

"You want to know about him? I'll tell you

whatever you need. In fact," Jerry added as he peeled back the towel and hurried to the counter where he kept bottles of scented oils and water, "let me buy you a drink or maybe lunch, and you can ask me anything you want to know. I don't know how much I could tell you that would be much help, but I'll sure give it a try."

"That covers one of the favors I meant to ask."

Jerry stood next to Nate's chair, staring at him with wide, overly eager eyes. Suddenly he spat out, "Oh! The shave? It's on the house."

"Not the shave."

"I'm always willing to help the law, so . . . when we meet up again you just let me know what I can do."

"I'll let you know right now," Nate said.

"No. I mean — it'd be better if — I've got a business to run here."

"Help me out right now and you'll be entitled to a very handsome finder's fee," Nate told him. "You make one more move toward that stick and you'll get something that ain't nearly as pleasant."

The barber froze with his hand poised less than a foot away from a length of wood leaning in a corner just behind a broom. One end of the wood was bound by twine to form something of a handle. Allowing his arm to droop at his side and his head to hang, Jerry shuffled to turn around and face the only chair that was occupied in his shop at the moment. "What do you want from me?" he groaned.

"How about a treatment of those nice, hot towels?"

28

The door to the barbershop was pushed open with enough force to make the bell connected to it sound more like a cat that had gotten its tail caught beneath a rocker. Its window was still rattling in its pane when the man who'd shoved it stomped the few short steps required to cross the room and dropped himself down into the largest of the chairs.

"Hello, Mr. Pescaterro," Jerry said. "The usual?"

"Can you toss in any extra services?" Dog Ear asked. "Like maybe have that pretty gal that sweeps yer floors give me a ride when yer done?"

Laughing nervously, Jerry said, "That's my niece —"

"Oh?"

"— and she doesn't work here regularly."

Pescaterro folded his hands across his belly and leaned back in his chair. "Then just the usual, I guess."

As Jerry took a moment to run his razor back and forth over a sharpening strip, Pescaterro looked over to the chair beside him where another customer lay quietly beneath several steaming towels wrapped over his face. "You ever seen that little squaw that sweeps the floors?" Pescaterro asked.

The customer shifted just enough to turn toward the sound of the other man's voice and then shook his head.

"Yeah, well yer missin' out," Pescaterro said. His bulky frame was almost too much for the chair in which he sat. His arms were thick with layer upon layer of muscle and his wrists were scarred with bands of gnarled skin marking the spots where he'd fought several battles against the various shackles that had been placed upon him. Apart from a nose that had been broken more times than the devil's promises, his most prominent feature were the burn scars running down one half of his mouth and chin like hot candle wax that had been drizzled over his face.

"She's not a squaw," Jerry said meekly.

"What did you just say?" Dog Ear snarled.

Holding his razor in a vaguely trembling hand, the barber told him, "My niece. She's part Spaniard."

"Fine," Pescaterro grunted. "I'd bend a Spanish bitch over and fuck her just as easily as I would a savage bitch. Now give me my goddamn shave."

Jerry's eyes darted over to the other chair. "I'm running a special today."

"What's that?"

"Hot towels for an extra ten cents. They soften the whiskers and are mighty relaxing."

"I don't want anything over my face," Pescaterro said.

Reaching for a wide metal box, Jerry pulled a lever that opened the lid to allow a gout of steam to rise from within. "Are you sure? It'll make you feel like a new man."

Pescaterro shifted in his seat contentedly. "To hell with yer special and to hell with that squaw sweeper of yers."

Jerry winced and eased the lid back down onto the box. "All right. Just thought I'd ask." After that, he whipped up a mug full of lather using a brush with long, soft bristles and began applying it to Pescaterro's face. At the same time, Nate peeled away the towels that had been piled onto his face and eased himself toward the edge of his chair.

Nate's boots had barely touched the floor when Pescaterro glanced over in his direction. The instant Pescaterro spotted him, Nate placed his hand on the grip of his holstered Remington and said, "You should've taken the special, Dog Ear. Would have been a nice treat before heading back to jail."

"Who the fuck are you?" Pescaterro grunted. "Some goddamn bounty hunter?"

"He's a lawman," Jerry said. "The best thing for you is to —"

In a swift set of movements, Pescaterro grabbed hold of Jerry's white jacket, pulled him between the two barber chairs and then swung him at Nate as if he were wielding a blackjack.

Nate had been expecting some sort of attack, but not this one. When he was thumped by the hapless barber, Nate rolled over the top of his chair to drop awkwardly onto the floor behind it. Sure enough, Pescaterro followed up with something much deadlier than his first attempt and a gunshot exploded in the little shop.

"I been waiting for someone like you to come along!" Pescaterro roared before sending another pair of rounds into the chair. "After nailing that sheriff up north to that tree, I was gettin' mighty bored."

Nate didn't know what Dog Ear was talking about, but assumed there was some poor lawman still rotting on a tree somewhere.

"You got one chance to go quietly, Pesca-terro," Nate said from behind his cover. "This is it."

"Yeah? How about you give me a second to consider that?"

A half second later, sounds of rending metal and screws being torn through the boards where they'd been mounted filled the air. Nate glanced around his chair to see Pescaterro's boots and the base of the larger chair just before it was ripped up from the floor. That chair was then lifted high and sent crashing down again.

The chair's backrest slammed against the portion of Nate's chair meant to support his feet. He tried to roll away from the collision, but Nate hit a wall before getting far enough away to clear. Not only did the uprooted chair fall toward him, but the chair that Nate had been sitting in also began tilting his way. The quickest method for him to avoid being buried under all of that padded metal was to crawl toward the side of the shop where the barber kept his tools and other wares in a series of small drawers.

"That's what I like to see!" Pescaterro said. "Crawl for me, little piggie! I'll have you squealin' in no time!"

Nate started climbing to his feet out of

reflex. Before he got one leg beneath him, he dropped back down again to press his chest flat against the floor. In the space of a heartbeat, a gunshot blasted through the shop to blast a piece from the cabinets where Nate would have been if he'd lifted his head any farther. Now that he'd gotten his bearings again, Nate lay on his side and drew the Remington. He sighted along the barrel for less than a second before squeezing his trigger. The pistol barked twice. One of those bullets sparked against what remained of the wide metal post where the larger chair had been moored and the other got Dog Ear hopping backward.

"Hooo-*wee*!" Pescaterro wailed. "Yer a nasty little bastard!"

Keeping his arm steady, Nate took careful aim and waited for another clear opportunity. As soon as he saw Pescaterro's feet shuffle into sight, he fired at them. Bits of leather tore from Dog Ear's boot, accompanied by a spray of blood. Pescaterro's only reaction was another wild howl. Instead of trying to find cover or get out of the barbershop altogether, the outlaw rushed around to the second chair to face Nate directly. If he felt any pain from getting hit, he wasn't about to show it.

Nate steeled himself with a deep breath

and clambered to his feet. As soon as he could, he crouched down low and circled around the upended chair so there was still something solid between him and Pescaterro. Dog Ear's shots came in a series of rapid pops. One after another, each round came within inches of putting Nate down. One of them scraped across Nate's back like a set of molten claws and was immediately followed by the metallic slap of a hammer against the back of an empty casing.

Nate stood up while firing a shot of his own. It was a rushed attempt, only meant to buy him another second or two. If he were facing someone who cared about life or death, it might have done just that. Against Pescaterro, however, it was simply a wasted bullet.

Dog Ear's face was covered with a sloppy, ear-to-ear grin. Charging forward, he stretched out one arm while cocking the other back. His fingertips slapped against the Remington's still-warm barrel to push it to one side so he could swing the straight razor he'd grabbed with his other hand. Nate barely had enough time to lean back and turn his head to one side before his face was sheared off the front of his skull. The blade sliced through the air in front of him, sending a cold chill raking down his spine.

"Not in here!" Jerry protested loudly from somewhere outside of Nate's sight.

When Nate tried to aim the Remington, he realized he couldn't move that entire arm. Pescaterro had clamped a solid grip around it and was holding it at a prime distance for his next swing with the razor. Before he could be eviscerated, Nate kicked Dog Ear anywhere he could. His boot pounded against his shin and even stomped down on the outlaw's feet, which only put a slight wince onto Pescaterro's face.

"I should'a gone for the special, huh?" the outlaw grunted as he pulled Nate in closer and butted heads with him. "That's funny."

Normally, Nate tried to avoid head butts simply because they only worked for animals with horns. For anyone else, it was generally a losing prospect no matter which end of it you were on. By the time Nate realized his arm had been released, Dog Ear's meaty hand had clamped around his throat.

"How long you been chasing me, bounty hunter?" Pescaterro asked as he pinned Nate against one of the large mirrors hanging on the wall. "Someone from that mining camp steer you my way?"

"It was . . . Keyes," Nate said desperately. "He told . . ."

"Uh-uh," Pescaterro grunted as he

brought the razor down toward the side of Nate's head. "Keyes may be a lot of things, but he ain't no backstabber."

"I swear! He —"

"Go on and keep screamin' if you like. I sure like it."

Instead of trying to talk his way out of his current predicament, Nate brought his knee up into a series of powerful blows. The first few thumped against what felt like a wall made of smoked ham hocks. Pescaterro didn't seem to feel much pain from the shots he'd taken and those knees hurt him even less. He was at least jostled enough for the razor to move a few inches away from its intended target. The next time, Nate drove his knee straight into Pescaterro's groin.

Dog Ear's eyes widened a bit and his lips curled into a reflexive snarl. That was the problem with trying to crack a man in the jewels. If he didn't drop right away, he'd just become a lot madder than when he'd started. Before Nate could try to follow up with another knee to the same spot, he was heaved to one side like a hay bale being tossed toward the back end of a barn. Nate's hip and leg knocked against something solid and the sound of shattering glass filled his ears. Suddenly, he knew where he was.

Too angered to form words, Pescaterro slashed with the razor. Nate twisted away while reaching out to grab whatever he could. As his hand closed around a tall jar, Nate felt a jab of pain in his face followed by the warm rush of blood. The razor had cut him and was so sharp that he'd barely noticed. He grabbed the hand that was still gripping his throat and dug his thumb as far as he could into Pescaterro's wrist.

"Slimy little fuck!" Dog Ear said through clenched teeth.

Nate swung his other hand around, smashing the jar against Dog Ear's shoulder.

"No!" Jerry hollered as if the jar had been broken against the side of his grandmother's head.

The air reeked of rosewater. Judging by the barber's continued mourning for the loss of his jar, it was fairly expensive rosewater. All Nate cared about was that the jar had indeed broken. Jagged portions of glass bit into his fingers and palm, which did nothing to keep him from hanging on tightly so he could drive the broken jar into Pescaterro's shoulder.

"Son of a bastard!" the outlaw roared as Nate twisted the broken shard of glass into his fresh wound.

The instant the grip around Nate's throat

loosened enough for him to draw a breath, Nate pulled away and jumped down from atop the counter where Pescaterro had tossed him. He tightened his grip on the broken jar while frantically looking for the pistol he'd dropped somewhere along the way.

He found it, but it was closer to Pescaterro's boot than his own.

Dog Ear straightened up to his full height, which put the top of his head within a scant couple inches of the ceiling. Reaching over one shoulder, he let out a throaty grunt which ended with a long exhale. "That's better," he said while showing Nate the wide shard of glass he'd dug from his flesh.

Nate couldn't help looking at the jar in his hand. Sure enough, he'd broken off a sizeable portion while stabbing Pescaterro. Suddenly, the remaining piece of bloody glass in his hand didn't seem so formidable. Pescaterro's eyes glazed over as he gleefully rushed toward Nate with his arms opened wide. Even if he'd seen the gun lying on the floor so close to him, it was doubtful he'd take the time to pick it up. Dog Ear was known for killing men in many ways, but standing and shooting like a regular murderer wasn't one of them.

Panic was a rare thing for Nate Sathow.

This, however, was one time when he could feel it nipping at his heels and climbing up his spine with its icy little fingers. Rather than give in to it, he grabbed the first thing he could from one of the nearby tables. His hopes rose when he realized he'd stumbled upon the spot where Jerry kept his more practical tools. As Pescaterro charged at him, Nate hopped aside and picked up a pair of long, narrow scissors. Pescaterro stopped short of slamming face-first into the wall and, before he could wheel around, Nate brought his fist down like a hammer.

The scissors dug deep into a meaty portion of Pescaterro's back near the shoulder. He'd been aiming for the fresh wound put there by the broken bottle and nearly hit his mark. Enraged, Pescaterro turned around while lashing out with a savage backfist. Not only did he thump Nate in the chest, but he did it so quickly that Nate dropped the scissors as he fell back.

"You're ruining my shop!" Jerry wailed from the corner in which he was huddled. "At least take this outside!"

Pescaterro turned toward the barber and said, "I know you set this up! You're dead as soon as I finish with this one here!"

Jerry shut his mouth and hunkered down in his corner.

When Pescaterro shifted his focus back to Nate, he got an eyeful of soapy water which was the next closest thing that Nate could grab. The outlaw howled as the soap stung his eyes. Balling up his fists, he stampeded in Nate's direction. At the last second, Nate dove aside so Pescaterro ran face-first into another set of low shelves. Nate stepped up to deliver a series of short, chopping punches to Dog Ear's ribs. His fists pounded into the same spot, tenderizing Pescaterro's side until the outlaw turned to take another swipe at him. Still partially blinded by the lather, he punched a hole into the barber's wall and sent his other fist crashing down onto a metal bin used to keep the day's special good and hot.

"Owwww!" Pescaterro cried as he scaled his hand with the metal container full of hot towels. The outlaw then wiped furiously at his face to clear his eyes.

Recognizing an advantage when he saw one, Nate looked around for something else he could put to use. There was another jar of clear liquid in an open cabinet. He picked it up, sniffed its contents and recognized the pungent scent of pure alcohol that was probably used to clean scissors and razor blades. He waited for Pescaterro to make some progress with the soap and when the outlaw finally spotted him, Nate tossed the alcohol into his face.

Since Pescaterro's eyes had been open wide, he got a full dose of the bitter liquid. He may have been mad before, but now he lost whatever was left of his mind. Clenching his eyes shut and gritting his teeth against the burning pain, Pescaterro lunged forward to get his hands on the man who'd sent him over the edge. Nate was lucky to step out of the way and hurried over to the length of wood that Jerry kept to use against unruly customers.

Before Nate could get a solid grip on the club, the barber grumbled into his hands. It had probably just been a complaint about the state of his shop, but the words were just loud enough to be heard. Pescaterro spun toward the sound of the rasping voice and stomped toward it while growling, "Found you, you bastard!"

"What?" Jerry squeaked. He couldn't get another word out before Pescaterro picked him up by one arm and the collar of his shirt. Squinting through a haze of pain and rage, the outlaw pivoted on both feet to throw Jerry out the front window.

Glass shattered loudly, and the barber let out a pained cry as he landed on the boardwalk outside. Passersby spoke in surprised voices and a few ladies screamed at the sight before them. Jerry pulled himself up on all fours, cut and bleeding in several places by glass that he'd broken with his body.

"I got you now," Pescaterro snarled as he wiped his eyes and stepped outside through the broken window. For a moment, he just stood there blinking furiously while using his sleeves to sop up as much of the alcohol and soap as he could. Half the time, he was clearing his eyes and the rest of the time he was wiping the mess back into them. When he was finally able to see again, he looked down at the barber in dazed confusion. "Where the hell is the bounty hunter?" he grunted.

Nate answered by cracking the barber's club against the back of Pescaterro's head. The outlaw staggered and turned around while collecting himself for a renewed attack. Rather than wait around for the fight to commence again, Nate drew back the club and swung it with all his might. Some of the impact was dulled by the mess of hair sprouting from Pescaterro's scalp as well as the general thickness of his skull, but that second knock combined with the first were enough to drop the outlaw to the ground.

The people who'd witnessed Jerry's exit through the window now stood to gawk at

Nate and Pescaterro in silence. Nate looked around just long enough to satisfy himself that none of the locals were about to enter the fray on Dog Ear's behalf. Then, he propped the length of wood on his shoulder and walked back into the barbershop to retrieve his pistol. When he returned, he found a familiar face among the astonished crowd outside.

"You sure took your sweet time in getting here!" Nate said to Frank.

"I was having a word with Grey," the preacher said. "What on earth happened here?"

"I'll explain it while we work. Now help me get this lunatic shackled good and tight."

29

The offices of Anstel & Joyner were located
in the newer section of Joplin's business
district. They were housed in a wide building with three floors, which made them
slightly larger than the bank which was
directly across the street. Black carriages
were lined up in front of the building,
tended by drivers who knew better than to
say a word to the well-dressed men who
walked in and out of the offices. They
scowled at Deaugrey as he passed them,
however. When he saw that, Deaugrey
tipped his hat and ambled toward the front
door.

"Do you have an appointment?" asked the
barrel-chested man who greeted Deaugrey
almost immediately upon entering the
building.

"I certainly do," Deaugrey announced.
"And I'd hate to be late for it because of a
well-meaning but troublesome lackey."

The man was somewhere in his thirties, had short brown hair, spectacles and a narrow, bushy beard that was reminiscent of a goat's. He raised one eyebrow and replied, "That'd be better than being late because you got tossed into the street and kicked beneath a set of wagon wheels."

After giving that a moment's consideration, Deaugrey said, "I suppose you're right. The name's Deaugrey Scott."

There was a set of stairs nearby. Two men stood there. The one who descended them first had a solid build and was slightly taller than average. His round face was smiling at the moment but had the potential for something much darker. Salt and pepper whiskers covered his chin and most everything below the neck was covered in an expensive dark blue suit. "There he is!" he declared. "I was hoping you'd arrive."

"Why wouldn't I?" Deaugrey replied.

"I realize my invitation wasn't exactly traditional."

"The most recent invitation was fairly straightforward." Looking past the first man toward the top of the stairs where Abraham Keyes stood, Deaugrey added, "It was the earlier introduction that left something to be desired."

Keyes smirked without saying anything.

"Yes," the man in the dark blue suit said. "But, considering the company you keep, you must understand why I'd be somewhat skeptical that you'd pay me a visit of your own accord."

Deaugrey opened his arms wide as if he meant to embrace the well-dressed man who was now walking toward him. "Well, here I am. See how far a man can get just by asking nicely?"

The well-dressed fellow nodded and offered his hand. "I'll tuck that lesson away for the future. I'm Preston Anstel."

Shaking Anstel's hand, Deaugrey said, "Pleased to meet you. Now let's talk business."

Anstel draped an arm around Deaugrey's shoulders and steered him toward the stairs. "Since time is a precious commodity to every man, I'll save both of ours by being blunt. I'm told that you've spent a fair amount of time in various sanitariums over the course of your years."

"*Fair* is hardly a word I would use to describe that time," Deaugrey said in a wounded tone of voice.

"Quite. Is my information correct?"

"It's correct, Mr. Anstel," Keyes said as the short procession passed him on the stairs. Falling in step behind them, he climbed the stairs while making less noise than a cat stalking an unsuspecting pigeon.

Deaugrey ignored Keyes and told the man beside him, "You are correct, sir."

"Good," Anstel replied. "Then I assume my information regarding you recently spending some of those unfortunate days in McKeag's Sanitarium is also correct."

"It is."

"Excellent. I, myself, have never seen the inside of one of those places. Please don't take that as an insult to you, but more of an admission of ignorance on my part."

"If only more men were so willing to admit that very thing," Deaugrey said wistfully.

As far as Deaugrey could tell, the second floor was filled mostly with shelves of books and an abundance of little desks where little men sat hunched while scribbling into large ledgers. There were hallways in the distance and several other doors, but he didn't have a chance to see much more before they'd climbed to the much quieter third floor. Just past that landing was a single hall that extended all the way back to a large door. There were only six other doors along the way, three on each side.

Anstel led the way to the second door on the left side of the hall, opened it and stepped inside. When Deaugrey paused before following, Keyes shoved him forward. The room was sparsely furnished, but comfortable. Its floor was carpeted. Two of its walls were papered. All three chairs situated there were padded. The shelves on the other two walls were filled with leather-bound volumes marked only with dates and Roman numerals.

Standing beside one of the chairs, Anstel propped an arm upon its backrest as if he were posing for a portrait beside his favorite Arabian stallion. "While you were in Mc-Keag's," he said after the lengthy pause he'd taken to enter the room, "did you have the opportunity to visit with any of the other . . . guests?"

"A few," Deaugrey said.

"What about a young woman by the name of Melanie Cavett?"

Deaugrey tapped his chin as he thought. He then lowered himself into one of the chairs, crossed his legs and turned his eyes upward as if to ponder the designs that had been etched into the wood trim along the upper corners of the room. "You know what might jog my memory? A glass of brandy."

"How about a knock to the head?" Keyes asked.

"You'll have to pardon my associate," Anstel told Deaugrey. "He is rather straight-forward."

"He's also had his chance to do things his way," Deaugrey pointed out. "And he made a mess of it."

"He did at that," Anstel replied while shooting a pointed glare at Keyes. "Abraham, fetch us both a glass of brandy, will you?"

Keyes stalked out of the room.

Once the door had been shut most of the way behind the lean gunman, Deaugrey asked, "Were you the one who sent him to that mining camp?"

"Yes," Anstel replied curtly. "But his orders were merely to bring you back here. I was quite dismayed when I heard how he attempted to accomplish his task."

Although Deaugrey didn't believe that for a second, he said, "It's nice to have a conversation with someone like yourself, Mr. Anstel. Or . . . should I call you Preston?"

"Either is fine with me. Now, does the name Melanie Cavett sound at all familiar?" When Deaugrey began tapping his chin again, Anstel asked, "What about Casey Pescaterro?"

"Now *that* name does strike a chord."

"I thought it might. He is one of many

men who will lead the charge against you. I daresay they won't be nearly as civilized as myself when they come calling."

Putting on a convincingly puzzled expression, Deaugrey asked, "Whatever would a known murderer like Pescaterro want with me?"

"He works for the Western Cartage Company. They have their spies throughout this town in an effort to cripple me and my prosperous business. Since you are now a guest of mine, thugs like Pescaterro and his ilk will tear after you just as viciously as they have torn after me."

"If only there was some way I could be protected from such a terrible fate," Deaugrey said drily.

Anstel grinned like a child who knew he had every adult that mattered wrapped around his little finger. "I'll admit, offering my protection is something I've done plenty of times in situations like this. However, considering your circumstances, I'd say you're already in need of a more secure arrangement. Otherwise, you wouldn't be here talking to me. Am I right?"

Keyes reentered the room carrying a half-full brandy glass in each hand. He gave one to Anstel and the other to Deaugrey.

Swirling the liquor in the curved glass,

Deaugrey sniffed it and then took a healthy sip. "Ahh. This does seem to jog my memory. I believe I did meet a certain girl named Melanie while I was in McKeag's house of horrors. Short in stature. Long, strawberry blond hair. Green eyes and quite a generous pair of —"

"That's her," Anstel cut in. "Was she still incarcerated the last you saw her?"

"Oh my, yes. The demons plaguing her aren't going to be letting go anytime soon."

"Then perhaps you might also know where patients at McKeag's are taken when they become particularly troublesome?"

Deaugrey took another sip of brandy. "I might."

"Would you care to include that as part of our civilized conversation?"

"Not for free. After all, isn't commerce the height of civilization?"

Anstel's face was an unreadable mask. Not a single feature twitched as he said, "My associate Mr. Keyes could always take you into another room and start breaking your bones until you tell me what I asked for."

"That wouldn't be very civil."

"Neither would some of the other things I could come up with. But, that's where we are if you want to stonewall me."

"Just coming here is a risk," Deaugrey said.

"You think your friend Nathan Sathow would try to kill you?"

"He doesn't appreciate it when his partners go behind his back."

"If it's money you want, I can offer you a tidy sum for telling me where next to look for Melanie Cavett," Anstel announced. "You see, she is no longer at McKeag's and I suspect she's been moved to an alternate location. Oftentimes, doctors have connections to more than one sanitarium, or there might be another place where the difficult patients are kept. I could eventually find this information out for myself, but I need to know right away. If you can provide me with this information, I can make it worth your while."

"How much are we talking about?" Deaugrey asked.

"Five hundred dollars and a ticket to anywhere you like as long as it's a suitable distance away from Joplin."

"I've got a better idea. Why don't you keep your money? It's really not that hard to come by and I'd rather have something else."

Although he didn't show any surprise, Anstel did seem genuinely interested the moment his offer of payment was refused. "What would you like?"

"Start by telling me why this idiot here tried to shoot me," Deaugrey said while flicking a hand toward Keyes, "when you could do the same thing very easily right now in this very room."

"And perhaps you could tell me why you came to this room," Anstel said, "when you must have been fairly certain that Mr. Keyes would be here."

"I didn't know anything of the sort," Deaugrey lied. As far as he could tell, his deception landed perfectly on everyone within earshot. "I know that your company and Western Cartage are locked in some sort of pissing contest, which means there's good opportunity for money to be made. When I came here yesterday, I merely asked to speak to the man in charge because I thought I could provide my services and get rich in the process."

"Rich? That depends on how far you're willing to go."

"What do you need her for?"

"Melanie Cavett is the sister of Samuel Cavett, the founder of the Western Cartage Company."

"Ahh," Deaugrey sighed. "So you want to find the buxom Miss Melanie for use as leverage against your competitor."

Anstel's nod was barely visible. Just another subtle nuance, like the bend of a single wisp of flame within a roaring fire, but Deaugrey's ever-searching eyes picked it up.

"One thousand," Deaugrey said while letting the brandy glass dangle between two fingers. "Pay me that much right here and now and I'll not only tell you where Melanie was taken, I'll have her brought to you."

Anstel's eyes narrowed suspiciously. "Why would you do that?"

"Because you're paying me."

"*How* could you do that?" Keyes asked.

"Let's just say Melanie and I were — are — more than just acquaintances," Deaugrey said. "When a woman as sweet as that one comes your way, any man should hang on to her." Licking his lips, he added, "And there are so many places on her that are just made for a man to hang on to."

Holding the brandy under his nose, Anstel drew a breath that was long enough to fill every bit of his lungs with the liquor's fragrance. His eyes stared straight ahead, but were clearly focused on nothing. His thoughts rolled around behind them before finally settling in the place they needed to be. "You'll get half now," he said after he'd snapped his focus back onto Deaugrey. "Half after you bring her here. I'll need to get a look at her to make absolutely certain she's the young woman I require."

"Of course. How long has it been since you've seen her?"

"A while."

Deaugrey winced. "You should know that spending time in any sanitarium will change a person. Both physically and spiritually."

"I don't give a damn about her spirit," Anstel said. "Just bring her to me." He walked over to one of the bookshelves and removed two wide volumes that looked to have been cut vertically so they were shorter than their neighbors. That way, they could fit on the shelf without hanging over while also covering the large handle hidden behind them. Anstel pulled the handle, which brought the entire shelf swinging outward on well-oiled hinges. Behind the shelf were not one, but four safes arranged two across and two high. Both safes on the top were similar and didn't seem extraordinary in the slightest. The one on the bottom left was taller and wider than the rest, mostly due to its walls, which looked thicker than the top two combined. The safe on the bottom right struck Deaugrey as downright peculiar. He caught sight of something etched into one corner of that one before Anstel opened one of the top safes and withdrew a stack of cash.

"Here you go," Anstel said as he closed the safe and spun the dial. "As I'm sure you've seen, I'm good for the rest and plenty more. If you prove to be a valuable enough asset in the days to come, I can indeed make you rich."

"If not," Keyes said, slapping his hand down onto Deaugrey's shoulder, "I can make you dead."

Deaugrey took the money and flipped through the stack while taking a long sniff. "Nothing smells better." With a grin, he added, "Except for certain bits and pieces of my dear Melanie."

Anstel's face remained a wall with no cracks. "Just bring her here." With that, he got up and walked out of the room. Once in the hall, he told someone, "Get him out of here," and walked away.

Before he knew what was happening, Deaugrey's glass was taken away. He was pulled from his chair and then shoved toward the stairs. He glanced over his shoulder and smirked at Keyes. "How'd you find me?"

"You came to us, remember?" Keyes replied.

"Not here. Back at that mining camp. How'd you find me?"

"Your friend Sathow and I have some history. I was already at that camp on other business when I saw him riding through there. He was preoccupied with something or other, but called you by name. He had to say it loudly because you couldn't take your eyes off of one of the whores trying to draw cowboys in off the street. I've seen that look in men's eyes plenty of times before. This time, it told me if I wanted to find you, all I had to do was keep an eye on that tent full of whores and you'd come along sooner or later. I was fairly certain it would be sooner."

"That doesn't explain why you put on such a display when you interrupted me in that cathouse," Deaugrey said while he and Keyes walked down the stairs. "Whatever history you had with Sathow doesn't explain that."

"You've had a price on your head well before making that escape from the nuthouse," Keyes told him. "The word of your recent liberation was put out through several counties, and it caught my attention since I know you've worked with my friend Nate Sathow."

Deaugrey could only guess at the sort of hell that would show in Nate's eyes if he knew Keyes had just referred to him as *friend.*

They were on the ground floor now and Keyes continued pushing Deaugrey along until they'd both stepped outside. "I wanted to put a bullet through your head," Keyes said in a voice that sounded like it had been dragged through a mess of wet gravel. "After what you pulled all throughout Linn County, the authorities didn't much care if you were brought in alive or dead."

"That was a memorable couple of weeks," Deaugrey mused.

"When he heard about you breaking out of McKeag's, Mr. Anstel got word to me the very next day that I should try to get to you as soon as possible. Between that and the reward being offered, I thought I should keep my eyes open. To be honest, I didn't really think I'd find you. Stumbling upon Sathow at that camp was a bit of luck. You being there with Sathow was an even nicer bit of luck."

That was a bit too much luck for Deaugrey's liking, but he wasn't about to let on. "Well, I appreciate you being so forthright with me."

Keyes filled the doorway with his tall frame and imposing stance. One hand was hooked over his gun belt and the other rested upon his holstered pistol. "Don't be too sentimental. There ain't nothing you can do with what I told you, and it was the quickest way to shut you up. Besides," he added as he stepped back and started closing the door, "you, Sathow and plenty of others I don't much care for will be dead soon anyways."

30

Pete had spent the last couple of days constantly thinking about what was happening in town. Part of that was because he didn't have much else to do while he lay on his belly in the weeds or sat against a tree with ants and every other kind of insect burrowing into his boots or nibbling at his sweaty skin. While he and Frank moved from one hiding spot to another watching the depot that he and Nate had found, the others were eating hot meals and sleeping in warm beds. Deaugrey probably hadn't left his favorite saloon and Nate was surely enjoying a hot meal and a nice shave.

"Not Pete Meyer," he grumbled as he lifted his field glasses to his eyes and used his free hand to smack a mosquito on the side of his neck. "Pete gets to sit in the dirt because that's what he does. Pete's a damn fool. He should've picked a more comfortable occupation. Maybe food taster," he groused. "Or gambler. Gamblers get the finest rooms and all the whores they can . . . What have we here?"

Throughout most of the time he'd been keeping watch on the depot, there hadn't been much to see. There were only a few guards. From what Nate had discovered, the place was locked up so tight that the depot didn't require many. But there was something in there, otherwise there wouldn't be any guards at all, and there certainly wouldn't be reinforced doors. Every so often, one of those guards might step into the old depot. So far, Pete hadn't been able to get much of a look inside when that happened but over the course of the last day, four men and a half dozen horses had trickled inside and had yet to come out. His luck might have changed, however, since the set of larger doors at the front of the big building were now being opened. He looked over to a spot about fifty yards away where Frank was hiding and signaled for him to sit tight.

Rusted hinges wailed and heavy wood scraped against the ground. Pete stared through the field glasses, smiling widely as he finally got a glimpse of what was being held within the old depot. It seemed a good portion of the building's innards had been scooped out to leave a hollow area. It took both guards to open the doors wide and four of the six horses to pull a long black wagon outside.

The wagon looked like it had once been a hearse. Now it was stripped down to the essentials and covered with bulky panels on the side with holes cut through at a passenger's eye level. Gun ports, most likely. As for the contraption bolted to the top of the wagon near the back of its roof, Pete could only guess.

"What in the hell?" he grunted while squinting through the field glasses.

Atop the wagon was some kind of large kettle with hoses and narrow pipes running along its sides. A handle was attached to a long nozzle fashioned from several pieces of various widths pointing behind the wagon. Thinking back to the specialty weapons commissioned from Caster Grunwaldt, Pete lowered the field glasses and cursed under his breath. Part of him had hoped the fire spout was just a fanciful lie, but that contraption on the wagon looked like anything but. After the wagon had been pulled far enough away, Pete looked for any more of the guards. They all seemed to be busy with the wagon and the horses, so he gave another signal to Frank. The preacher nodded to acknowledge the command and moved in to get inside the depot for an even closer look.

As much as he hated to leave Frank to his own devices, Pete knew the preacher could take care of himself. They'd already argued about what to do next, and the consensus had ended in favor of the greater good. Still, he didn't feel good about hurrying back to the spot where he'd tied his horse. Behind him, the team tied to the wagon was straining to get it moving. Its wheels were turning and it would surely gain some momentum, but it wouldn't be a quick ride into town or wherever they were headed.

When he got to his horse, Pete didn't give a damn about making noise. Attracting the guards' attention would only give Frank a better chance to infiltrate the depot, so he snapped his reins, tapped his heels against the horse's sides and took off like a shot toward Joplin.

Nate wasn't much for strolling and it was even rarer for him to do so while wearing the simple, contented smile of a man half his age. The source for that smile was easy enough to see. Of course, any man in the vicinity would probably not even notice Nate at all since the woman on his arm was so naturally captivating.

"So," the woman said, "this is Joplin. I've heard good things about it."

"Perhaps we can take in some sights when this job is over," he said while shifting his weight to compensate for the heavy bag he carried in his free hand.

Even when Angelica Corday frowned, she was beautiful. Her smooth skin seemed positively luminous in contrast to the raven-black hair framing her face. Thin, red lips formed the frown, which had more playfulness in it than anything close to sorrow. "It's always a job with you, Nate. When are you going to take better care of yourself? Or," she added while leaning in closer to him, "you could let me take care of you."

"We might have had time for that if you hadn't gotten yourself locked away, Angelica."

"I've been out of jail for a month! Where have you been?"

"Keeping busy. And since I had to send telegrams to four different places if I was to have any chance of reaching you, it seems you've been keeping plenty busy yourself."

Angelica wore a simple black dress with a white lace collar and matching cuffs. The red ribbons woven into the bodice created a set of lines that nicely accentuated the trim curves beneath her clothing. Smiling, she put a spring in her step which made it seem more like she was playing dress-up as she took hold of her skirt and gave it a little twirl. "I have been busy," she said. "I was also very flattered that you took such pains to bring me here. Your message sounded so . . . urgent."

"I need you, Angelica."

Her eyes widened and she sighed. "I like the sound of that."

"You're the best in your line of work. If you sign on to this job with me, you'll be more than happy with your share of the pay."

"Back to jobs again," she pouted. Before she could get too worked up, her other arm was taken by a second man who fell in step with them. Her smile returned as she un-hooked herself from Nate so she could cling to the second man's arm like he was saving her from drowning. "Hello, Deaugrey," she purred. "At least there's someone here I can rely on for a good time."

"Indeed, you can," Deaugrey said. "And I've already started to fill your dance card."

"See, Nathan?" she said. "Someone around here knows how to treat a lady."

"I'll let you spend every waking hour with the crazy man," Nate said. "We'll see how long you last."

"That," Deaugrey said as he tightened his grip on her arm, "is what I believe is referred to as a verbal contract. From what I hear, they're quite binding."

Angelica laughed with him and continued to rake Nate over the coals while the three of them walked back to the Joplin Grand Hotel. They were about five long strides away from the wide front porch when the hotel's doors opened and Pete frantically hurried outside. The tracker looked to either side and was about to take off running in another direction when he finally spotted the threesome headed his way.

"Thank God!" Pete said as he hurried over to them. "I just tried looking for you inside . . ."

"Let me guess," Deaugrey said. "We weren't in there."

"What is it, Pete?" Nate asked. "What's wrong?"

"Over the last few days, a few men have taken their horses into that old depot," Pete explained. "Just like I told you when I saw you last time. Those horses are hitched to some kind of wagon that looks to be too damn heavy to be carrying just a bunch of men. It left the depot and there was something bolted to the top of it that could very well be that fire spout that Caster put together."

"Fire spout?" Angelica asked. "What is that?"

"Much like it sounds, actually," Deaugrey told her.

"I'll tell you about it later," Nate said. "Pete, where were they headed?"

"Don't know yet. I knew I could get to town and warn you before the wagon got here. It took a bit longer than I thought to find you, though. We gotta find that wagon and put it down."

Deaugrey and Angelica were staring at something farther down the street. "Finding it may not be a problem," she said.

Nate and Pete followed their line of sight as the crowd on both sides of the street began to look and point as well. Smoke was rising from another part of town that was smearing the sky with thick black trails.

"Putting it down, however," Deaugrey said, "may not be so easy."

31

Nate wasn't very familiar with the streets of Joplin and he didn't need to be. All he had to do was follow the smell of smoke and the sounds of screams to bring him closer to the source of the fire. When he was about to turn the next corner, gunshots were added to the mix.

"How many men were on that wagon?" Nate asked.

Pete was still beside him and replied, "At least six went into that depot over the last day or so along with two guards on the outside. I don't know how many are here now because as soon as I saw that wagon roll out, I got back here to warn you as quickly as I could."

"Where's Frank?" Nate asked.

"He slipped into the depot to get a look at the place."

"Good. Now's the perfect chance for that."

Around the next corner, Nate found a scene of total chaos. People huddled on both sides of the street, watching three nearby buildings consumed by a growing fire. There were already men tossing water onto one of the larger buildings and a bucket brigade was forming to keep the blaze from spreading any farther. Two smaller groups of men stood facing each other in the street. Although they were near the groups that were fighting the fire, they were definitely not a part of them.

"Climb down from that wagon and keep your hands where I can see them!" one of the men shouted.

Two gunmen faced his group near the black wagon that had been parked in the middle of the street. "Stay where you are, Jake!" one of those fellows shouted. It wasn't until that moment that Nate spotted the man who sat perched atop the wagon behind the contraption that had been bolted near the back end. Jake must have been the one up there because he waved at the two near the wagon from behind the contraption.

"You know what we're after," the second man near the wagon said.

"That's the sheriff," Pete said as he and Nate did their best to get closer to the confrontation without attracting attention. "That place across the street from all them flames is his office."

"Jesus," Nate sighed.

"There's still time to put a stop to this, Hastings!" the sheriff shouted. "I don't give a damn who you work for. You're not getting away with this."

Hastings was the oldest of the men near or on the wagon. He wore a duster that had been pulled back to grant him easy access to his holster, and a bandanna covered a good portion of his mouth. "It's already done, Sheriff," he said. "Turn our man loose and we'll be on our way. Keep us waiting any longer and you'll have a whole lot more to worry about!"

To emphasize Hastings's point, Jake pointed the nozzle of the contraption toward one of the buildings that hadn't started burning yet and sent a stream of fire toward it. Nate could smell kerosene in the air and saw the spark at the tip of the nozzle that had set it alight. The fiery stream grew longer and shorter in time to how Jake worked the pump on the side of the contraption. When the stream was at its lowest, the flame got dangerously close to his hand and was finally cut off when Jake flipped an iron shutter that closed the top portion of the device.

People had scattered at the sight of all that fire, and the men fighting the blaze worked even harder. The flames that had just spewed from the nozzle had singed part of an awning, but hadn't done much more than that.

Nate turned toward the two people who'd followed him and Pete this far. Pointing to Angelica, he said, "Grey, get her out of here."

Deaugrey nodded quickly. "Of course."

Digging her feet into the ground, Angelica kept herself from being moved. "You wanted me here to help, Nate," she said. "So let me help."

"This isn't why you're here," Nate told her while shoving her toward Deaugrey. "And if you get burnt to a crisp, you won't be much use to me whatsoever. Go with Grey and stay safe. Pete and I will handle this."

The lawmen who'd taken a stand against the wagon had backed up a few steps but were still facing the men who'd started the fire. "You make one more move to work that machine and we'll start shooting!" the sheriff warned.

Hastings stood his ground. "You hit the

wrong part of that wagon and this whole block goes up in smoke."

"The longer we stand here and talk, the more of this town will burn around us!"

"Your town," Hastings said. "Not mine. And if you don't want it to burn, then I suggest you do what we asked."

The sheriff thought about his options for a few more seconds. He made up his mind real quick when the front portion of the bucket brigade hollered an alarm as a portion of one burning building's roof collapsed. "Wesley," the sheriff said. "Bring that prisoner out here."

"Goddamn it," Nate snarled from within the crowd.

Pete was still beside him and asked, "What are we gonna do? We can't let them burn this whole place to the ground."

"It won't come to that. If they wanted to destroy this town, they could have doused more of it in kerosene while driving up and down every street."

Nate didn't have to tell Pete what that reason was and if there was any question in either man's mind, it was answered by a wild howl coming from within the sheriff's office.

Pescaterro came out of the sheriff's office hot on the heels of a barrage of gunshots that were fired randomly through the front window. The crowd that had been outside waiting to see how they might be able to help with the fire now scattered like a flock of birds that had been flushed from a bush. As he stepped outside, the outlaw shoved the younger deputy in front of him.

"Nobody come near me, you hear?" Pescaterro shouted.

The sheriff held his hands out to show they were empty. "Take it easy. You got what you want."

Until now, Nate had hung back so as not to make things worse. Since they'd already gone straight to hell, he rushed toward the lawmen and said, "Get away from that wagon!"

The sheriff turned, recognized Nate from when he'd brought Pescaterro in after subduing him at the barbershop and started to motion for him to stay back when the wagon's driver snapped his reins. Already nervous from the nearby fire and the excitement surrounding them, the team of horses lurched into motion to pull the wagon down the street away from the fires and the group of lawmen. Pescaterro reveled in the sheer chaos filling the street and laughed maniacally while running to catch up to the black wagon. Before he could get to it, the wagon's back gate fell open to reveal the multiple barrels of a Gatling gun. The man inside the wagon turned the gun's crank and sent a barrage of lead into the street.

Nate and Pete had been hurrying to the lawmen's side and split apart to get out of the street as the first shots came. Even if they'd charged straight ahead, they wouldn't have gotten to the lawmen in time before they were cut down by the Gatling gun's hellish spitfire. Dropping to one knee, Nate drew his Remington and held one arm out so he could prop the gun on it for support. Knowing the pistol's range all too well, he took aim while trying to ignore the stream of hot lead that was working its way toward him.

Once he had his line of fire set, Nate slowly let out his breath and squeezed his trigger. The Remington bucked against his palm to spit a round at the back of the wagon and knock the man behind the Gatling gun straight back into the shadows. The mechanized weapon's barrels stopped turning, and the wagon kept rolling down the street.

Not all of the lawmen had been hit. One of them nursed a grazing wound on one arm while another seemed to have made it through the ordeal without a scratch. That one was already tending to the sheriff, who was lying in a pool of blood in the dirt. Since he couldn't do any good for the lawmen, Nate ran to catch up with the wagon.

"What the hell do you think you're doing?" Pete asked as he ran behind him.

"I brought that maniac in once," Nate said between huffing breaths. "I won't let him get away now."

"There's more than the damn wagon to worry about!"

As soon as Nate thought about something other than Pescaterro, he realized the thunder of hooves wasn't just coming from the team in front of the wagon. It also came from directly behind him. Nate turned to look over one shoulder and was just in time to see Hastings charging toward him with pistol in hand. After clearing a path by hopping up onto the boardwalk running alongside the street, Nate swung the Remington to pound it against the mounted gunman's chest. Hastings slumped in his saddle to catch his breath when Nate grabbed his arm and pulled him down from the horse.

Hastings was twisted around by the combination of Nate pulling him in one direction and the horse pulling in the other. Thanks to the nearby flames spitting cinders onto the horse's back, the animal wasn't about to show one bit of care for its rider. It reared and then thundered onward after shaking Hastings loose from the stirrups. All of this took place in a matter of seconds, ending with Hastings hitting the boardwalk on his side.

Since he already had a firm grip on the gunman's arm, Nate stomped his boot into the other man's armpit and wrenched with all of his might. Hastings let out a pained yelp as his arm popped out of joint. After that, it only took one good twist for Nate to turn Hastings into a wailing, pathetic creature writhing on the boardwalk and pleading in a string of nonsense syllables.

Nate bent down to take the pistol that Hastings had just dropped and collected his horse, which was still fidgeting nearby. As soon as he was in the saddle, Nate saw another gunman who'd been near the wagon rein his horse to a stop while sighting along the top of a Peacemaker. Two shots blasted through the air, both of which were fired from behind the rider to drill fresh holes through his upper chest. His eyes rolled up into his head and he started to loll forward before he was pulled back over the opposite side of the horse. Pete looked over the top of the horse, still holding his smoking pistol in hand.

"I suppose you aim to ride straight at them like a damn fool?" Pete asked.

Nate was situated now and had gotten the horse under control. "More or less, yeah," he said.

"Just try not to get too close. I'd rather not be the one to hand Angelica your ashes."

"Don't worry," Nate said as he snapped the reins and raced after the wagon. "I'm sure Deaugrey wouldn't mind doing it for you."

32

The wagon wasn't exactly racing through the streets of Joplin, but it wasn't nearly as slow as Nate had expected. He caught up to it in short order, his path lit by the few sporadic fires set along the way. When he rounded a corner, Nate got a better look at the wagon and the infernal contraption bolted on top of it. A narrow stream of fire erupted from the nozzle, licking an awning and the front of another shop as the wagon trundled along. Folks screamed at the sight of it and scattered in every direction, but the fire itself was confined to the very edges of the buildings it had touched. By the time Nate rode past them, the owners of the buildings had already come outside to get a good start at dousing the flames.

"Get a little closer if you like!" Pescaterro shouted from his station atop the wagon. The outlaw turned the contraption to face directly behind the wagon and added, "We'll even slow down for ya!"

Nate smelled the pungent odor of kerosene scant moments before he felt a wave of heat wash over the front of his body. He gripped his reins tightly and steered his horse toward an alley on the left side of the street. When the horse got a sample of the flame on its hind end, it charged down the alley at nearly a full gallop. Fortunately, Nate was able to get it calmed down before his commands were ignored altogether. When he reached the end of the alley, Nate circled behind that building and charged down the next alley so he could meet up with the street once again. He saw the wagon roll past the mouth of the alley before he'd made it halfway down the narrow space.

Holding his Remington in a steady grasp, Nate waited until he got a clear shot at Pescaterro and then took it. Between the motion of his horse, the rocking of the wagon and the outlaw's erratic movements, Nate's shot had little chance of success. Even so, he managed to get close enough to draw Pescaterro's attention before he could set fire to whatever was in his sights at the moment.

"There you are!" Dog Ear said as he cranked the upper portion of the contraption around. "Stop this thing, Talman!"

Apparently, Talman was the wagon's driver because after Pescaterro's order, the team was brought to a noisy stop.

Nate took quick aim and fired a shot meant to pick Dog Ear from his perch. Instead, it hissed through the air above Pescaterro's head. The outlaw grinned like the madman he was and started working the pump connected to the fire-spewing device bolted to the wagon. Nate's next shot clipped that device in a spot that sent a thin fan of fire spraying from one side instead of through the nozzle.

Pescaterro bared his teeth and ducked behind the contraption while drawing a pistol from his holster. Before he could pull his trigger, he was reminded of Pete's presence when Pete fired a shot behind him. Pescaterro grunted in pain, but refused to drop. Wherever he'd been hit, it didn't wound him enough to keep him from twisting around to fire a series of shots at the alley on the opposite side of the street from Nate's.

"Get 'er movin' again, goddamn it!" Pescaterro roared.

Talman snapped his reins to get the wagon lurching forward. Pete took his chance to fire again. At least one of his bullets found its mark because a pained groan came from the front of the wagon as it was drawn down the street and out of Nate's immediate line of sight.

Pulling back on his reins, Nate slowed his horse without bringing it to a stop. Whatever Pescaterro had in store for him, he wasn't about to charge straight into it without giving himself at least a little time to react. He emerged from the alley and was almost immediately joined by Pete.

"I've got a plan," Nate said to the tracker.

Pete nodded once and fired a shot at the wagon. "I was hoping to hear something like that."

"I believe there's a nice open spot a few streets down where a corral or two butt up against an empty lot. You know the one I mean?"

"Yeah."

"We need to get that wagon into that spot," Nate said, "and then hit the fire spout with all we've got. Should blow that thing to hell without taking any more of this town along with it."

"Good plan," Pete replied. "Except for one part. That lot is in the other direction."

"Can you think of any other place we can bring that wagon?"

Pete didn't have to think for very long

before he shook his head and said, "Nope."

"Then since you know where that lot is, you can drive the wagon there. I'll deal with Pescaterro."

Pete snapped his reins and rode ahead.

Nate urged some more speed from his horse and easily caught up to the wagon. Ever since Pete had fired at the driver, Pescaterro was nowhere to be found. The top of the wagon was empty except for the contraption that rattled and shook like so many spare parts piled on top of a mess of copper tubes. When he got a little closer, Nate could see the outlaw climbing over the front of the wagon to drop down into the driver's seat.

"Hey, asshole!" Nate shouted as he drew up alongside the wagon. "You about ready to turn yourself over and face the rest of your jail sentence like a man?"

Pescaterro had been tending to the slouching driver. As soon as he heard that question, he stood up in the driver's seat and pointed his pistol at Nate. Dog Ear unleashed a torrent of obscenities which couldn't be heard since he'd also unleashed a barrage of gunfire at about the same time.

Ducking down over his horse's neck, Nate steered down another street and tapped his heels against its sides for a bit more incentive. The bullets from Pescaterro's gun burned through the air, each one getting closer to drawing blood before Nate was finally out of the outlaw's range. Instead of waiting to get another shot or even steering the wagon to follow his target, Pescaterro climbed right back on top of the wagon and allowed Talman to slump over.

While Pete had also been hunched over his horse, he rode forward instead of following Nate. Now that Pescaterro had found something else to do, Pete drew up until he was even with the driver's seat. Then, he pulled one foot from his stirrups and pushed off of the other to leap from his saddle. He reached out with both hands to catch the handle on the side of the wagon meant for the driver to pull himself up when climbing into his seat. One of Pete's boots rattled against the front wheel and came dangerously close to getting snagged before his other foot found something more stable that he could use as a step. Using muscles fueled by a good amount of desperation, he hauled himself up and onto the wagon.

Talman turned to look at the uninvited passenger. Although he attempted to lift a shotgun to repel the boarder, he was too weak to raise the weapon more than a few inches before allowing it to fall from his grasp. He groaned and pressed a hand to a bloody wound on his right side.

"Looks like you got hit pretty good," Pete said as he sat down beside the driver. "If you want to see a doctor, you'll have to do what I say. Otherwise I'll toss you from this wagon right here and now."

Letting out a breath that seemed to have been the only thing filling his body, Talman shuddered and started to roll toward the open side of the wagon. Before he could fall to the street, Pete grabbed his shirt and pulled the driver back up beside him. "Not just yet, friend," the tracker said. "I got a question or two to ask."

Nate might have been able to pick off the outlaw from the top of the wagon if he could take a moment to aim. Instead, he was forced to control his horse while charging down a slender portion of a busy street. The wagon took up most of the path through town, which left Nate with precious little space to maneuver. When he wasn't forced to weave between folks trying to walk on the boardwalk, he was doing his best to keep his horse from getting tripped up by a water trough or a poorly placed barrel.

When he finally found a stretch of road that was mostly clear, Nate raised his

Remington to fire. Pescaterro had made it to the contraption on top of the wagon and begun furiously working the pump. Only a trickle of kerosene was being fed to the nozzle, so he reached down to fiddle with the tubing connected to something near his feet. Just as Nate found his shot, the contraption on the wagon spewed a long tongue of flame toward the street directly behind them. Nate fired up at the outlaw and saw his bullet spark against the side of the contraption.

"You're a persistent cuss, I'll give you that!" Pescaterro shouted while he brought the nozzle around toward Nate.

The road widened as it crossed another street. Since he only had another second or two before he would need to break off and circle around again, Nate aimed the Remington as if he were pointing his finger and fired up at Dog Ear. His bullet snapped Pescaterro's head back, but the outlaw quickly recovered. When he brought his head up again, he was wearing a wide smile as blood flowed from the grazing wound he'd been given on his left cheek. Pescaterro swung the fire spout around with renewed vigor and was only distracted when the entire wagon lurched to one side.

"Watch it up there!" he shouted at the

driver's seat.

The team of horses was verging on turning wild and it was all Pete could do to keep them from stampeding out of control as he convinced them to round the next corner. Once they'd completed the sharp turn, Pete flicked his reins and shouted for anyone walking the street nearby to clear a path for him.

All this time, Nate had drawn up close enough to the wagon to get a better look at the contraption on top of it. As far as he could tell, it was basically just a pump connected to a supply of kerosene with some sort of flint near the end of the nozzle. Like any weapon, it wasn't very complicated once it was seen as a machine instead of something terrible in itself. Nate didn't know all there was to know about Caster Grunwaldt's contraption, but he had a good idea of how to keep it from working. Pulling back on his reins, Nate slowed his horse just enough to get a look at the fire spout from a different angle.

"Where you goin'?" Pescaterro shouted as he turned the nozzle to keep Nate in his sights. "We ain't through yet, bounty hunter!"

Nate watched Pescaterro carefully. When the outlaw started working the handle that

356

would get the kerosene flowing, Nate took aim and fired every last one of his bullets into the pump that drew the combustive liquid from its supply. His first round sparked against a copper pipe. The next punched a hole through a small metal cylinder. The next hit the top of that same cylinder, doing enough damage for the pump to come out in Pescaterro's hand.

"What in the hell?" Pescaterro said while looking at the broken pump handle as if it were a severed limb. Before he could say much of anything else, the wagon turned sharply again onto a course heading back in the direction from which it had come.

Since the flames had stopped spewing from the contraption, Nate allowed his horse to slow down while he reloaded the Remington. When Pescaterro looked at him from atop the wagon, Nate gave him a casual wave. That was more than Pescaterro could take, and he threw the handle away so he could draw the pistol tucked under his belt. He fired a few shots at Nate, none of which came close to hitting him. When the wagon slowed to make another turn, the outlaw shifted his attention toward the driver.

"All right," Nate said while snapping the Remington shut. "Let's put an end to this madness."

Pete kept his head down, his grip tight on the reins and both feet propped against the boards in front of him. When Pescaterro shouted at him, he acted as though he hadn't heard anything. Soon, there was no possible way to ignore the raving killer as he pounded his pistol on top of the wagon like a crazed judge with a gavel.

"I said stop this damn wagon!" Dog Ear hollered. When the wagon kept rolling, he crawled toward the front to get a look at the driver. "You ain't Talman!" he said.

Sneaking a quick glance over his shoulder, Pete replied, "And you ain't very bright."

The road in front of the wagon was now clear. Pete had driven off the busier street onto a path that provided easy access to the backs of several of Joplin's liveries and feed stores. Now that he had a wider road in front of him and didn't need to worry about as many people crossing in front of him, Pete snapped the reins to get the team working as hard as they could. That first surge not only shook the wagon, but also sent Pescaterro sliding back toward the contraption that was now so much useless metal.

"You're dead!" Pescaterro swore.

Pete had heard that threat several times while riding with Nate Sathow, and he figured he'd hear it a few more before he decided to part ways with him for good. Hearing it from someone like Dog Ear, however, didn't sit well with any man who put much of a value on his life. Pete's spirits lifted somewhat when he spotted the old fence surrounding the open lot coming up on his right. The only reason that spot had stuck in Pete's mind at all was because it had seemed like a nice little bit of quiet in the middle of a thriving town. He'd passed it by when scouting Joplin on his first day there and thought he might come back if he needed somewhere to stash everyone's horses in a pinch. Now, he leaned forward in his seat and gauged how much longer he could allow the team to go full steam before reining them in.

Behind him, Pescaterro scraped at the roof of the wagon while pulling himself closer to the front. Pete took that as his cue to pull back hard on the reins. Dog Ear cursed one more time as he flopped onto his side and dropped his pistol while scrambling to grab hold of something so as not to fall off the wagon completely.

Nate thundered into the lot and circled around the wagon so his horse could burn through its last bit of steam before coming to a stop. Its hooves were still kicking up dust when Nate swung down from the saddle and reached for the rope hanging near his right leg. He kept his eyes on Pescaterro while easing out the lasso and giving the rope a few twirls.

"What the hell you gonna do, bounty hunter?" Dog Ear snarled as he reached for his pistol. "Take me in like a calf?"

Without a word, Nate threw the lasso, dropped the rope over Pescaterro's head on the first try and pulled with all his strength. It wasn't enough to bring the big outlaw down on the first try, but he made Pescaterro wobbly enough to be dragged off the wagon on the second. The outlaw howled like an animal and grunted loudly when he hit the ground on his side. Blood was still streaming from the nick he'd gotten from one of Nate's bullets, and he wasn't faring any better after his awkward landing. It was the pure crazy inside of him that pulled the outlaw to his feet and sheer muscle that allowed him to free himself from the lasso.

Pescaterro bared his teeth. He'd dropped his pistol on the way down, but scooped it up while snarling, "You couldn't kill me before and you ain't about to now!"

Nate's answer to that was to draw his Remington and fire from the hip in a lightning-fast motion. His round cut a trail through the air and burned a hole through Pescaterro's left shin.

"God*damn*!" Dog Ear screamed.

"Toss the pistol and come along quietly," Nate warned.

Pescaterro's face barely looked human when he looked up. Shifting his weight from his wounded leg, he started to bring up his pistol once more. Although he didn't seem to feel it when his other shin took a bullet, the outlaw's legs could no longer hold him and he fell over in a heap. Nate strode over to him, kicked the pistol from Pescaterro's hand and then stomped him twice in the head. For a moment, it seemed as if the outlaw still had some fight in him. After another second, though, his body went limp and he passed out.

Looking down at the fallen outlaw, Nate felt the entire ride through town catch up to him at once. His head drooped slightly and his bones began to ache with every bump he'd weathered. The stench of all that kerosene made his head throb, and his ears rang from the thunder of gunfire. When he heard the sound of movement coming from the wagon, Nate snapped his Remington up to aim at the driver's seat.

"Easy," Pete said as he raised his hands a bit. "It's only me."

Once again, Nate allowed himself to relax. "What can you see from up there? Anyone coming?"

"I'd say the law and a good portion of the rest of the town is still busy with the fires." Pete climbed over the back of the driver's seat and onto the wagon's roof where he could examine the contraption bolted there. "This fire spout is simple enough, really. Just a pump and something to make a spark. Not even very efficient at getting the job done."

"It sure created a hell of a commotion, which I believe is all it was intended to do," Nate said as he used the rope to hogtie the unconscious Pescaterro.

Pete climbed down from the wagon's roof and walked around the back to get a look inside. "Just the Gatling gun in here," he reported, "and what's left of the man who was turning the crank."

"What about those armor plates?" Nate asked.

"They're not in here. I guessed that as soon as I saw how fast this wagon was moving. They must've dumped them off somewhere. Doesn't make sense as to why they'd do something like that, especially when they knew Dog Ear was gonna lead them straight through hell and back."

"That's just the thing. I don't think they were supposed to make it back."

Pete walked around to join Nate a few yards away from the wagon. "Pescaterro may be crazy, but he didn't strike me as someone with a death wish."

"This man's not a partner in what's going on here. He's just another weapon. The man at the top of this gang just pointed him in the right direction, wound him up and turned him loose. You going to give me a hand with this?" Nate asked as he started dragging Pescaterro by the ropes binding the outlaw's hands and feet.

Pete hurried over to Nate's side and grabbed part of the rope as well. Between the two of them, they managed to drag Pescaterro at a fairly steady rate. "You think Keyes is the one in charge?" Pete asked.

"Keyes is a conniving, cold-blooded lizard. Of course he's the one behind this mess."

"To what end? This all can't just be about carving off a piece of that railroad pie."

"I've got my suspicions," Nate said. "And we're real close to proving them right. For now, I'd like to tie up the two loose ends we got right here."

Pete looked down at the first loose end which was still trussed up like a prize heifer. When he looked to Nate again, he found the other man pointing his Remington at the wagon. "Wait!" Pete said. "Since that thing stopped moving, all that kerosene ain't been getting spilled off. It's all soaked in!"

"That wagon wasn't supposed to make it through the night," Nate said. "Considering what's on it, I'm inclined to agree with that decision. Get that team unhitched."

Hurrying to the front of the wagon, Pete rushed through the motions of freeing the four horses from the wagon. He managed to keep hold of two of them, but lost the others when the frightened animals bolted for the street. Leading the remaining horses toward Nate, Pete said, "We might be able to get some use out of that wagon."

"It's caused too much damage already."

"Yeah, but —"

Nate didn't wait around to discuss the matter before firing. His bullet punched straight through the container of kerosene beside the pump and his next cut the support holding the nozzle which dropped it and the flame inside onto the wagon's roof. Although a fire did start, Nate sped it along by sending another bullet to nick the edge of the contraption and send a bunch of sparks flying. As Pete had suspected, the wagon had absorbed a good amount of spilled kerosene and went up like a bonfire when the sparks touched down.

Standing with Nate to admire the growing blaze, Pete said, "It might take more to destroy that thing."

"Before anyone can get to it, the law will collect what's left. Also, this'll create a nice diversion for us to get away from here without having to answer a whole bunch of damned questions."

When the fire reached a larger supply of kerosene, it sent a loud blast straight up into the starry sky. Heat washed over both of the men standing over the prone outlaw. "This doesn't make much sense," Pete said. "Why go through so much trouble just to let Pescaterro have a night's fun?"

"This wasn't for Pescaterro, and it wasn't just to strike at the town law. This was to rattle a whole bunch of people all at once."

"Why?"

"Because someone stands to gain from it," Nate replied. "Someone stands to make a whole load of money. More money than can be gained by getting paid by either company to hurt the other. That's all this kind of thing is ever about. When something is just about blood, it's much easier to see."

Pete helped drag Pescaterro away from the fire toward the spot where the horses were waiting. "If you say so. You know," Pete grunted while staring down at the outlaw, "it would have been easier if you'd allowed him to walk on his own."

"No," Nate replied. "This bastard's done enough running free."

"So we've got to take him all the way back into western Kansas?"

"That's where the men who funded our little venture want him brought."

"He'd surely cause a lot less trouble for us if you'd shot him somewhere other than the legs," Pete said.

"This one's bound for the noose and that's where he'll go. No matter how tough they talk, all wild dogs like this one will piss themselves when that rope goes around their neck. I'm not the only one who'll like to see that."

"Just trying to think of a way to make the ride easier," Pete grunted as he strained to keep dragging Pescaterro along.

After letting out a tired wheeze of his own, Nate said, "We'll get another wagon."

33

Two hours later, Nate was lying in a tub of hot water with one leg dangling over the side and his head resting upon the smooth, curved surface. Steam rose from all around him, and he let out a long, contented breath. When he opened his eyes, he was treated to the sight of Angelica sitting directly across from him. Her skin glistened with water that wasn't quite high enough within the large tub to conceal her breasts. She smiled and used both hands to get her hair wet.

"You've changed, Nate," she said.

"How so?"

"Used to be you'd be more anxious after a night like this one."

Nate shrugged and shifted within the tub. "We need to lay low for a spell. I don't see why we can't enjoy ourselves a bit while we do."

Angelica's foot slid against his leg and

moved up along Nate's inner thigh. "I couldn't agree more. I'm just saying it wasn't so long ago that you wouldn't have thought that way."

"Well then," he said with a growing smirk. "Let's just see if I can surprise you again."

Reclining and arching her back a little, Angelica draped both arms along the sides of the tub. Just as she was going to cash in on the promise Nate had made, someone knocked on the door.

"Get the hell out of here," Nate said while leaning toward Angelica.

The doorknob rattled before another series of quick knocks came. From the other side of the door, a voice said, "Open up. It's Frank."

"Leave. Now!"

Angelica grabbed the sides of the tub and stood up. Water dripped from every beautiful curve of her slender figure. For a moment, she stood there and grinned down at Nate. "We're here to do a job," she said. "Best get to it."

"That's what *I* should be saying," Nate said, drinking in the sight of her naked body.

"I know," she said as she stepped out of the tub and grabbed a towel to hold against the front of her body. "But someone needs to tend to important matters. There'll be time for diversion later." When Angelica walked to the door, she moved nice and slow. Although she kept her front covered, she allowed Nate to get a good long look at her taut backside. Opening the door, she looked outside and said, "Hello, Frank."

"Umm, hello, Angelica. We need to talk. All of us."

He wasn't standing alone out there. Both Pete and Deaugrey were behind Frank and anxious to get a look past him.

"Give us a moment, will you?" she asked.

"Of course."

She closed the door and dropped her towel at the same time, knowing exactly what she would or would not show the men outside. Turning on the balls of her feet, she strode across the room with all the confidence of someone wrapped in full riding gear and a double rig holster. "I'm not trying to torture you, Nate. We just don't have time for much else apart from business right now and you know that as well as I do."

Nate stood up from the tub and walked over to his clothes. "I know, but you can't honestly tell me you're not trying to torture me."

"All right," she replied with a grin. "Maybe just a little."

Both of them pulled on enough clothing

to be presentable and, in less than a minute, the other three who'd been waiting in the hall joined them. The hotel room was a fairly good size, but most of it was taken up by the bed and bathtub that had been brought up by special request. Frank walked straight over to the small table by a window where a pitcher of water was situated near two glasses. After pouring himself a drink, he pulled aside a curtain to look down at the street below.

Pete remained near the door with one hand resting upon the grip of his holstered pistol.

Deaugrey made his way to the first chair he could find and sat down. Although his gaze lingered on some very specific parts of Angelica for a few moments, he raised it to look her in the eyes before too long.

"Where have you been?" Nate asked.

When Frank turned around to face him, there wasn't an ounce of the warmth he showed to his congregations. His face was dirty. His clothes were stained with sweat. His hand clutched the water glass as if he were about to shatter it within his grip. "I've been getting a look inside that depot," he said.

"What did you find?"

"Most of the specialty weapons Grunwaldt talked about were on that wagon. A few were still in the depot. Other than that, just a small stockpile of rifles, pistols and enough ammunition to wound half of Joplin."

"Not exactly worth the trouble they took to fortify that place," Nate said. "They could have done the job a lot easier by posting a few more guards instead of reinforcing those doors and walls."

"Exactly what I was thinking," Frank said. "But there was something even stranger. That wagon rolled out to free Dog Ear Pescaterro from the town jail, right?"

"Most definitely."

"And Dog Ear is on the Western Cartage payroll."

"That's right," Nate replied.

Frank drank the rest of his water before pouring some from the pitcher into one hand so he could splash it on his face. Although he was a bit cleaner, Frank still had a steely edge when he said, "Most of those weapons and ammunition I mentioned were in boxes marked with the names Anstel and Joyner."

After letting that sink in for a few seconds, Deaugrey asked, "Shouldn't they be marked as Western Cartage property?"

"Yep," Nate said.

"And why don't you seem very surprised about that?"

"Because those weapons, this feud between these two companies, Dog Ear running wild through the streets, it's all just a big show."

"This ain't a show I'm enjoying too much," Pete said from his post near the door.

Nate looked over to the tracker and said, "That's because it's not being put on for our benefit."

As Nate talked, Angelica had been straightening her clothes and running a brush through her hair. "Whose benefit is it for?" she asked.

"That's something I imagine you'll find out. At least, you will once I get you close enough to do what you do best."

Deaugrey looked over at her with a smirk that had nothing to do with Angelica's rumpled appearance or the disheveled state of her clothing. "I'll be able to help with that. I managed to have a chat with Mr. Anstel. Things have been mighty hectic around here lately and I haven't gotten a chance to tell you all about it."

"*Hectic* doesn't quite cover it," Nate said. "Go on."

"Our mutual friend Abraham Keyes

seemed most anxious to have a word with me back at that mining camp," Deaugrey explained. "And by that, I mean he wanted to put a few bullets into me."

"Wouldn't be the first one who wanted that," Pete grunted.

Deaugrey tipped his hat to the tracker. "And he won't be the last. Anyway, since Keyes appeared to be working for Anstel and Joyner, I went to have a talk with them."

"You could've gotten yourself killed!" Frank said.

Nate was quick to jump in. "Let him talk."

Although Frank was troubled by what he'd heard, he held on to what he was going to say for now.

"Preston Anstel is anxious to gather some dirt on his competitor," Deaugrey continued. "Apparently, one of the more attractive ladies who shared the hospitality of McKeag's Sanitarium with me is the sister of Western Cartage's owner, Sam Cavett. I said I could arrange for her to meet Mr. Anstel and have a little chat by tomorrow."

"And you want me to play the part of the sister?" Angelica asked.

"You'd look better in a dress than any of us," Deaugrey replied.

Rubbing his chin, Nate asked, "How will you explain getting her here from McKeag's so quickly?"

"I did have relations with the buxom Melanie Cavett before she was taken elsewhere," Deaugrey said. "She didn't have anyone else to talk to so she became rather chatty in the late hours of the evening. Between the bits and pieces I learned from her and my own powers of persuasion, I should be able to come up with a convincing enough story. Besides, all we need to do is get Angelica into Anstel's building. Preston wanted to impress upon me how rich and influential he was and, in doing so, showed me a wall of safes he seemed particularly proud of. One of them bore the seal Pete described upon his return from Nagle. Grunwaldt's two overlapping sideways *V*s."

"Grunwaldt?" Angelica asked. "As in, Caster Grunwaldt?"

"The same."

"You know him?" Nate asked.

She laughed as if someone had asked if she knew where to find the sky. "Caster Grunwaldt has made some of the best safes ever sold. You don't see many of them around because they're usually more expensive than whatever is inside them."

"Can you open one?" Deaugrey asked.

"I wasn't brought here just to give you

boys something to look at."

"She can crack open any safe there is," Nate said. "That's why I wanted to bring her in on this job." Looking back to Angelica, he asked, "You can crack open one of Grunwaldt's safes, right?"

"I got into three of them a year ago when I was still living in London. It wasn't easy," she said, "but it can be done."

"What makes them so special?" Pete asked.

She shrugged. "Depends on what it's for. Grunwaldt is an artist. He can put together anything a customer might want. He's known for a few different things. When I get a look at it, I should be able to tell you plenty more."

" 'Should'?"

"That's good enough for me," Nate said. "Keyes is the one who wanted that safe, which means whatever's inside is damn important. If the safe is as special as Angelica is saying, it could very well hold the piece that clears this whole picture up for us."

"Last I heard," Deaugrey said, "our dear Angelica was in a spot of trouble."

"There was a problem or two in Nebraska," she admitted. "Had to keep my head down for a while, but it'll pass. Nate always comes along to sweep me away when I need it most."

"That's real sweet," Deaugrey snipped.

"What's that got to do with anything?" she asked.

"If you got caught, it must mean you slipped up," Deaugrey pointed out. "This job has already had enough surprises. We don't need to get this far only to realize one of us can't deliver."

"If you're so worried, then you can toss a saddle onto your horse and leave town," Nate said. "I'll deliver your cut of the profits myself when I get a chance."

Deaugrey was quick to reply, "Don't get your nose bent the wrong way. I'm just saying that Anstel has plenty of hired guns protecting his interests. Keyes is among them, and he's dangerous enough on his own."

"I'll worry about Keyes," Nate said. "Frank and Pete will help me. Grey, you and Angelica will get into Anstel's office to crack open that safe. I'll see to it that Anstel will have bigger problems than you two."

"How quiet do we have to be?" Deaugrey asked.

"You'll have some time to work those persuasive powers and get as close as you can to that safe. When the three of us arrive to make some waves, you should have a bit more elbow room."

"I like the sound of that."

"Are you certain it might not be a bit soon to start making our presence felt in such a way?" Frank asked.

Pete chuckled once. "I'd say it's been felt pretty good so far."

Nodding, Nate added, "And we arrived at the game too late in the first place. Things have already moved along too far for us to try and work many more angles than we already have."

"Then I suggest we take Pescaterro and go," Frank said. "That's what we were paid to do in the first place in case you've forgotten."

"I haven't forgotten, Frank. I think I've got a notion of what's going on and Keyes is way too close to getting rich off of the blood that was spilt. After all he's done, I can't abide by letting him get what he wants."

"So this is about revenge?"

Everyone in the room looked over to Nate for the few seconds he took before saying, "Yeah. Part of it is revenge . . . in the name of the marshal Keyes killed and dragged through the mud. The other part is simply because we're here and we're in a real good spot to be the one faulty cog that causes an entire machine to burst apart at the seams. None of you have to go along. That's always been our deal. But if you do, you'll have a cut of the price that's got to be on Keyes's head as well."

"I came this far," Pete said. "Also, Keyes and them others have taken too many shots at all of us. Riding away without making them sorry for that don't set well with me at all."

When Nate looked over at him, Deaugrey said, "These sound like long odds. I'm never going to turn away from a chance to thumb my nose at the odds."

"I just got here," Angelica said when it was her turn to opt in or out. "I barely got to enjoy myself yet. Also, cracking open another Grunwaldt safe will be a feather in my cap that money can't buy."

"Frank?" Nate asked. "You in?"

"As long as you promise one thing," the preacher replied. "If this safe doesn't give you the answers you're after, we're through with this whole affair. You're right in saying we're late in coming to this game. Any town tempted by railroad money in any way is going to have companies scraping to get as much of it as they can. That's just the way of the world. Trying to cleanse all of that is a fool's errand."

"Spoken like a true preacher," Deaugrey grumbled.

Ignoring Deaugrey's snide remark, Nate said, "I'm not trying to cleanse anything, and I don't hold out much hope in figuring out everything that's been going on here. My concern was Pescaterro. He's wrapped up tight and gagged in the dry goods store being used as a sheriff's office for the time being. The sheriff's hurt real bad and the deputies have no qualms with us taking Pescaterro out of their sight when we leave Joplin. We stumbled upon Keyes and I ain't about to let him go. After that — this town can sort itself out."

Frank's eyes narrowed as he studied his friend carefully. Finally, he nodded and said, "All right then. I'm in."

34

It was a half hour before noon the next day when Deaugrey marched Angelica into the offices of Anstel & Joyner. They were immediately greeted by a pair of tired-looking gunmen who stopped them before they could get past the main desk situated at the bottom of the stairs. A few minutes later, Preston Anstel appeared at the top of the stairs looking much less polished than he had at his and Deaugrey's previous meeting.

"What's this?" Anstel grunted.

Deaugrey nodded toward Angelica and said, "This is Melanie Cavett."

Making no attempt to hide the path his eyes took as he drank in the sight of her, Anstel said, "She's quite beautiful, but not quite as . . . ample as you'd described her."

Angelica adjusted her posture and arched her back while every man in the room stared at her chest.

"Tastes vary," Deaugrey said. "Also, the selection within McKeag's walls isn't exactly as good as one might find around here."

Anstel waved them up and turned to walk away. After Deaugrey's guns were taken from him, he and Angelica were ushered up the stairs to the familiar hallway on the third floor. Having already opened the first door on the right, Anstel held it open so they could step inside. It was a modest office with a rolltop desk against one wall, a map of the state on another wall and enough books piled onto a pair of shelves and a couple of tables to stock a small library. Sitting at the desk, Anstel began rustling through the narrow drawers as he said, "That was fast."

"I'm a little early," Deaugrey said. "But not by much."

"No. I mean finding Miss Cavett there. Was she already in town?"

"Close."

The drawer he'd been looking for contained a pair of spectacles which Anstel placed upon the bridge of his nose. After the wire frames were looped behind his ears, he took a longer look at Angelica.

"If you don't believe I could get her here," Deaugrey said, "then you should have set a longer deadline."

"Honestly, I thought you'd come back with some sort of excuse telling me why you couldn't get to her just yet."

Deaugrey smirked. "And during my explanation, I'd part with a few details that would allow you to go and retrieve her yourself without having to pay me. Or, after you graciously gave me more time, you'd knock down my fee. Am I close?"

Anstel smirked and opened one final drawer. "I did have a word with someone else who'd met Miss Cavett some time ago. They gave me a few things that would help me identify her. They should be around here somewhere."

"Or you could talk to me," Angelica said. "I'm standing right here, you know."

All this time, Anstel had barely acknowledged her presence. He didn't do much to change that except to look at her for less than a second and getting up from his seat. "Where are those damn pictures?" he shouted into the hallway. He then stepped outside and slammed the door shut behind him.

Deaugrey looked over to Angelica and said, "He was much more polite the last time we spoke."

"He's an ass. Where's the safe?"

"Across the hall."

"So," she said impatiently. "Let's go."

After waiting for the sound of Anstel's steps to fade, Deaugrey stepped up to the door and took a look outside. It was barely open a crack and when he peeked through, he froze for a few moments and then stepped back. "There's a man outside."

"There's probably a lot of them," she said. Since Deaugrey didn't say anything to that, she let out a heavy sigh, pushed him out of her way and pulled open the door. "Could you come in here?" she asked the burly fellow standing just outside the door. Smiling sweetly and giving him a look that could have started a war, she added, "Please?"

The man who stepped through the door was one of the biggest ones they'd passed on their way up from the lobby. The pistol holstered at his side seemed like an afterthought since he could probably crush just about any living thing in his bare hands. As soon as he was in the room, he looked expectantly at Angelica and she looked expectantly at Deaugrey.

"What, umm, do you need?" the gunman asked.

Angelica may not have been saying much, but she looked awfully good doing it. She chewed on her lower lip and swayed a bit as if she was pondering the mysteries of the universe. She eventually glanced over to Deaugrey, only to find him watching her just as intently as the gunman. "I was hoping you might help me with something," she said in a voice that was smoother than fine satin against warm skin.

"Sure," the gunman said.

When he stepped toward her unimpeded, Angelica grabbed a candlestick from the desk and cracked it against the gunman's forehead. His brow twisted in pain before his eyes rolled up into his head. Angelica grabbed his lapels so she could guide his fall toward the floor without knocking anything over on the way down. The gunman hit the floor heavily, leaving her standing over him with the candlestick.

"When I distracted him, you were supposed to knock him out!" she scolded.

Deaugrey blinked in surprise. "Did we make that plan on the way in?"

"No, but you should have seen what I was doing."

"Oh. That sounds more like something Nate would have seen."

Angelica shook her head and plucked the pistol from the gunman's holster. "Show me to that safe," she said while handing Deaugrey the pistol.

"We're supposed to wait for Nate to make

his move."

"Is the hallway clear?"

Deaugrey took a look outside. "More or less," he said.

"Then let's go! Christ Almighty, when did you become so timid?"

"I'm not timid, but I'm also not crazy! There are only two of us with significantly more killers and assorted brutes in here with us."

Pulling quickly away from the door, Angelica shut it tight and put her back against it. "Someone's coming," she said, "and they're in a hurry. Hide that man."

Deaugrey looked from the gunman taking up a good portion of the floor to the limited amount of remaining space in the room. "Where should I put him?" he hissed. "In one of those little drawers? Perhaps under the desk where anyone larger than a child would have trouble fitting their damn knees?"

The floor shook with several approaching feet until it sounded like a stampede was making its way down the hall. Deaugrey held his gun at the ready and set his sights on the door. Rather than burst through it, however, the men in the hall charged straight past the door and continued to the stairs. When they'd gone, Angelica took another look outside.

"It's clear," she whispered. "Let's go."

As soon as they were both in the hall, Deaugrey began to smile. "This promises to be a very interesting afternoon."

As it turned out, Nate didn't need to make an appointment to get a meeting with Preston Anstel. All he had to do was walk up to the front of his offices and shout his name along with a few other colorful phrases that sent the locals scattering away from him. In less than a minute, men came running out the front door to fan out in front of the building. A few even stepped onto the second-floor balcony, which was where Nate kept his eyes pointed.

When he spotted a familiar face on that balcony, Nate smiled widely enough for it to be seen even if someone were looking down from the roof. "There you are, Keyes! I figured you'd want to stay as far from me as possible."

Preston Anstel stood next to Keyes with his hands on his hips like an emperor surveying his lands. "I'm the one you called for, mister! What's the meaning of this?"

"I came to ask that you release Abraham Keyes into my custody," Nate replied. "He's wanted for killing a lawman and plenty of others."

"I was cleared of that killing," Keyes said proudly. "Get your ass out of my sight."

Anstel extended an arm to hold Keyes back without taking his eyes off of Nate. "What if I refuse your request?" he asked.

"Then I'll change it from a request to a demand," Nate said. "Send that murdering son of a bitch down to me. Now."

"I don't have to do anything you ask," Anstel said. "In fact, I'm within my legal rights to have you shot."

"Since I imagine you've got a few lawmen in your pocket, I reckon that's so. Do you know who Casey Pescaterro is?"

"Of course. He's that wild dog Sam Cavett busted out of jail. Nearly burned down half of Joplin in the process."

"Him and that son of a bitch," Nate said while pointing a steady hand at Keyes, "are partners and they're setting your company and Western Cartage against each other so they can swindle as much money as they can from both sides."

"That's preposterous!"

"I can prove it."

"How?"

Keeping his finger pointed at Keyes, Nate said, "Send that one down here and I'll

387

make him squeal."

Keyes grinned as well when he said, "Gladly."

"No," Anstel said. His one arm proved too weak to keep Keyes from moving toward the door that would take him back inside, so he grabbed Keyes and said, "No! I'm a businessman, not a killer. These are insane accusations, nothing more."

"Then where's the law?" Nate asked.

"Probably dealing with the hell that was unleashed last night. Probably still looking for that Pescaterro fellow. Probably questioning Sam Cavett about his part in setting that animal free!"

Nate nodded. "I imagine you're right. So that just leaves you right here with me and I ain't about to go away."

"Let me go," Keyes said.

Too frustrated to contain himself, Anstel not only let Keyes go but shoved him toward the door. "You want to take care of this?" he said in a low, rumbling voice. "Then end it here and now before any lawmen do show up."

Keyes nodded and stormed through the door that would take him inside so he could get to the stairs.

"This isn't good," Deaugrey said as he hurried back into the room they'd just snuck into. "He seems upset. They seem real upset."

Angelica knelt in front of the safes that had been hidden behind a set of shelves. As soon as Deaugrey had brought her to that room and showed her the stack of iron boxes hidden behind the shelves on one wall, she'd known which safe required her attention. Judging by the way she'd caressed the dial and even touched the hinges on the door, she didn't even need to see the maker's mark stamped into the corner. "Which is it?" she asked, keeping one ear pressed against the front of the safe. " 'He' or 'they'?"

"It was he, now it's they. And they seem rather close to trading blows . . . or bullets."

She paid no attention to the pounding of steps directly below them. Instead, she kept her eyes closed while slowly turning the dial. "Are they coming up the stairs?"

Deaugrey cracked the door open, peeked outside and closed it again. "No. I believe they're headed down."

"Good. Let me know if anyone comes this way. I've almost got this open."

"Really?"

"Yes," Angelica said before she turned the handle and opened the safe. "Really."

Although there was plenty of money to be found as well as a few bundles of folded papers held together with twine inside the safe, she pushed all that aside so she could run her fingertips along the interior walls and bottom of the safe itself.

"That seemed fairly easy," Deaugrey said. "I suppose that's why you're the expert in such things."

"That wasn't the real lock," she said.

"Seemed locked to me."

"It was, but it's just a regular lock. There's got to be more. With a Grunwaldt safe, there always is."

"Obviously, Nate is creating some kind of stir outside but I wouldn't count on it lasting forever."

"That's why you're here, isn't it?" she asked. "To guard me?"

"Yeah, well hurry it along all the same."

Angelica's eyes snapped open wider as if she'd just awoken from a deep sleep. "Got it!"

Rushing to her side, Deaugrey hunkered down to get a look. "What is it? What did you find?"

"The second lock."

Beneath the papers she'd pushed aside was a subtle crosshatch pattern that had been etched into the bottom of the safe's interior. After a little more searching, Angelica's fingers ran along the continuation of that pattern going up along one of the safe's walls.

"Where's the lock?" Deaugrey asked.

"This is it," she told him. Pressing down between two of the lines etched into the safe's interior, Angelica slid a thin strip down and to the side before putting it back where she'd found it. "Have you ever seen a Chinese puzzle box?"

"Yes."

"This is sort of like that. These panels slide around and when they're put into the right shape or order, the box opens."

"So get it open and we can get the hell out of here," Deaugrey snapped.

"It's not going to be that easy. Grunwaldt is a master craftsman."

"If you can't do it, tell me right now."

Angelica scowled as she manipulated the panels embedded within the safe. For every one she moved, another was revealed. "I've opened one like this before. It's going to take a little time."

"That may be in short supply, darlin'."

Abraham Keyes stepped out of the front door of the building and came to a stop at the edge of the boardwalk. Even though several men watched from within the building and plenty more watched from the streets or windows nearby, it seemed he and Nate were alone.

"You got some nerve, Sathow," Keyes said. "Throwing accusations at me when you ain't nothing more than a bounty hunter with more kills to his name than any of the men you go after."

"And you're too full of yourself after twisting the law into some foul thing just to suit your purposes."

"You're spouting off about the law? Are you still waving around them stolen badges whenever the mood strikes you?"

"This ain't about me," Nate said. "It's about you and Pescaterro. Dog Ear is already finished. That means it's your turn."

Holding his arms out, Keyes declared, "I'm just a man doing his job, and this whole town stands to benefit."

Nate shook his head. "I don't give a damn what you say or what you got cooking around here. I've already seen what you are. Anything after that doesn't matter. You should have been strung up a long time ago."

"Then by all means — bring me to justice so I can say my piece to a judge."

Nate stood tall and stared at Keyes until

the other man's calm demeanor melted away.

"Got it!" Angelica said proudly. "It wasn't easy, but it wasn't as bad as I thought it would be. Turned out it was just a more complicated variance on a pattern used in the other Grunwaldt safe. Part of it was a jumbled version of his maker's mark and another part was —"

"Save it for when I buy you a drink," Deaugrey said while rushing back to look over her shoulder. "What did you find?"

"More papers," she said, handing them over so she could turn her attention back to the safe. "They mean anything to you?"

Deaugrey flipped through the folded bundle and quickly read through a few papers. "Why, yes," he said as he selected a few to take from the bundle before handing the rest back to Angelica. "I believe they do. More importantly, I imagine I know someone who might be interested in knowing what we've discovered. Can you find your way out of here on your own?"

"I don't want to leave you here."

"You're not leaving me. You're getting the rest of those papers away from this place. Now can you do it or not?"

She nodded and brushed her hand gently

against Deaugrey's cheek as she passed him. "I've slipped out of tighter spots than this one. See you soon."

"Yeah. Hopefully."

"You think you're gonna walk away from this, Sathow?" Keyes roared. "You don't even know what you stumbled into!"

"You're still breathin'," Nate said. "That's all I need to know. The rest can work itself out."

Keyes chuckled and looked around to find a half dozen of Anstel's men behind him.

"All of you," Anstel shouted from the balcony. "Get back in here!"

"One moment, Preston," Keyes said. "Just about through with this."

"No, Abraham. Now!"

Nate smirked. "Sounds like you're in trouble again."

Whether it was the grin or the sly remark that pushed Keyes past his limit would remain a mystery. He bared his teeth like an animal that had been backed into a corner and drew the .44 hanging at his hip.

With no wasted movements, Nate pulled his Remington and fired two quick shots.

Half of the other gunmen behind Keyes stood frozen in their tracks. Two of them reflexively tried to answer the gunshots using their own weapons, but were held in check by a short series of shots fired at the building from across the street. Their eyes went to the storefront opposite the Anstel & Joyner offices to find a single man stepping through the shop's front door. Pete held a Sharps rifle to his shoulder, its barrel still smoking and his finger on the trigger.

"Move away or fight," Pete said. "Choose right now."

All of the remaining gunmen made their choice known by moving into the building.

Keyes let out a shaky breath and dropped to one knee. Two crimson stains grew on his shirt, one at his heart and the other a few inches to the right of it. "I . . . already paid for what I did to . . . that marshal."

"No," Nate said. "But you're about to."

The pistol fell from his hand a second before Keyes fell over.

35

While the covered wagon may have been small, it was the best Frank could find on short notice that was within their means to purchase. Its function was to carry a small amount of supplies or possibly a load of hay which meant it was just right to hold one large outlaw wrapped in several lengths of rope with an old bandanna stuffed into his mouth. Frank had parked the wagon in a livery near the southern edge of town. Frank sat on a stool beside it with a shotgun resting across his lap and a Bible in his hands. When he heard a group of people pulling open the livery's door, he put one down so he could pick up the other.

The door swung open so Nate, Angelica, Pete and Deaugrey could stumble inside. Frank stood up with the shotgun still in his grasp. "How did everything go?" he asked. "What happened with Keyes?"

"I shot him," Nate declared.

"You left four hours ago! It's almost five o'clock! Where have you been?"

"Celebrating," Deaugrey replied in a way that sounded more like "shell-a-brating."

Frank scowled at them, one by one. "Have you been drinking?"

"Yes," Angelica said in a voice that had barely been touched by the influence of liquor. "Preston Anstel had some of the finest wine I've ever tasted."

"His whiskey weren't too bad, either," Deaugrey slurred.

"Someone tell me what happened."

Nate took a quick look inside the covered wagon to find Pescaterro in there. Compared to the small size of the wagon, Dog Ear seemed even more like a giant than usual. "I called out Keyes and got him to overplay his hand. He thought he had a small posse behind him to back his play. He didn't and now he's dead."

"And Mr. Anstel, along with all his hired guns, just let you kill him?" Frank asked.

Deaugrey stumbled forward. "He was more than willing to watch . . . to see . . . to let . . ."

"How much did he have to drink?" Frank asked while scowling at Deaugrey.

"At least triple the amount the rest of us did," Nate replied.

Angelica patted Deaugrey on the shoulder, which was enough to force him to sit down on a pile of straw with his legs stretched in front of him. "I opened that safe and found a stash of papers inside," she told Frank. "It turns out they were deeds and legal documents for the ownership of the Joplin Mercantile Company."

"Good Lord," Frank sighed. "Another company."

"I never heard of it either," Nate said. "What matters is that Preston Anstel had heard of it. Joplin Mercantile has been trying to get some of the money being brought in by the railroad expansions, but are third in line behind Anstel's company and Western Cartage."

"So why would Preston Anstel have an interest in owning a company that's already being beaten by his own?"

"He doesn't," Angelica told him. "He didn't even know about the papers. Preston didn't even know about the compartment in his safe or that it was a Grunwaldt. Keyes must have switched it out with one of the safes that were already in Anstel's office. Also, it was Keyes who'd signed those papers to gain controlling interest of Joplin Mercantile."

"I was right about Keyes playing both

sides against each other," Nate explained. "Him and Pescaterro were in with the two leading companies so they could chip away at them both from the inside while keeping them at each other's throats. While Western Cartage was being set up to look like a bunch of heavily armed outlaws willing to burn this place to the ground to spring Dog Ear out of jail, Anstel was going to be exposed as a blackmailer in possession of all the dirt Keyes himself collected. Both companies would either be run out of town by the law or tear each other down, clearing the path for Joplin Mercantile to sweep up the profits once the railroad made their big expansion."

"And Keyes is the owner of Joplin Mercantile," Frank said.

"Not anymore. He's dead so it reverts back to Michael Jamieson, the founder of Joplin Mercantile, who was pushed out by a particularly nasty bit of blackmail used by Keyes."

"Which is all now burnt to cinders after I dug it out of the papers that were hidden in that beautiful safe," Angelica said.

"What was he being blackmailed with?" Frank asked.

She shrugged her shoulders. "Don't know.

Don't care. My job was just to open the safe."

"Which she did incredibly *well*!" Nate said as he planted a kiss onto Angelica's lips.

"So Keyes was hiding his documents in Anstel's own safe?" Frank asked.

"Not just any safe," Angelica told him. "A Grunwaldt. If I hadn't already seen one exactly like it, I might have missed the panels hidden inside that thing. Anyone without a trained eye would have never noticed them. And the only reason I got the second compartment open is because I'm the best you're likely to find who isn't Grunwaldt himself. When it was time for Keyes to finish what he was doing, all he needed to do was go up to that office and get his papers. Until then, Anstel would do all the work of guarding them for him."

"Not a bad way to go, actually," Frank admitted. "Hopefully the town law finds this story interesting as well. I doubt we'll be able to avoid meeting up with them before leaving Joplin."

"Already taken care of," Pete said. "We scrounged up the sheriff after Keyes went down."

"Any trouble with the company's hired guns?"

"It's funny how timid men like that get

when they see the biggest and baddest of them gunned down right in front of them like a dog in the street. By the time I came back with the law, I believe Anstel was damn close to tears."

"Quite a sight, really," Angelica said.

Nate chuckled. "Don't feel too bad for him. He may have lost everything he had, but he was also the one doing his best to force another company out of business through intimidation and blackmail."

"What about the owner of that other company?" Frank asked. "Western Cartage?"

Deaugrey sat with his back against a wall. "Sam Cavett. He's already in a jail cell after funding last night's fire. Of course, he says he didn't give any order to bust Dog Ear out of jail, but it don't really matter now. He's through in this town and every other."

"I don't feel bad for any of those businessmen," Angelica said. "It was quite a sight to see a man as imposing as Preston Anstel get worn down to a nub."

Frank hooked his thumb back toward the wagon where Pescaterro was stewing in his own juices. "And this one?"

"He's ours for the taking," Nate said. "After he got a look at everything in those safes and heard what witnesses said about me defending myself against Keyes, the acting sheriff was looking for a way to thank me for doing his job for him."

"We're the ones that get to drag Dog Ear Pescaterro back to Kansas," Frank pointed out. "I wouldn't exactly call that a reward."

"Then you can forsake your cut of the money that's due to us and ask for a nice pat on the back instead."

Frank waved that off and took the mostly empty bottle of whiskey from Nate's hand. After removing the cork, he sniffed the liquor and nodded in approval. "Rich men do have the best whiskey. Wait a second. This whiskey and that wine were given to you by Preston Anstel?"

"I said they were from Anstel's office," Deaugrey corrected. "I never said he *gave* them to us."

"Well then," Frank declared as he raised the bottle, "here's to finally leaving a town without being chased out of it."

None of the others were as happy about that as Frank. Finally, Nate said, "We're actually supposed to leave Joplin as soon as we can."

"You mean . . . in the morning?"

"No. I mean now. The sheriff doesn't want to see any of our faces again."

"Ain't that what happened after the last

job you hired me for?" Pete asked.

Nate didn't have to think very long before saying, "Yep. More or less."

Raising his bottle even higher, Frank said, "Then here's to consistency."

ABOUT THE AUTHOR

Marcus Galloway is the author of numerous Ralph Compton novels, including *Ralph Compton Hard Ride to Wichita,* and *Ralph Compton One Man's Fire.* He is also author of The Man From Boot Hill novels and The Accomplice novels.

The employees of Thorndike Press hope you have enjoyed this Large Print book. All our Thorndike, Wheeler, and Kennebec Large Print titles are designed for easy reading, and all our books are made to last. Other Thorndike Press Large Print books are available at your library, through selected bookstores, or directly from us.

For information about titles, please call:
(800) 223-1244

or visit our Web site at:
http://gale.cengage.com/thorndike

To share your comments, please write:
Publisher
Thorndike Press
10 Water St., Suite 310
Waterville, ME 04901

CPSIA information can be obtained
at www.ICGtesting.com
Printed in the USA
FFOW02n0009080515
13297FF